Danger. Danger. Danger.

Sabrin whipped her head toward Ryder as he reached over and cinched her safety belt tighter.

His eyes never left the road.

And then she saw it: up ahead, two men were in the black sedan.

"You see them? Two more in the yellow one behind us. They just sandwiched us in."

Sabrin looked around at where Voodoo was strapped to the passenger seat, his K-9 safety belt in place. "Voodoo, lie down."

"I'm going to get away from them as soon as we reach that intersection," Ryder said. "Be ready. Three. Two. Here we go." With his feet playing both the gas and brake pedals, Ryder spun the wheel, and they turned a one-eighty.

Sabrin was tossed about on her seat as she gripped the armrest.

"Still coming. Here we go. Three. Two." He slammed on the brakes and threw them into reverse, backing into an alley.

Seconds later, the yellow sedan whizzed by. Sabrin knew that one car could wait at the crossroads and the other could simply circle the block and come up behind them.

She didn't want to be caught in this alley with no escape.

Surely, Ryder knew what he was doing.

Fiona Quinn is a six-time *USA TODAY* bestselling author, a Kindle Scout winner and an Amazon All-Star.

Quinn writes suspense in her Iniquus world of books, including the Lynx, Strike Force, Uncommon Enemies, Kate Hamilton Mysteries, FBI Joint Task Force, Cerberus Tactical K-9 Team Alpha and Delta Force Echo series, with more to come.

She writes urban fantasy as Fiona Angelica Quinn for her Elemental Witches series.

And, just for fun, she writes the Badge Bunny Booze Mystery Collection of raucous, bawdy humor with her dear friend Tina Glasneck as Quinn Glasneck.

Quinn is rooted in the Old Dominion, where she lives with her husband. There, she pops chocolates, devours books and taps continuously on her laptop.

Facebook, Twitter, Pinterest: Fiona Quinn Books

DEFENDER'S INSTINCT

USA TODAY Bestselling Author

FIONA QUINN

HARLEQUIN

This book is dedicated with gratitude to Michele Carlon—
a generous and gifted friend

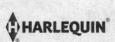

Recycling programs
for this product may
not exist in your area.

ISBN-13: 978-1-335-42998-8

Defender's Instinct

First published in 2020 by Fiona Quinn. This edition published in 2022.

For questions and comments about the quality of this book, please contact us at CustomerService@Harlequin.com.

Harlequin Enterprises ULC
22 Adelaide St. West, 41st Floor
Toronto, Ontario M5H 4E3, Canada
www.Harlequin.com

Printed in U.S.A.

DEFENDER'S INSTINCT

Acknowledgments

My great appreciation—

To my editor Kathleen Payne.

To my publicist Margaret Daly.

To my Australian specialist Elisa Hordon.

To my Beta Force, who are always honest and kind at the same time: C. Villani, M. Carlon.

To my Street Force, who support me and my writing with such enthusiasm and kindness.

To the real-world K-9 professionals who serve and protect us.

To all the wonderful professionals whom I called on to get the details right—

> Dr. K. Connor for her consistent K-9 inspiration, both through her stories and her amazing photographs.
>
> Virginia K-9 search and rescue teams for their work in our community, their dedication and professionalism. Every time I search and train with you, I'm inspired.

Please note: This is a work of fiction, and while I always try my best to get all the details correct, there are times when it serves the story to go slightly to the left or right of perfection. Please understand that any mistakes or discrepancies are my authorial decision-making alone and sit squarely on my shoulders.

Thank you to my family.

I send my love to my husband, along with my great appreciation. T, a life with you is one of my very best decisions. Thank you for giving me a solid foundation on which to grow.

And of course, thank *you* for reading my stories. I'm smiling joyfully as I type this. I so appreciate you!

Chapter 1

Ryder

The crowd exploded in a riot of cheers.

Ryder could just make out his Cerberus teammate, Ridge, with his hand in the air, accepting the admiration at the other end of the K9 trial course.

The gathering of international working dog professionals had nestled into an otherwise quiet Moravian valley in Czechia near the borders of the Slovak Republic and Austria, just northeast of Vienna.

Glorious terrain. Hilly. With a green so vibrant, a smell so fresh, it overwhelmed his senses.

This was nothing like being out on the station where Ryder had grown up. In the Australian Outback's flat open lands, the air on his father's ranch was dusty dry, leaving a powder on his skin and grit in his teeth.

There, he'd waved off flies instead of waving at the excited crowd.

Ryder lifted his head to check Ridge's course time on the massive digital clock. K9 Zeus had moved through in record time. He sat at the top of the leader board.

"See that, Voodoo?"

Ryder's Malinois looked up at him and tipped his head as if asking for more information. Then turned back to stare into the crowd.

Ryder followed his dog's gaze.

Yup, there *she* was again.

She fit in, for the most part. Ryder guessed she was early thirties. Her hair pulled back into a distracted ponytail told him she wasn't here to flirt. Her clothes were the typical European dark jeans with a snug white T-shirt over a curvy body. Thin leather straps traced over her shoulders, one of those backpack-style purses. Those kinds of bags were easily pickpocketed, and no one in the defense field would carry one.

So not a security professional.

Daytripper? K9 fangirl? Tourist who wanted to see what was happening down here in the valley? The tickets to spectate cost a hundred and fifty US dollars per day. You had to really want to be here to be here.

Even if she were just rich and didn't care about the money, they were at least an hour from anything Ryder would deem touristy.

The International Working Dog Competition aimed for remote and difficult to attend in an effort to dissuade the general public from participating.

Here, qualified K9s fought for the titles and gained certifications, upping their price on the wider market.

Besides the competitors, there were also the buyers who came here to scope out possible working dogs for their kennels.

Ryder had spotted several American buying teams here over the last few days. They'd compete on price for the dogs they thought might make the grade for United States Military special operations forces like the Green Berets, the Deltas, and the SEALs.

Cairo, the K9 who took down Osama bin Laden, was culled from competitors like the dogs Ryder and Voodoo were up against today.

Here, the buyers looked for athleticism, courage, and the secret sauce that set certain dogs apart—intelligence, personality, and *sanity*.

Ryder had seen some amazing dogs on the course over the last four days. Some of them, though, he would never consider as future working dogs. They were just too high-strung, and frankly, terrifying.

No doubt, all the dogs on the course today had the capacity to kill. Quickly. Effectively. *Happily.*

What was needed was a K9 with an off switch. K9s like Zeus and Voodoo, here. Ryder dropped his hand to his dog's head. Voodoo would go to battle with Ryder by day and curl up with his blankie on Ryder's bed at night, snoring and wagging his tail to some happy dream he was having.

Neither Voodoo nor his teammate Ridge's German shepherd-Malinois mix breed Zeus was available for sale.

Their task at this competition was to show what Iniquus trained K9s could do. It was all about prestige on the world stage.

That prestige translated into high-dollar security contracts.

Ryder lifted his gaze. Voodoo still had his focus on the woman.

She wasn't a buyer. At least she didn't have the look. No pad and pencil for notetaking. She wasn't wearing sunglasses to hide her interest.

Ryder stroked a hand over his beard. Had he run an Iniquus mission that involved her?

Iniquus was a clandestine group. They kept their heads down—their eyes on the prize. And they never willingly exposed anything they did publicly.

Even here, under tight protocol and security, Ryder and Ridge had grown out full beards, wore mirrored aviator glasses, and pulled the brims of their ball caps low. If a photo got out of either of them, the only thing that would be recognizable would be their K9s and their Iniquus uniforms.

So that this lady seemed to know him was a head-scratcher.

She didn't know Voodoo; Ryder was reasonably sure of that. Voodoo and Zeus both came out of a rescue raid on a Honduran detention center—private prison—a couple years back. Voodoo had been a seven-month-old puppy. Ryder had trained Voodoo, and when Voodoo had passed all of his certification trials, they had deployed together. Typically, Ryder and Voodoo were sent out to do mission support, and that was always clandestine.

There was the close protection he'd done in May with Hollywood starlet Berlin Tracy. But she'd always called him Kiwi, not Ryder, and the K9 he was handling had been his cousin's pet Chewie Barka.

As the staff reset the course for Voodoo's trial, Ryder kept his head on a swivel, so it didn't look like he'd homed in on the woman, though she unabashedly stared right at him.

Ryder definitely wanted to know why Voodoo was locked on to her, his body rigid, ears forward, like all he wanted was a release command so he could sprint toward her.

She held up a hot pink water bottle with Voodoo's name in bold black letters and gave it a hello waggle.

Ryder pretended he didn't see it.

Nope. This didn't read like "fangirl."

It wasn't like she was trying to get him to come over to her.

She was making herself visible to him.

The whole thing struck him as…off.

Voodoo stomped his foot and looked up at Ryder, then back at the woman.

"Yeah, I *see* her, mate." Ryder wished he could read his dog's thoughts. "We're going to focus on this contest, though, hey?"

Ryder knelt beside Voodoo. "Listen up. The old man has the top score today. Now, we know that Zeus is a chess player. He does everything with intention, so he shaves off the time most teams know will be taken up with hesitation. You're last running this course. If Zeus is at the number one place, and we don't get into the semifinals, well… I'm not saying it would set you and me back with our reputations, but we'd be hard at it to regain face."

Voodoo pawed the air and made a whining sound.

"Here's the thing. You're not Zeus. Not yet, anyway.

You're too young to have his wisdom. But—and this is a big but—you have me on your side."

Voodoo stared Ryder hard in the eye, opened his mouth, panting with tension. His muscles bunching, his body primed. He wanted to go!

"If you listen to my commands, and we work this together, your brawn and your bravery, well, you and me, mate, we'll be sitting at the top of that leader board, too." Ryder gave Voodoo a nod, then gathered his leash. They made their way toward the starting line.

"Moving up to the starting position is Iniquus's Cerberus Tactical K9 team Ryder and Voodoo." The heavily accented English came over the loudspeaker. "This is Voodoo's first international competition." They repeated all of this in French and then in Czech. "Voodoo is a two-year-old Malinois rescue who has been trained by Ryder at the Cerberus campus in the United States of America. Can he catch up with the exceptional score of his fellow Cerberus semifinals qualifier, team Ridge-Zeus?"

"You and me, mate." Ryder unclasped the lead. He stepped a foot back, crouching down, up on his toes in a runner's stance, ready to catapult them into action.

The buzzer sounded.

Ryder raced forward.

In this round, the judges weren't just watching speed and handler control; they wanted to know how the K9s did when confronted with challenges that weren't necessarily part of the dogs' happy list.

Ryder's task was to keep Voodoo calm and focused. That would be key.

If riled, Voodoo would try to go fast and hard. That had its place in their world of Iniquus security, but here that would lead to frustration and a poor time on the end clock.

Voodoo was wearing the requisite equipment: the bullet-resistant vest and a radio collar. The set up weighed a little less than two kilograms—or about four pounds as the Yanks would say. It was fine for the run. It might make Voodoo a little more hesitant as he reached the water obstacle.

This course was a serious test of the K9 teams' skills and relationships. First, there were the challenges known to be difficult for dogs, open staircases into darkness, blacked-out slender passageways for crawling by voice command. It was this maze where Zeus had made spectacular time. The handlers were on the ground listening to the dogs' movements, then using the radio to indicate which direction to travel to get out of the maze. A single wrong turn could leave the K9 at a dead end.

Backing up in a crawl was always tough.

The entrance to the maze was blocked with a gate. The K9 needed to push that over to make a bridge to the building.

Running at full speed, Ryder yelled, "Tackle barricade."

While most of the dogs were commanded in German, Czech, or Dutch, Ryder thought it was safer to have his own set of commands. Words were just sounds. The trainer gave the sounds meaning through repetition. "Tackle" was the term Ryder typically used when he wanted Voodoo to knock someone down but not get in a bite. But Voodoo had also been trained to use it to shut gates and the like. Tackle meant a leap and a push.

Voodoo thrust off his back legs and sailed through the air, extending out so that as his weight forced the barrier over, Voodoo landed on all fours.

Ryder made sure he was right there beside his partner to give him the next command.

"Giddy up," Ryder said to get Voodoo climbing up the open staircase toward the door that had been left open a crack.

The crowd cheered.

Voodoo had trained to ignore loud noises like gunfire, truck rumbles, and explosions. He'd had some experience with crowds as they'd done patrols for parades and sporting events. But these high-pitched whistles, and the crowd yelling Voodoo's name, were making Voodoo skittery as he moved away from his handler up the stairs.

This next challenge required radio command over the comms unit that Voodoo wore on his collar.

Ryder lifted his radio and depressed the button. "Good job, Voodoo. Good boy. Open sesame," he said. Ryder worked to get his own adrenaline from infecting his voice. Voodoo needed calm and cool. He needed to hear a simple work command. An agitated handler sparked the nerves of his K9. Emotions ran down the lead. They also traveled the airwaves.

Voodoo stuck his nose into the crack between the door and the wall. With a flip of his head to the side, he exposed a fence and a tunnel.

"Smooth and easy, mate. Focus on my voice. In you go. Snake."

Voodoo backed up a step, bent, and looked. He wasn't a fan of pitch black.

"Good job. I'm right here with you. In you go. Snake yourself in there, bloke. Here we go. Snake."

Voodoo squatted into a low crouch. His tongue stretched out as he gave a loud yawn. Then inched forward. Inched some more. Another yawn of distress, and he got all of himself in.

Ryder stood underneath the structure. If he reached up, Ryder could just touch the wide pipe above his head.

"Forward. Snake forward."

Ryder could hear bumping and scratching as Voodoo complied.

"Head right. Right. Right. Right."

Voodoo turned down the correct pipe and stopped at the branch.

Perfect. That was precisely what Ryder wanted to happen. Voodoo wasn't going to freak out in there and try to get himself out. He was going to trust Ryder to direct him. "Good job, mate. Now head left. Left. Left. Left."

It was an arduous time in the maze. The course designers hadn't chosen this obstacle on a whim. It was an essential task in the military working dogs' repertoire. Ryder had been deployed on a search and rescue mission where Voodoo's ability to transport comms, food, water, and medical supplies—crawling back and forth through a jumble of debris—meant the team was able to save the lives of thirty students trapped in their classroom by a mudslide.

This was a harrowing business.

Lives were often at stake.

The K9s had to be solid.

Voodoo was out of the maze, and it didn't go any

easier from there. He had to step off onto a rope bridge with uneven planks and a lot of air between them. Voodoo was sure-footed as the bridge swayed and moaned with Voodoo's weight and movement.

"Slow and steady there. Slow...steady...good boy!"

At the end, instead of having Voodoo run down the ramp. Voodoo simply leaped the six feet to the ground.

In English, the loudspeaker called, "Cerberus Tactical K9's Ryder with his dog, Voodoo, racing toward the water obstacle now. Voodoo is a Malinois. While many Malinois enjoy swimming and are strong swimmers, they tend to hesitate, if not balk, at dock diving events. So far, Voodoo has proven to be fearless. For a dog just out of adolescence, he's a solid performer."

Ryder and Voodoo ran side by side to the water test. This was where Voodoo could get hung up. It wasn't the water; it was the jump in that was the problem, especially since this water was dark. A swimming pool would have had no stopping effect on Voodoo, but muddy water was a place he resisted.

Ryder sprinted beside Voodoo as they climbed the steps onto the wooden dock, then commanded, "Into the drink," as Ryder dove off the dock.

At a challenge, the handler wasn't allowed to touch their K9 until the K9 had hesitated or failed for thirty seconds. At that point, if the dog was stuck on a task, the handler could put hands on the dog to get the needed task accomplished. One team, for example, had to wait until the handler could push over the beginning ramp.

That thirty seconds was too precious for Ryder to wait if he needed to throw his dog into the pond.

So, Ryder set the example with a surface dive that allowed him to keep his hat and sunglasses in place.

The pond was deep and shockingly cold. But as Ryder turned onto his side, he heard the splash right behind him. "Good boy! Good boy, Voodoo. Paddle for it."

Luckily, it wasn't far to the other side. "Paddle." Just enough to test the dogs' willingness to do what was needed.

Ryder pulled himself, streaming with water, out onto the dock on the other side.

Voodoo scrambled up the stairs to stand beside him.

As Ryder pounded his fist onto the button to stop the timer, Voodoo shook his coat, showering Ryder with pond water. "Yeah, serves me right. I don't blame you a bit."

Just moments later, Ryder stood on the platform with Voodoo panting at his side. Their names boomed over the speaker system, and Ryder raised his arm to accept the crowd's cheers. They'd reached the semifinals of the International Competition for Working K9s just behind Ridge and Zeus's scores.

Six teams total stood in a semi-circle. "Ladies and gentlemen, these are the K9s advancing to the semi-final round!"

Ridge ducked his chin. "Five o'clock." He indicated the direction of interest.

"Got her."

"She's had her eyes on you."

"Yup." Ryder reached up and scratched the top of his beard. He couldn't wait to shave it off.

"Fangirl?" Ridge asked. "She's got that hot pink Voodoo water bottle."

"Voodoo's man enough not to worry about his name on hot pink. You jealous she isn't a Zeus gal?"

"Zeus has all the gals he needs. I'm telling you, this woman has stalker vibes. She wants you to see her and acknowledge her."

"What do you think will happen if I do?"

"Don't know." Ridge chuckled. "Bigger question, do you have the stones to find out?"

Chapter 2

Ryder

Ryder was the only one chafing in wet tactical pants as they jogged down the road, heading for their campsite.

During their turn in the competition, Ridge had pulled Zeus's rubber ball from his pocket—fully within the rules—and tossed it into the pond. Zeus leaped in to rescue his toy. Decks and water didn't faze Zeus a bit. And Ridge stayed dry as a bone.

Still, Voodoo was his partner, and Ryder willingly dove into the water with him. No worries.

With precautionary leads attaching the dogs to their handler's belt, Voodoo and Zeus trotted happily along, sniffing at the air that was growing heavier with moisture.

A storm was rolling in.

They were two miles down the road. Another two, and they'd reach their Winnebago—the word used for any RV where he grew up in Australia—tucked under the sweeping branches of a walnut tree. About the size of an extended delivery van with enough headroom for walking around, these campers were a little tight inside for a guy his size to maneuver around but provided the basics well enough.

A farmer had rented them the spot for camping during the weeklong K9 trials.

Privacy and space were key here. It gave the dogs a rest from the crowds.

Hotel rooms were scarce in the village. Many of the attendees were staying in rooms rented out by local families. With the dogs, Ridge and Ryder didn't think that was a good idea. They were better off out here with the fields around them, where their K9s could exercise to help work off their excess energy.

It was a picture-perfect landscape that offered some comfortable downtime without the worries that the dogs would bark and wake everyone. The operators wouldn't have to shoo away people who wanted to put their hands too close to the dogs' sharp teeth.

Security working dogs were *not* pets.

Ryder and Ridge had each rented an RV. They were comfortable enough. The July days here were in the high seventies. The nights in the fifties. With a campfire crackling, they'd been comfortable and happy.

A storm was heading in. That might put a damper on tomorrow. Though, the contest wouldn't be called for rain. The K9s had to perform just like the operators did—no matter the weather.

When Iniquus sent them in for search and rescue

in disaster zones, the weather was dependably shite. They trained for it. Expected it.

A motor rumbled behind them.

Ridge looked over his shoulder as they moved off the road. "It's your girlfriend."

Ryder didn't turn his head. He'd wait and see what happened next. Not much cover out here on the country road. Nowhere to run, nowhere to hide. He didn't get the vibe from her that she was assassin material, though.

"Hey, guys." Her window was rolled all the way down, and she was barely inching forward. "Need a ride?" She had a lovely smile.

Obviously American from her accent.

"Thanks," Ridge said. "The dogs are covered in mud. We wouldn't want to get your vehicle dirty."

"It's a rental. I don't mind." She looked directly at Ryder as she said it. She wasn't flirtatious at all. Friendly. He still couldn't place her, though it was starting to bother him, because—even with the beard, glasses, and hat—she seemed to know him.

"The dogs are still riled from all the excitement today," Ryder said. "Better we should let them work that off, hey?"

"Oh." Her face turned serious as she offered a nod of understanding. "Yes." Her bright blue eyes lacked the hard edge that would cue military-style training. She looked…innocuous was the word that came to mind. He'd guess she had some desk job somewhere and looked at computer screens all day. "Okay. Well, I'll see you in a little bit then." She finger waved and headed down the road.

"She'll see us in a bit?" Ridge asked.

"Dunno, mate."

"Did you tell her where we're camped?"

"Never spoke to her." Ryder wasn't carrying his phone to snap a picture and send it back to Washington, DC, for their operations commander, Bob, to run through the Iniquus AI systems. This contest was explicitly and purposefully in a cell tower dead spot.

It was meant as a security measure.

In order to attend, each person—contestant or spectator—had to sign an agreement stipulating that no photography or video would be taken at the competition.

Professional video of individual K9 runs would be provided to the handlers at the end of the contest. The handlers could use the information to study for fine-tuning their K9's training. If the videos were impressive, the tapes would be placed in the dog's file along with his vet record, certifications, competition scores, and other information relevant to the job.

Keeping tight hold on security was paramount since these K9s were the best in the world, heading for sale to world tactical facilities, including the US special forces. If the K9s had their name, image, command language, hand signal record, skills, and limitations available for study on the web, that created risks for deployed teams.

In his time with the Australian Commandos—tier-one special forces operators—Ryder would never publicly use his K9 partner's name while working where the enemy was listening. It just wasn't safe. Hence the personal command language Ryder had developed for Voodoo.

Ridge bumped Ryder's arm and nodded.

Ryder changed his vantage point. The mystery

woman was turning in on the farm road that led to their campsite. "She seemed nice enough." Ryder shrugged.

"You're usually in hot zones and not working close protection," Ridge said. "'She seemed nice enough' can get you killed. What did Voodoo think about her?"

"He paid close attention. Could be that he sensed something there. Could be she rubs sirloin behind her ears. We weren't close enough for me to tell. If you're frightened, mate, I could hold your hand."

The walk from that point was a silent one.

Both operators watched their dogs for signs.

Zeus and Voodoo loped along with long tongues, seeming to take their new-found celebrity in stride as they climbed the elevation toward their camp.

There was her car, right next to their Winnebagos.

Ridge lifted his chin. "Company."

"I see."

"Someone sent her to us specifically." Ridge pitched his voice so it wouldn't carry with the breeze that was kicking up.

"Agreed." Now that the sun was going down, Ryder pulled off his sunglasses. Tucking the earpiece into the neck opening on his shirt, he spun his ball cap around to wear it backward.

"She's got the campfire going."

"Hospitable. Maybe she's got steaks to toss on the barbie." Ryder had been kidding, but as they approached, he noticed that she'd spread what looked like dinner on the folding table he and Ridge had been using as an outdoor kitchen.

"Hey there!" she called over her shoulder as she opened a food container, smelled it, then arranged it with the others. "I ordered this from a cute little mom-

and-pop place on my way in. It smells delicious. It's still steaming hot."

Ridge and Ryder advanced toward the fire circle. Ryder noticed she had a tarp and tent on the ground next to her car. It looked like she thought she was moving in.

She put her hand on her chest. "Sabrin." As if that explained everything.

"Okay," Ryder said to Ridge. "I'll let you sort this. I'm going to get cleaned up and get Voodoo fed."

Ridge ducked his head and raised his brows. "We talked about stones."

"You've got Zeus with you in case you need backup, mate." He looked toward his RV with its external antennae. "While I'm in there, I'm going to get on the satellite phone and see if this isn't a care package from home." He smacked a hand on Ridge's chest then lifted it toward Sabrin. "G'day. I'm just going in to get out of my wet togs."

"That's fine. You look confused. I guess you haven't gotten a message today, but I'm here because of Honey."

Ryder paused with his hand on the Winnebago door. "Honey, yeah?"

Honey Honig was an Iniquus Panther Force operator; his specialty was hostage negotiations.

"He asked me to pair up with the short-straw." She looked directly at Ryder. "I guess that would be you."

Ryder looked across at Ridge. At six foot three, the two men were almost exactly the same height. "How do you figure?"

"Ridge bested your score at the competition today." She skated a hand out as if to soothe any wound. "Not to say that your score isn't stellar. I mean, you came in second. And not a very distant second. Hmm." She seemed to try to change from that line of thinking. "You're wet. Why don't we talk when you're cleaned up?" She tipped her head to the side and did a little lift to her shoulders.

Ryder bobbed his head toward her, then he sent Ridge a glance. "I'll be out in a jiff."

Inside, Ryder's RV was efficient, modern, and comfortable. It had a queen-size bed across the back that was just long enough to accommodate his height if he lay at an angle. That left a wide corner, plenty of room for Voodoo to curl up with his blanket.

Even though a bunk could fold down over the foot end of the bed, running longways down the RV, it was too short for either Ridge or Ryder to sleep on comfortably. Besides, it would never do to have both dogs together in such tight confines. The last thing they needed was a fight to display dominance of the RV.

The two Winnebagos had worked out fine this week.

Ryder clicked on the automatic hot water heater in the micro-bathroom and signaled Voodoo in to get a spritz from the hose to clean his muddy paws. He'd feed Voodoo, then jump in the shower.

Feeding Voodoo was a bit of a trick.

When Voodoo was brought to Iniquus, along with Zeus and a dozen or so other dogs, it was to make sure they were safe. The prison where they'd worked was destroyed during a kidnapping rescue mission of one of Iniquus's Strike Force members. Voodoo was still a puppy. Food at the prison had been scarce, and Voodoo had learned to fight for survival. Voodoo's relation-

ship with food was the only dark place that remained
in his psyche.

Ryder had worked to get Voodoo's territorial re-
flex over his food bowl calmed. Still… Ryder had to
be cautious. Voodoo would never eat except from his
bowl. He never scavenged. But once the kibble hit his
bowl, he could turn vicious quickly. Ryder never fed
Voodoo around other dogs. He certainly never fed Voodoo around other people. Even Ryder had to be careful
around Voodoo's teeth at mealtime.

"Feel better, mate?" Ryder asked as Voodoo stepped
back into the hall space. "No more grit between the
toes?"

Responding to a hand signal, Voodoo walked over
the towel to dry his paws.

Ryder fastened the lead to Voodoo's collar. In a very
calm voice, he said, "Time to tuck in, yeah?" He slowly
pulled the bowl from the cabinet and placed it on the
counter. "Sit tight." Ryder opened the bag and scooped
out the kibble. Ryder could feel the strain from Voodoo as he fought against his past to do the right thing,
sit and wait for the signal.

Ryder carefully laid the bowl on the ground as he
stepped into the shower. "Tuck in," he said in a happy
sing-song voice.

As Voodoo leaped forward, Ryder slid the shower
door closed.

Ryder peeled off his cold, damp clothes that clung
to his skin.

While the shower water was adequately hot, the tank
was small. Ryder was used to getting cleaned up while
out on deployment. Just enough water to get damp,
then with the faucet turned off, a good scrub with the

liquid soap head to toe, a final spritz to clean the suds off, and call it done.

Ryder opened the shower door just enough to make sure that Cujo was gone. Voodoo was back to his loving self before Ryder exited to dry himself off. He turned and looked out the front window. There was Sabrin, a pack hugged in her arms, wide-eyed and blinking at him as he stood there, towel in hand, full monty.

Chapter 3

Sabrin

*H*ooboy.

If she'd had her druthers, Sabrin wouldn't have seen Ryder naked.

And worse, Ryder wouldn't have seen her standing there, mouth agape, staring in through the windshield at him.

Just how was she supposed to scrub the image of Ryder's body from her memory?

Okay, sure, when he was hefting himself out of the water at the competition, she might have let her imagination run a little wild, allowed a stray fantasy a moment of attention. Because, honestly, what woman wouldn't?

The Iniquus uniform compression shirts didn't leave much to the imagination. Those shirts were explicitly chosen—Sabrin would surmise—because they displayed the strength and athleticism of the operators who wore them. The broad shoulders, the defined pecs...the washboard abs.

Rock hard.

Mmmm—that's not a good thought, don't think "rock hard." Don't. Just...move on to something different.

Sabrin picked up her newly purchased flashlight. She momentarily stalled, looking down at it, lying in her curved fingers, noticing the length and the heft. She exhaled through pursed lips, set the light aside, and rummaged through her luggage for absolutely no reason other than she needed to get her head screwed on straight.

Not head. And *no* screwing.

What the heck was wrong with her?

She closed the lid on the case.

Not everything had to be a double entendre. Sabrin could just have a normal thought.

She was here in a professional capacity. *Act accordingly.*

This had never happened to her before—seeing a colleague naked.

Not true, Sabrin reminded herself. She'd seen plenty of her female colleagues unclothed over the years in the locker rooms.

Women, though, had never done anything for Sabrin's libido.

Reaching around the back of her case, Sabrin tugged at the zipper that didn't want to budge.

Ryder, though...

Sabrin pushed down at the corner with her left hand, and the zipper started to slide.

She was an adult woman who had seen many, *many* men's bodies in her private life.

Okay, not *that* many. But certainly *some*.

Granted, none of those men had bodies like Ryder's. *He* was sin on a plate.

And, okay, it had been a while.

So maybe her hormones had gotten a heads up.

Nope. *Remember? Not doing double entendres?*

No heads were up.

His "head" was down.

Her head was…short-circuiting.

She raked her fingers over her scalp. Pulling the elastic band from her dark brown hair, she gave the natural waves a shake, then scraped the strands back into a new ponytail.

Ryder had a beard. Focus on *that*.

Beards were not Sabrin's thing. In fact, she actively disliked them. After a friend of hers had told her how erotic it was for a guy to make love to her with a full beard—how it had felt on her sensitive skin—Sabrin had been curious. So when Sabrin met a bearded man that she clicked with, she'd overcome her visual distaste and started dating him in the hopes that her experience would be equally "mind-blowing" as it had been for her friend.

It had *not* been.

Actually, for her, it was scratchy and unpleasant.

Beard rash, she discovered, was a thing.

Sabrin moved the bearded guy from lover to friend-zone.

He was nice enough, and he made really good lasagna.

After that, Sabrin crossed "bearded men" off her list of things she wanted to experience.

Broad chest, Adonis thighs, and the quite magnificent…yes. Sabrin cleared her throat, well *that*, notwithstanding, she didn't need to replicate past sexual disappointments by experiencing a beard, again.

Case closed.

No need for further speculation or fantasy.

She smoothed down her shirt. Good? Yes. Good.

Sabrin was thrown off; that was all. This morning, she was picking up her suitcase in Bratislava, the capital of Slovakia, getting ready to surprise her grandmother, Babka, with a birthday visit when she got a call from her superior. She was needed for a mission with lives on the line.

She'd agreed to forego her vacation and help—of course, she did.

Lives over birthday cake—a no-brainer.

The intelligence on this case was thin so far. The one thing that was crystal clear was that—*emphatically*—there could be no governmental fingerprints on her involvement. She was here on vacation. That was it.

To that end, there were a couple of Iniquus operators on the ground, over the border in the Czech Republic, just an hour or so northwest of Babka's house.

Iniquus was a private security group. Squeaky clean. Dependably good at what they did. One of them—the short straw—would help her develop a cover as she followed her orders.

Ryder didn't have a short straw, that was for sure.

We weren't going there, remember? Lives on the line…

In this case, the short straw meant that Sabrin could

have the number two man at the competition at the end of today. After reviewing the qualifications of the K9s they were handling, Sabrin had decided that Zeus, the more mature K9, the one with more operations under his collar, would come out on top.

She'd bought the hot pink water bottle to signal to Ryder that she'd arrived, but he looked decidedly past her as she'd tried to acknowledge him.

It seemed she was a surprise package.

When Ryder emerged from the RV, Sabrin slammed the trunk shut and rounded her car. Brushing her hands together as if to remove some dirt, she squared her shoulders and plastered on a professional nice-to-meet-you smile.

Ryder's face was unreadable.

Sabrin guessed that was one of the reasons that operators often wore beards. They not only disguised their faces; they helped hide emotions. Good for poker.

She nodded at the tactical computer system in Ryder's hands. "Did you get through by satellite?" *Good, she sounded normal, professional, indifferent.*

"Yes, ma'am." Ryder set the computer on an auxiliary table that Ridge had set up.

There was a man's face on the screen. She didn't recognize him.

"Sabrin, this is Bob. He's Cerberus Tactical K9 Team Alpha's chief of operations." Ryder nodded toward Ridge. "And you've met our commander, Ridge Hansen?"

"I have. Thank you. Hello, Bob."

They pulled up the camp chairs, so they could all participate in the video call.

Zeus and Voodoo lay beside their handlers. Sabrin wanted to pet them, but she'd wait and ask later.

"Gentlemen, you've met our counterpart, Sabrin Harris. I'm glad she hooked up with you without any problems. Sabrin represents the State Department. She landed this morning in Bratislava for a family visit when she got tapped for this assignment." He focused on Sabrin. "Thank you for your willingness to switch gears."

Sabrin gave him a nod.

"She'll be getting her feet under her just like we are. Ryder, you and Voodoo will be partnering with Sabrin on this assignment."

"State is our contractor?" Ryder had changed into over-washed jeans that looked butter-soft. When he stretched his legs out to cross them at the ankle, Sabrin could see peeps of his tanned skin through the worn spots that had given way to frayed rips.

"Negative," Bob said. "Iniquus has a private contract paid for through a K and R insurance policy. This is Honey's show."

K-kidnap and R-ransom.

Iniquus was often hired by the four international insurance providers covering entities like universities and private industries to intervene when their people were snatched off the board.

Honey Honig—an ex-Delta Force operator who signed on with Iniquus after retirement from the military—was reputed in the intelligence community as one of the best hostage negotiators in the world.

If things went south, and he was unable to strike a deal, Honey had the backup of one of the operational forces at Iniquus to go in and tactically retrieve the hostages. Tactical was always a last-ditch effort. There were too many ways that things could go wrong.

Reclaiming a body was not the goal.

Besides Honey's work on negotiations, what Sabrin's involvement meant, along with Ryder and Voodoo's, wasn't apparent. Sabrin could help if translations were needed. She had a good command of local politics in Slovakia and customs.

Sabrin hoped that as Iniquus brought their team up to speed, she'd glean some much-needed information, as well.

In her job, the secrecy and compartmentalization were the pieces she disliked most.

For example, why was Iniquus being told that she represented the State Department when, in reality, she did no such thing?

Bob caught her eye. "For your information and comfort, Ms. Harris—"

"Sabrin, please."

"Yes, ma'am. For your information, Sabrin, we are speaking through end to end encryption."

"Thank you."

"K and R?" Ryder asked.

"K anyway," Bob said. A black German shepherd sat between his knees and was watching them on the screen. "We have no information about ransom demands. That doesn't mean they don't exist and are being held in someone else's hands."

"How many people were kidnapped? And how many of those are covered under the contract?" Ryder asked.

"Twenty-five international researchers, and the Slovakian driver. Four of them are under contract with Iniquus. Those four, of course, are our priorities. If

Iniquus can help the others, that's a bonus. For us, we're focused on two males." Bob picked up a piece of paper. "Aged twenty-two and twenty-four, environmental sciences graduate students. A female aged sixty, professor of environmental sciences, ornithology. Female aged thirty-six, assistant professor, environmental sciences, her focus is on changing air patterns." He laid the paper down. "All of the clients have outdoor experience. All are in good health with no life-threatening health conditions or life-sustaining medications."

"Ambulation issues?" Ryder asked. They needed to know if the victims could walk out of a bad situation.

"No known deficits." Bob emphasized the word "known."

In Sabrin's experience, these situations were fluid and bad things changed outcomes and exfil plans.

As usual, she'd plan for the worst and hope for the best.

Sabrin had felt her shoulders arch back at the last description of the female assistant professor. A female was often assumed to be innocuous by her gender alone. Authority, but not the top authority. Young, but not too young. Very "middle of the road." Nothing that would capture particular attention. Sabrin would bet anything that her involvement was over the thirty-six-year-old female. A possibility. Something had to be unusual here…or Sabrin wouldn't have been put in play; her superiors would have left this to the capable hands of Iniquus.

"This is where?" Ryder asked.

"They were last identified as being in the Tatras Mountains in northern Slovakia. According to satellite information, they are nowhere near there now." He scratched at his silver hair.

"I'm grabbing a map." Ridge stood.

"Do we know why they were in the Tatras, to begin with?" Sabrin asked as Ridge strode toward his RV. It was parked at a right angle to Ryder's, making a cozy camp set up with the fire circle in the middle.

"The researchers were participating in a study of bird migration and the impacts of climate change on their populations. The research group was placing data collecting apparatus in advance of the fall migration cycle."

The Tatras mountains made a natural boundary between Slovakia and Poland to the north. The mountains were quite high, impacting the movement of air masses, so that made sense to Sabrin.

They sat in silence until Ridge returned with a map in hand.

"We believe the researchers were taken hostage on their bus," Bob continued as Ridge took his seat. "Politically, the Slovakian government is worried about too many cooks in the kitchen and told the United States government to stand down. Slovakia will handle the negotiations, tracking, apprehension, and rescue."

"We have only four Americans of the twenty-six on the research expedition?" Sabrin asked. "What are the other nationalities?"

"That's all the information I have for you. Honey will have more."

"How did the US government respond, other than to send us Sabrin?" Ryder asked. He looked down as Voodoo stood, turned, and lay back at his feet facing the opposite direction, tongue out, panting.

Sabrin noticed that Zeus changed his angle, too.

"Sabrin flew here on vacation to be with her family. She's not in the area as a government official. That should read clean since she bought her plane tickets a while back. Is that right, Sabrin?"

"Yes, about two months ago."

Bob leaned back in his seat. There was tension at the corners of his mouth. "Look, the Slovakian government understands that insurance companies and security firms exist and that our respective countries have little control. The request to stand down was sent to Washington. I'm sure the Slovakian government hopes for a trickledown effect—that Washington would pressure any entities like us to stay away." He raised his eyebrows as he inhaled deeply. "In any case, the Slovakian government would perceive any action on our part to be aggravating to their handling of this situation. We certainly don't want to be a disruptive force, and we still have contractual obligations to the university." He focused on Ryder. "You should be aware that's the case and stay as clandestine in your operation as possible. Trumped up charges are always a possibility to get you out of their hair. It becomes problematic all around if either you or Sabrin lands behind bars."

"Roger that," Ryder said.

"Ryder, you have your Australian passport?" Bob asked.

"I do."

"You'll leave any American identification or papers with Ridge to bring home. You'll be traveling on your Australian identification. You can work out with Sabrin what your back story is and how you two became a couple." He turned to Sabrin. "State said you two would be traveling as a romantic couple, is that correct?"

Sabrin cleared her throat. "Yes, while I have a reason to be in Slovakia, my introducing Ryder to my family gives him a better cover than his just deciding to show up. It safeguards our working together. When presented with this scenario, I concurred."

"And the official American stance?" Ridge asked. "State sent us Sabrin. Why did they send Sabrin?" He turned toward her. "No offense meant. I'm trying to understand the terrain. Your being attached to Iniquus efforts is a little unusual."

Sabrin sent him a tight-lipped smile. She'd like to understand her involvement, too.

Bob said, "Our government respects the sovereignty of Slovakia."

"And our government sent us Sabrin," Ridge repeated.

"Sabrin is here to surprise her grandmother for her grandmother's ninetieth birthday. It's been on the books for months. She's bringing her *boyfriend* Ryder Kelly, who had been over the Czech Republic border with his K9 at a dog contest. Now, they're going to visit the family and take a lovely vacation, hiking, and camping as they explore."

"Got it," Ryder said. "And Honey?"

"Will be wheels down within the hour. He prefers to work in the same country where the hostages are held. He can get a flavor for what's happening around him, and that makes a difference. You will be communicating with him over encrypted channels as we're doing now. You will not be meeting up with him in person."

"Roger that," Ryder said. "Who's in my chain of command?"

"Honey."

"All right." Ryder pulled off his ballcap, ran his hand through his wavy brown hair, then put the cap back in place. "So we sit tight?"

"For tonight. Tomorrow, I understand, is the birthday party. Is that right, Sabrin?"

"Uhm, yes. A dinner. Should I still go?"

"We'd appreciate it. That way, your family knows why you're around and can back you up if you run into legal issues. Tell them your plans to tour and enjoy natural Slovakia. They can let you know if anything is happening locally that you should be aware of as you head out to the woods."

"Right. That's right." She nodded vigorously. She was going to have to bring Ryder to meet her family.

A first.

They'd read into it.

Hooboy.

Feign attraction and a relationship with this bearded man? She could certainly do that if it meant helping to save lives.

Even if it complicated her own. Right?

Chapter 4

Sabrin

"Lots of bordering countries—Poland to the north, Hungary to the south, Austria…" Ridge said, looking down at the road map he'd spread on his lap.

Bob chewed his upper lip as if contemplating, then nodded. "No indication that they crossed any of them. But as you know, we never say never."

Sabrin quirked her head. "You know for sure the bus's disappearance is a kidnapping, not simply the bus being late, an accident of some sort?"

"Yes." Bob leaned forward again. His face took up the whole screen; she could see intelligence and sincerity in his eyes. And concern. He knew there was something off about her attachment to Iniquus. She could see that he had questions of his own. Expectations that she'd be forthcoming.

Even if she were willing to, she had nothing to share.

Though Bob was obviously from a military background, he had an inclusive, warm way of speaking. It was quite family-like—nice. Sabrin felt enfolded into the team and not like the sore thumb she'd assumed would be the case. "Ryder," Bob said. "I need you to bow out of tomorrow's competition, make it reasonable and aboveboard. Got it?"

"Wilco."

"We'll have you keep the RV as you head to Sabrin's grandmother's birthday party. Then you two can use it camping, keep you out of the hotel computer systems, keep up the vacation feel to your roving around." Bob turned his focus on her. "We wish your grandmother many happy and healthy years to come."

"Thank you." Sabrin watched both Ridge and Ryder focus down on their dogs.

There was a new alertness to them. Both K9s stared out over the field.

Sabrin wondered if there might be deer or farm animals that had moved into the dogs' awareness.

Ridge lifted his chin toward her. "Is anyone meeting you here?"

"Me?" She shook her head. "No."

Ryder reached out for the laptop. "Bob, I'm putting you up until we have this sorted. FYI, there's a storm moving into the area. It might affect the satellite connection. We'll reach out when we can."

"I have nothing more. You'll be run through Honey and Panther Force," Bob said. "Good luck to you both. Out." The screen went black.

Ryder took the laptop inside, chirruping for Voodoo, who tagged at his heels.

When Ryder emerged again, Sabrin noticed that he left the door open an inch as he moved his chair in front and sat down.

Ridge did the same with Zeus at his RV.

Sabrin turned to scan where the dogs had focused. Now she could see the roof of a car heading their way.

Company.

But who would be driving through a field out here in the middle of nowhere?

Whoever they were, it was best if the group wasn't sitting here staring at them as if primed for a fight. Natural. Calm.

She stood and walked over to the table. "I mentioned that I ordered some food on my way out here. I thought you might like to experience cultural cuisine instead of what I imagined you have planned for dinner. What did you have for tonight? Steaks and potatoes?"

"Pretty close," Ridge said with a smile.

"This looks like it's still piping hot." The restaurant had included little packets of utensils. Sabrin opened the plastic wrapper to get a spoon to scoop the food onto the thick paper plates that came with their order.

"*Das Sag*," Ridge said through the door, a German dog command that Sabrin recognized as "stay." Ridge sauntered over to stand beside her at the table. "It smells amazing. Thank you for thinking of us. What's it called?"

"It's *Moravský vrabec*, Moravian sparrow." She made a plate for Ridge. Sabrin assumed that the men's configuration meant that the dogs were out of sight and contained by having their handlers bodily in front of the doors. But, since the doors were not closed and latched, the dogs could arrive on the scene should they be needed. Maybe Ridge had gotten up because Zeus had better control under such circumstances.

Either way, in this part of the world, a woman serving the food to the men was more in keeping with customary roles. "This is a regional dish that I thought you might enjoy trying. It's not sparrow, though. It's actually pork. Here you see, it's served with the traditional dumplings and sauerkraut. And I have cold beers in the cooler." She pointed toward her car. "It's typical to have a beer with this dish."

"Nice," Ryder said, then lifted his chin toward her car. "I see you brought your tent."

"When my plane landed..." She let that thought drift off. "Why don't you start with this." She handed the plate to Ridge. "As you see, I bought plenty, but if you don't like it, you might want to go back to your planned dinner. I won't be offended at all."

The cars were getting closer.

"They're almost here," Sabrin said. "Should I keep pretending we don't see them?"

"Affirmative." Ridge picked up a utensil packet. "We'll just keep going about our business. I'm going to sit down with this. Can you serve Ryder, please?"

She sent a tight smile to Ryder, then picked up another plate.

"What is it you do for State?" Ryder asked.

What do I do for State? Nothing. "Mostly, my work is about clear communications." Yeah, that was a good line to take. "I do a lot of translation. Explaining how culture impacts word choice and actions." She felt a wiggle in her system. It didn't sit right with her to obfuscate with these men.

This sensation was a first. Playing a role was just part and parcel with her duties.

"Anyway, I arranged to rent my car. I was trying to get someplace close by to stay. There was nothing in the area. This is a very secluded place to have a K9 competition. I'm sure the organizers had their reasons." She walked the plate over to Ryder. "Would you like a beer?"

Ryder was looking over her shoulder. "How about you fix yourself something to eat and come sit beside me?"

She nodded and continued on. "Since I was told you two had RVs here, I stopped by an outdoor shop and bought basic camping gear and some extra outdoor wear on my way here." She gestured toward her tarp. "I was hoping you might invite me to join you."

"Storms coming in," Ryder said. "High winds. Heavy rains."

She put a dollop of each dish on her plate then balanced it in one hand. "I saw that on the radar on my weather app while I was still in Slovakia. It's the season for thunderstorms." Lifting a folding chair with her free hand, Sabrin stepped carefully as she made her way over to Ryder. Close enough to look like a couple. Positioned, though, in such a way that she wouldn't be in either Ryder's or Voodoo's way should this car turn out to be a problem.

But why in the world would that be the case?

"My iPhone doesn't work out here. I didn't bring a satellite phone with me." Sabrin settled back in her chair. "I hadn't seen a need when visiting my family." She lifted a hand. "All that's to say, I haven't looked at the weather since this morning. If the storm rolls in, my back up plan is to sleep in my car." She stuck her thumb in her mouth to clean away the drip of sauce she'd picked up from the plate. "Mmmm. So good. I think you'll like this. I hope so." She glanced toward the RV door, where she could hear Voodoo whining to get out. "Going forward with the mission, I figured either you'd have working comms, or I could buy what I needed once we got into Slovakia. I didn't want to purchase anything that would seem…unnecessary." She shoveled a bite into her mouth and held a hand in front of her lips, so she could speak before she swallowed. "Good thing you could communicate with your base, though, or my being here, even with dinner in hand, would seem odd." She looked over as the car came to a stop.

Four men. Big men.

The only weapon she had on her was a knife she had in an ankle holster under her jeans.

"If the weather isn't as bad as it looked on the Doppler," she said. "I'd rather not sleep in my car."

"Not much of a car," Ryder said as the men got out.

She shrugged. It got her from Point A to Point B. She'd chosen a small car to get around the city with ease. Sabrin hadn't considered needing to sleep in the car when she reserved it last week.

"Hello!" one of the men said in Slovak, looking directly at her.

She lifted her chin. "Hello."

"The old man said he was renting camping space to some Americans down here."

Sabrin translated. Neither operator gave a response. She picked up her fork and took a bite of food.

"You're here for the dogs?" he asked.

She translated.

The men nodded as they ate.

"I like dogs."

She didn't translate, and she didn't respond.

"It's polite in this part of the world to welcome people to come, sit."

"We're eating dinner," Sabrin said.

"I see that." The man tipped his head at her. "We've just gotten up from the table. Now we drink. We will share." He lifted a bottle of vodka and gave it a shake of enticement.

Sabrin translated, then switched to Slovak, "We don't drink, but thanks anyway." She translated that back to English.

Neither operator had said a word. Just quietly ate their food.

"What kind of man doesn't drink?" he asked.

It was strange, Sabrin thought, that none of the other men spoke to her or to each other. It made this guy the leader. The leader of what?

Maybe just the town thugs.

They felt like bullies, trying to pick a fight. This guy wanted Sabrin to translate the taunt. It was emasculating that Ridge and Ryder would depend on a woman to do their translations and then to add in that they were unmanly not to drink? In this part of the world, that would end in fisticuffs, especially if booze were involved.

Drinking here was a sport. The liter per person per annum was higher than almost anywhere in the world.

Sabrin took another bite.

"What are you doing here all by yourself, little lady?" He went for a different tack.

"How is it that I'm alone?"

"The old man said he rented to two Americans with their RVs. You just showed up. I was watching you up at the dog contest. All by yourself." He nodded back to her tent. "And you don't have a warm bed." He put his hand on his chest. "I have a very comfortable bed. You are welcome to share it with me."

Again, the man was trying to rile the operators. Why?

She chose not to translate. Instead, she put her hand on Ryder's knee. With affection in her eyes, she looked at him, then back to the leader. "You're mistaken. I have a warm bed tonight. I bought that tent because we might be doing some camping this week. I wanted to practice getting it set up to make sure all the pieces were there and that there was no manufacturer's defect. Let it air out. But then, as you said, the storm is coming in. So I changed my mind." As if on cue, thunder rumbled off in the distance.

She told Ridge and Ryder in English the gist of what was going on.

That the man here was speaking to her in Slovak, that didn't mean that he or one of his cohorts didn't speak English. They might be holding back to hear what was said between them when the operators thought it was safe to speak freely. Surely, the Iniquus men knew this. But Sabrin made sure to call Ryder sweetheart so they'd be cautious.

"Even so." The leader put his foot on a tree stump and leaned his forearm onto his knee. It made his jacket swing open, and she spotted what could be the grip of a pistol at his hip. "An RV is no place to be in a storm such as this." As her gaze drifted down to his waist, he pulled his jacket forward to cover his weapon. The move was graceful and nonchalant. So he hadn't been threatening her by showing her that he was packing. He'd made a mistake. "The wind," he gestured widely, "it can blow an RV right over. My four walls are stout and strong." He waggled his eyebrows, so she knew this was a metaphor.

Men could be so gross.

"I can take good care of you there."

Laughter twitched on his friends' lips.

She turned to Ryder. "Delicious, huh? Can I get you some more?"

"Thank you," Ryder said.

She set her plate in her chair and took his plate in her two hands, bending down to give him a kiss. He accepted it with no surprise and no hesitation. It looked natural.

His mustache prickled against her lips. Yup. That facial hair was an excellent deterrent to getting her panties in a bunch over her new colleague.

If only she could scrub the memory of him fresh from the shower from her mind.

Focus!

These guys wanted something.

A conversation? Information? A fight? Her? It wasn't readily apparent. Sabrin liked the way the operators were handling it, though. Just not engaging. She'd follow suit.

As she filled the plate, the man tried again. "You're too pretty for that caveman. You should come drink with me."

She looked over her shoulder at him. "My doctor said I shouldn't drink." She touched her stomach then walked over to Ryder with the plate. "It's bad for the baby."

"What was that?" Ryder mumbled under his breath, then said louder, "Thank you," as he accepted the plate.

"He's inviting me into his bed." She picked up her plate and retook her spot.

"With me right here?"

She swirled her fork into the sauce. "He doesn't think I'll translate what he's saying." She smiled indulgently at him, putting as much warmth and love into her eyes as she could. She took her napkin and wiped some sauce from his whiskers.

Beards were food traps. *Blech.*

"Thank you," he said for others to hear. He took the napkin from her hand and, as he wiped it across his lips, said under his breath, "They're right, though, aren't they? You're not translating. We're getting the cleaned-up version."

She turned to the leader. "Where is your mother? I'd like to ask her about the best place is to shop for baby clothes. It would be so nice to have something special for my little one from the beautiful Czech Republic. Perhaps a doll." She made a sour face. "Oh dear, the morning sickness just goes on and on, doesn't it?"

The dynamic shifted.

The leader guy said, "Enjoy your meal." They turned, got back in their car, and headed off.

"What was that you said to get them gone?" Ridge asked.

"I let them know I'm pregnant and morning sick."

Ridge's face took on a dark cast.

Ryder stiffened beside her. "Are you?"

"No, of course not—do you think the US would send a pregnant woman out on a field assignment?"

The men relaxed again.

"Still," Ridge said in between bites. "In case they come back, looking for trouble. I don't want you sleeping in that tent tonight."

Ryder hitched a thumb back over his shoulder. "There's an extra bed in my Winnebago."

She didn't want to get off on "damsel in distress" footing. She could hold her own. "So, you can protect me?" She batted her eyelashes, hoping it came off as sarcastic.

"Well, my dog can, anyway." Ryder's lips twitched into a smile. "My apologies in advance, though. Voodoo passes gas at night, and it's offensive."

Lightning flashed, and a few seconds later, the sky rumbled again.

"Take a look-see," Ryder said.

She set her plate down to follow him through the RV's door.

It was nice. Clean lines and cool tones made the space look much larger than it was. Her gaze moved over the bathroom, the kitchen, an eating area, and the queen-size bed.

Everything neat and clean. It smelled faintly like room deodorizer with a name like Summer Breeze on the label.

Ryder leaned over his bed and jerked down on the folding bunk.

It certainly looked more comfortable than sleeping upright in her car or in the tent with a thin mat under her sleeping bag, especially in a storm.

"Thanks, I appreciate the invitation." She'd be sleeping with him—well, in the same space as he was—after tonight, anyway.

Sabrin frowned as she looked out the window at the bruised sky.

Her mind was on the twenty-six people held by the kidnapper. Would *they* be okay in the impending storm?

Chapter 5

Ryder

When Ryder woke in the morning, he reached out to find Voodoo and give him a rub. His arm swung wide, no Voodoo. Pushing himself up on one elbow, Ryder looked up at the bunk where Sabrin slept. In the dim light that sifted through the window shades, Ryder found his dog had managed to get himself up there with Sabrin, curling into a ball in the little nest she'd made by bending her leg.

Sabrin circled an arm over Voodoo, holding him up against her.

Voodoo opened one eye to look down at Ryder, then thumped his tail happily. But he didn't budge from his spot.

Can't much blame you there, mate. That looks like a comfortable place to be.

Ryder scrubbed his palms into his eyes, scratched at his beard as he rolled over. At least with the new assignment, he'd be able to get rid of the beard. He lifted the edge of the shade to get a look outside without disturbing Sabrin's sleep.

The storm had raged last night. The ground was covered with branches and leaf debris. The heavy rains left the field a bloody mess.

Now the sky was still dim—the sun hadn't come up yet—the worst of the bad weather had seemed to have passed.

Inside the Winnebago, it was warm and cozy. Ryder felt at peace.

That was an interesting thought; peace hadn't been part of Ryder's personal vocabulary in over a decade. Well, at any point, really. He'd always felt like he needed to get up and get moving, heading somewhere. Doing something.

That "get on it" energy sprang him out of bed every day of his adult life.

This morning, with the droplets from the overhead leaves tapping hypnotically at the Winnebago's roof, Ryder was contented. He'd be willing to have a bit of a lie-in to listen to the rain.

And yet, Ryder reminded himself—throwing back his covers—there were things that needed doing.

The K9 contest continued this morning, and he and Voodoo had to make a good showing so as not to raise suspicions before they dropped out.

Ryder scooted to the end of his bed. He'd slept in sweatpants and a t-shirt. It was more than he liked, but he was sharing his space with a lady. The pants did an adequate job of concealing his morning wood.

Sabrin had slept in a shorts set, and now one bare leg wrapped over the top of the covers. Long and shapely. He bet it would feel nice to run his hand along the smooth-as-satin length up to her shorts. To wrap his fingers around her ankle and—

He shook his head. *Keep it clean, mate.*

Ryder quietly started a pot of coffee, then went into the tiny bathroom with his clothes in hand to get himself ready for the day.

With the door shut, Ryder's shoulders filled the space. But he wasn't going to be ungentlemanly for the sake of comfort and get dressed in the hall. That look of shock on Sabrin's face yesterday when she'd looked through the window right when he'd been standing there, after his shower…

Aussies didn't much think about being naked. Once he'd moved back to the United States, though, Ryder had had to get used to the prudishness of the Yanks.

Yeah, he'd seen her face flame red.

Yeah, he knew it had made her uncomfortable.

It didn't stop her from kissing him.

Line of duty, obviously.

Ryder put toothpaste on his brush and cleaned his teeth.

Funny thing about that kiss… When she'd bent down, it felt reflexive for him to tip back and accept it. Natural. It wasn't a "first kiss" kind of kiss. It was the kind that a lover would drop in offhanded affection. She'd played it well, he thought. It seemed to him that Sabrin was used to fieldwork, which made her work for "State" seem bogus. *Who was she really?*

He spat, rinsed, then stood to look himself in the mirror.

That kiss…

Ryder picked up his comb.

That kiss had made his lips buzz. He'd licked them to make the vibration stop, and he could taste her. Could *still* taste her these many hours later. Warmth had slid through his system, something he'd never experienced before. And he wanted more. Wanted to experiment with the sensations. It might even be the reason why, Ryder admitted to himself, he woke up this morning feeling contented.

Ryder didn't like that thought, so he buried it immediately. Lives were on the line. This wasn't a dating game. And even if it were…

One of the first cover stories that had popped into Sabrin's pretty head was that she was pregnant. That meant it was a thought that hovered near the surface, easily fished up to meet the need.

Ryder had met women like that. They were ready for rings and vows. They wanted to pick paint colors for nursery walls and thumb through baby name books.

It was all good.

Just as long as that kind of energy was directed at some other guy.

On the dating scene, if there was even a hint of the woman wanting to put down roots, Ryder was saying goodbye. He just wasn't the guy for *that* job.

After watching his dad's serial marital failures, Ryder wanted none of it.

So even though a chemistry experiment with Sabrin looked like it would be a good time, Ryder would take a pass.

Not that the invitation was being extended to him. In fact, Ryder got the impression that it was decidedly not.

Granted, that made him a little curious.

It wasn't like Ryder had ever found his bed cold when he needed a little heat.

Do you hear yourself, mate?

He didn't need to swipe right or swipe left here. She was State, and he was Security.

Twenty-six lives were on the line.

This morning, up at the contest field, the competitors waited in a barn. It was an okay barn. Nothing special. Clean.

Odd, though.

Ryder had been in plenty of trials and competitions over the years, and this was the first time he'd seen something like this organized.

It wasn't because of the rain—that was over.

Ryder decided that the organizers had something planned that was meant to surprise the competitors. Something that might give an advantage to those who had time to develop a strategy and see the shortcomings of those who preceded them.

Today, they were tracking a human scent trail, and there was supposed to be a takedown component.

Voodoo was going to have a blast.

There was nothing he liked better in life than to bite the bad guy.

Each team had their own stall here in the barn, piled with a bed of fresh straw, smelling sweet and clean. There was a camp chair for the handler and a bowl of water for the dog.

Spartan.

Dull.

Fieldwork, in Ryder's experience, was made up of

high-adrenaline peaks between long periods of boredom. A whole lot of hurry up and wait. It was good practice for both him and Voodoo to sit quietly.

There was a hazy space that Ryder had worked out. A kind of alert meditation. It reminded him of the snakes back at the station lying out on the rocks, absorbing the warmth, eyes half shut, restful but aware. Regardless of their state of apparent sleep, they were prepared for the time the hawk swooped down to grab them up as a late-afternoon snack. They'd get away, though. That shadow would pass between their eyes and the sun, and *zoop,* zero to sixty in a nano-second. They'd be off down a crack in the rocks.

Ryder eased his chair back, perching on the rear two legs, his head against the rough boards of the barn's wall. He could hear the crowds cheering in the distance. It seemed to swell upward; he'd guess that they were in some kind of indentation in the land.

For some reason, he'd imagined that they'd be trailing their mark through the woods. But no, it didn't have that kind of sound to the crowd.

Voodoo stood. Circled. Plopped down, then plunked his chin onto the toe of Ryder's boot. Voodoo didn't like lying around here much. He was a high energy dog who wanted to get going.

Ridge was in the stall next to theirs. He moved over to the half-wall that separated their stalls, crossing his arms over the ledge. "Save the best for last, I guess. My ass is falling asleep."

Ryder had a piece of straw in the corner of his mouth that he was idly chewing. He settled his chair back on all four legs, stood, and scuffed over to Ridge, so they could talk without worrying about being overheard.

Even if few people in this part of Czechia spoke English, there was no point in taking chances.

Ridge leaned in until his mouth was near Ryder's ear. "You've got a plan?" The two teammates hadn't had a good time to talk since Sabrin had entered the picture.

She'd set out some breakfast rolls from her cooler this morning. They'd warmed them up in the oven. Filled with meat and cheese, they were much more pleasant than the protein bars Ryder had planned to eat. The three had sat around the table, gobbling them down and drinking their coffee in silence.

Sabrin had been there. Not menacingly. Not obviously. Just sort of…constantly. Then she'd given them a ride up to the competition fields this morning.

"I've been going over the scene with the men last night," Ryder said.

Ridge nodded. "Me too. I wish Sabrin had given us a clear translation as things were unfolding, but I trusted she handled it fine. We weren't in a campsite, just set there at the edge of the tree line. How'd they know to show up that way?"

"Seemed like we were the destination, not the curiosity out the side window. I agree. The question here is, why?" Ryder asked.

"Could be that they were exactly as they appeared—some local hooligans wanting to rile things up who got the information from the farmer." Ridge paused. "That doesn't feel right."

"Could be they were Sabrin's contacts…?" Ryder offered. "After all, she said she was translating, but how could we tell one way or the other? I'd keep a wary eye out after we leave. No one will have your back." He glanced down at Voodoo, panting in the bed of straw. "We're going to bow out because of injury," Ryder said. "Today, since they're doing a scent and a bite, I'd like to give Voodoo a chance at getting a chomp in. Once he's had his good time, I'll let the judges know we're taking a yellow card."

Ridge nodded solemnly. "Sorry about this." He knew the amount of work it took getting the dogs ready for a contest like this. "I'm sure Iniquus will make it up to you."

"No worries." Ryder lifted his chin, acknowledging the sentiment behind Ridge's words. "Afterward, I'll have Sabrin drive us back to the campsite. I've already got everything loaded up. My plan is to head-on in order to get into Bratislava in time to clean up for the party. Maybe Honey will reach out, clear things up a bit."

Ridge lifted his brows as he ducked his chin. "It's important you make a good impression on Sabrin's family. You know they're going to think they're your future in-laws."

"As long as they feed me, mate. I'm happy to get my cheeks pinched."

Ridge nodded but looked like he wanted to say more.

"I'm just not sure what to make of her." Ryder canted his head. "Have you ever heard of State attaching to a private op like this before?"

Ridge pursed his lips as he shook his head. "Never. But Honey might have a different answer."

"Her language skills, connections, and a pretty solid cover story can be helpful," Ryder said speculatively. "Still." He rocked back on his heels. "It doesn't sit right."

"Just so you're aware going in that things aren't what they seem."

"So what you're saying is that I should Sharpie the consulate's phone number on my arm?"

"Can't say that's a bad idea." Ridge grinned. "But, you realize that the embassy is State. So she's their guy."

"I'm Australian. I haven't got anyone from my embassy tagging along."

"Ryder Kelly?" A man walked in from the open door.

"Here." He raised his hand high enough to attract the guy's attention.

The man called over, "I'll drive you to the competition site and explain the course."

Ryder reached a hand out to shake with Ridge.

"Safe travels. Good luck to you," Ridge said as they clasped hands.

"You as well, mate." Ryder chirruped to let Voodoo know they were on the move. As Voodoo came up beside him, Ryder clipped on his lead, and they followed along with the man who'd called his name.

They were led over to a pickup with the engine idling. A woman with a sparse bun sat in the passenger's seat. Hay lined the bed of the truck. "You can climb around back here," the man offered. His English was thickly accented.

"Alley-oop," Ryder said as he posted a hand on the side of the truck and sprang over the side. Voodoo leaped gracefully in, then sat beside Ryder, tongue hanging out, eyes bright, knowing he was heading toward a job. There was nothing that Voodoo liked better than a physical challenge. "Rough and ready, yeah, mate?" He gave his dog a wink.

Since they'd shrouded this event in secrecy, it was bound to be good.

After a short drive, they pulled up to what looked like a village constructed of particleboard. It was the kind of thing that they used to train for a high impact mission back when he was an Australian Commando. They'd erect a mock-up of the building they were going to infiltrate, and they'd practice it over and over until it was muscle memory—when they didn't need to count steps under his breath anymore, his arms, his legs, his eyes, knew exactly what to do. It made the team smooth. They were the tip of the spear, inserting with surgical precision.

It made sense to Ryder that the contestants had been sequestered away from this structure.

Even now, as he walked over the dirt paths strewn with straw to keep boots out of the mud, he was reflexively counting. Windows. Doors. Mapping what he thought might be inside.

He guessed that they'd give him a scent to offer Voodoo, and he'd have to clear the building. It was going to seem odd without a weapon in his hand. He'd already reached for his AK three times by habit.

On the other side of the building was a herd of sheep in what looked like a corral. Voodoo was very interested in those smells. His nose was in the air. His body was rigid with concentration.

Back on the station, Ryder had grown up with big powerful dogs. They were handy at catching snakes and shaking them to death. Good at keeping the predators at a distance. They used herding dogs for the livestock. Voodoo didn't have this background. Ryder didn't think Voodoo had ever had contact with any kind of livestock except for police equine teams. He put that on a mental list of things he wanted to work on with Voodoo.

All right. This was going to be interesting.

Ryder's gaze passed over the audience.

There was Sabrin at the front, waggling her hot pink Voodoo water bottle and cheering.

He raised a hand in her direction. In return, she blew him a kiss, and he heard, "Good luck, baby!" called out.

Ryder would have thought that play-acting was unnecessary until he saw that to her left and one row back were the guys from last night. So he touched his heart and gave her a boyfriend grin.

Ryder didn't like the look of those men. He was glad that he and Sabrin would be driving away today. They were the kind of guys who liked to muck things up just for the jollies of it. The kind of men who thought— while buttressed by a shot or two—that they could take on an operator and come out the victor.

Heck, weirder things had happened. A lucky punch, and you could lose your tooth.

Fight for the greater good against an enemy? Yeah, Ryder would put them on the ground.

Go at it to help some guy make a show of his gonads? That wasn't worth the scraped knuckles.

It wasn't a stretch to think that these guys wanted to make some show in front of Sabrin. Could be that because she spoke like a native, that the men were feeling territorial over one of their women and didn't want a foreigner on their turf. Ryder knew men like that. Men who hadn't evolved much from their caveman roots.

Pregnant. That was a great way to make them

back down. But either these guys didn't believe her or didn't care.

Standing here, looking objectively, Ryder could un-derstand it. She was a very pretty woman. A natural kind of beauty. Not the polished and manipulating kind of pretty that he'd dealt with when he was on a mission with Hollywood's Berlin Tracy.

There was a sexy lushness to Sabrin that…the image of her in his arms came full-blown to his imagination. Holding her against his body, her breasts pressing into his chest, palming the curve of her ass. He shook his head to clear that picture.

She was comfortingly womanly.

But there was more to her than that. She looked kind and intelligent with none of the aseptic vibes that he'd come to associate with women in the intelligence field.

State.

Nah. That didn't sit right. But neither did any of the other affiliations he could think of. There was no in-stitutional militancy about her.

Even Voodoo, who was aloof to strangers, was act-ing funny.

Ryder wondered if there was a man in Sabrin's life. People who worked for State—flying back and forth between continents—were often married to their jobs.

Bloody hell, he needed to get his head right about her. This was no way to set off on a mission.

Chapter 6

Ryder

"Ryder."

He turned his head toward the same man who had driven him to the site in the pickup.

An older man stood beside him and was saying things in short sentences. The driver was translating. "Here is your scent." He held out a PVC pipe with a stopper at the bottom and a screw-on cap. "You are to find and apprehend this man." He tapped the PVC. "*This* man and no other." His finger waggled side to side. "You'll be judged on time. However, there is a five-minute penalty for each person that your dog takes down who is incorrect."

Ryder stroked a hand down his beard. "All right. But these folks acting as decoys, they're wearing bite suits?"

The driver passed Ryder's question on, listened, and turned back to Ryder. "Yes, everyone has safety equipment. After the takedown, you will proceed west." The man spun around until the sun was on his back and extended his arm outward. He drew it back in and turned to face Ryder. "There's an agility trial and two walls. After you cross over the second wall, you will find the timer's stop button. Press that to end your task."

Ryder nodded.

"You may take your mark." He gestured toward a white line spray-painted on the dirt in front of the particleboard house.

Unleashing Voodoo, they stood at the line. Ryder could well imagine that those who had come before him would dip down into a runner's crouch, ready to sprint forward. Ryder did not.

Nose work was Voodoo's least favorite job. Learning to follow a scent was a perishable skill that they practiced daily. It took a lot of concentration.

If Ryder got Voodoo amped with go-energy, it would make it hard for Voodoo to focus.

Once Voodoo was presented with the scent, he'd know they were after a human, not a drug or an explosive.

Knowing there were decoys to get his dog in trouble, it was better to go at this slowly and methodically.

The horn sounded.

Targets stuck their heads out of various windows to watch them launch off the starting line. *Sorry, folks, not happening.*

Voodoo looked to Ryder for his green light.

Ryder knelt and took a moment to rub Voodoo's ears and talk to him soothingly. When Voodoo was concentrating better, Ryder pulled the cap off the tube and held it out for Voodoo. "Scent. Scent. Scent." He repeated while Voodoo had his nose in the tube, letting Voodoo know that he should absorb that signature for his next command. When Voodoo looked up, focusing on him, Ryder knew that Voodoo had the imprint. "Get it."

Voodoo's tail wagged.

"Get it" was the "seek, find, bite" command. It was oh so much more fun than "Find it," which was his search command.

Voodoo's nose was in the air.

Ryder looked toward the door, wondering what they might have in there to pull the dogs off their task. If it were him trying to make a dog forget their job, he'd put out some dog biscuits, some tennis balls, maybe a raw steak.

Voodoo took two slow paces forward, his nose in the air, his eye on an upper window where a man could be seen just inside the shadows.

Voodoo's head oscillated like a fan.

Ryder gave him space to do his work.

Voodoo took off at a lope rounding the building, heading right toward the sheep.

Bullocks.

The crowd was laughing.

Whatever, Ryder thought. He was going to throw this at the end anyway. Ryder wouldn't try to redirect Voodoo. Heck, let him have some fun with the sheep.

Voodoo snaked under the fence that penned the herd. Ryder was swinging his leg over when he saw Voodoo put his front paws up on a sheep's back. Man, if Voodoo got a bite in and tasted sheep's blood, this was going to go badly. He felt apprehension glisten over his skin and forced those thoughts out of his mind.

Voodoo was back on all fours, winding through the sheep. Ryder was glad that Voodoo would occasionally stop and put his snout in the air. It helped Ryder keep up, though the sheep leaned into his legs, pressing him off his direct path.

The smell was overwhelming, even for Ryder. He'd been years away from the scent of wet wool and lanolin. It was unctuous and sticky. Ryder knew it would cling to his clothes and his skin. Just the way to meet his new "in-laws" and make a good impression on Sabrin's family. To that thought, Ryder tacked on the clarifier so they'd solidify their cover story and have local support if it was needed.

Grabbing handfuls of thick fleece, Ryder tried to keep the sheep from grinding their hooves onto his feet. He was grateful that his steel-toed boots—that had weighed him down in yesterday's swim—were doing their duty protecting his toes today.

A vicious growl turned the sheep's bleats to screams of fear.

Voodoo had disappeared from sight.

Ryder thought that either his dog was being trampled, or he'd given in to the scent of sheep and gone wild, catching and killing his own supper. Ryder waded as fast as he could toward the noise.

The sheep, acting as a herd, panicked and ran for the fence line.

A man's yell went up. Pain and fear.

Bloody hell, someone was out there.

With the sheep riled, a man could easily be trampled

to death. Had the course designers not taken that into consideration?

Ryder fought toward the sound of growls and human pleas for help.

When Ryder finally got over to the man, he found his dog clamped on to a padded arm, trying to drag the guy from under a protective structure. A large bull's-eye, pinned to his shirt, indicated that he was indeed the mark.

"Away," Ryder said. That command had started off as a game to get Voodoo to put his toys away when he was a puppy, but Voodoo had interpreted it as the command for release and step back. Ryder went with it. And that was now his command for releasing a bite. "Away!" Ryder said more forcefully.

Reluctantly, Voodoo complied.

"Team Voodoo has found the mark in record time. He is our first and only K9 to not search the structure but to follow an air scent through the sheep straight to our target. Well done to Voodoo and his trainer, Iniquus's Ryder Kelly. They will now follow through to the obstacle course."

Ryder was pleased that they had an obstacle course next; it was Voodoo's second favorite thing to do. This would allow Voodoo to calm a bit from his predatory nature. Ryder pressed through the sheep, chirruping to get Voodoo to move with him toward the west and the trail.

Over the ramps, through the tunnels, leaping, jumping, balancing. Tongue draping down, slobbery, and pink. Tail wagging joyfully, Voodoo arrived back at Ryder's side.

Over near a tree, a man yanked a pulley to bring a

red disk up in the air, well above his reach. Oh, ho ho! This was a favorite Voodoo game.

Voodoo watched as Ryder gave him a hand signal, then he darted forward gathering speed, leaped into the air, and snatched the disk from where it hung a good eight feet off the ground.

Back at Iniquus, Voodoo held the record. He could jump nine feet into the air and could sail twenty feet from one side of a bush-filled median to the other.

Voodoo trotted back to hand it to Ryder, then looked from toy to tree and back again, as if asking Ryder to put it in the tree so he could do it again.

"Away," Ryder said. He accepted the disk and put it on the ground. He turned, and they sprinted toward the first wall.

Voodoo sailed over while Ryder ran around to meet him on the other side.

"Come on. Alley-oop!" The jumping command. There, the second wall was quickly in their rearview mirror.

This time when Ryder met Voodoo on the other side of the wall. Voodoo looked for his next command, and Ryder lifted his wrist in the air for just a nano-second, letting his hand droop down.

Up came Voodoo's paw.

"Are you hurt, mate?" It wasn't a question of concern. It was a command. A practiced trick that Ryder had worked on when Voodoo wanted to learn something new.

Voodoo hobbled forward on three legs, whining.

The crowd gasped and made empathetic moaning and clucking noises.

Voodoo, in his pitiful three-legged hobble, followed Ryder across the finish line. Ryder hit the stop button, then knelt and inspected the leg that Voodoo had kept aloft, dangling pitifully. Who knew that ruse would come in so handy? "Come on, lamby pie," another command. This one told Voodoo that Ryder would carry him, and Voodoo should rest easy across Ryder's shoulders.

Ryder strode toward the judge's table. Their score was top of the board.

Shaking hands with each of the judges, Ryder said he'd yellow card Voodoo.

Sabrin was by his side, helping with translations. Her worried hand rested on Voodoo's neck. She had no idea this was a farce. Her whole body held the tension of worry and pity.

Ryder hated to do this to her. But from her body language, no one would guess he and Voodoo were acting. He stepped clear of the judges' table as they set up for Ridge and Zeus's run.

When Ryder stopped to adjust Voodoo, Sabrin lowered her forehead to rest against Voodoo's as she rubbed Voodoo's ears. Her face was red, and there were tears in her eyes when she came up on her toes and kissed Ryder. This time it was a much longer, much more satisfying kiss than the peck she'd given him last night. "Let's find a good vet."

She reached her arm around his back, Voodoo relaxed across his shoulders, they walked toward her car together.

The tears and emotion were for Voodoo, he thought. The kiss *wasn't* for him, though.

Ryder scanned the area. Sure enough, there were

three of the men from last night, watching Sabrin's every move.

He pulled down his mirrored sunglasses. With hard eyes, Ryder sent them a very direct, very easily read Neanderthal message: *She's mine.*

Chapter 7

Sabrin

Every time Ryder wanted to speak to her, Sabrin pinched him and glared. It took three times until he got the message. If he couldn't tune in to her better, they'd be butting heads during this mission.

Too much was at stake.

She wasn't sure how to manage him; they didn't know each other well enough yet that they could dance without stepping on each other's toes.

They arrived at her car, and she fobbed open the hatch.

Ryder carefully placed Voodoo in the back, crooning to him, using words that were wrapped in a thicker accent than he usually used, words she didn't understand. If this was some kind of payback for her speaking foreign languages around him, then he was acting like a juvenile. If this was just how he spoke to his dog in a childhood love language, well, that was more understandable.

She made sure Ryder was watching her when she pulled the cellophane encapsulated wires, the size of a quarter, from her back pocket and laid it on her palm.

He looked down at it, stared hard, caught her gaze, and gave her a slight nod.

Hidden by the hatch and the bulk of Ryder's body, Sabrin slid the comms wire back in her pocket.

Along the way, someone had slipped it into her pocket. Obviously, they were interested in what she had to say.

With cell towers being ineffectual in this area, it meant the spy was listening in on a radio close by. Sabrin wanted whoever this was to think they were successful in hearing them, so she could cement her alibi. If she and Ryder could establish a clean image, whoever this was tagging along might pull their manpower back to use elsewhere, giving her team relief from scrutiny.

"Ryder, what *happened*?" She put her hands on his waist and tilted her head back to talk. "I saw Voodoo coming over the wall. He looked great all the way through the agility challenge."

"It's that same tendon." He pulled his hat off, turned the bill around backward, and put it back on, smooth and natural.

Sabrin felt hyper-aware of anything that could be read as "off." She felt eyes on her. It made her flesh crawl. She fought to keep herself from looking too stiff—a cardboard cutout, a caricature. She hoped her agitation would come off as concern for Voodoo.

Which she, for sure, was feeling. She looked down at him, lying there, tongue out, panting.

He didn't look like he was in distress. Dogs, though, could hide their pain.

Ryder slid his sunglasses off and hung them from the earpiece in the neck opening of his shirt. He followed her gaze down to Voodoo and waited for her to look back at him before he said, "You know the vet was worried we were pushing it coming here."

"Yes, but she said to watch for tenderness. You said Voodoo's been solid through the whole event."

"I guess that last bit was too much." His hands came down and rested on her hips, and she liked them there a little too much.

"Do we need to find a vet, or do you have a local name?" She looked toward the barn. "I can go back and ask for recommendations. Surely they know someone who works with athletic dogs."

"No." He pulled her into a hug. His head on a swivel, he was using the move to hide his search for prying eyes; Sabrin felt sure. "We know what this is. Voodoo is calm with his weight off the injury. We just let him rest."

"He hates that." Sabrin spotted three of the men from the night before, lacing through the field of uniformly parked cars. There were four men last night. One had to be sitting in their vehicle, acting as ears. She pressed into Ryder's left side to get him turned in the right direction; with his height, he'd be able to see better.

"Yeah." He tapped his thumb into her back three times then dropped a kiss onto her forehead. "Well, we were heading to Babka's house right after the finals.

This takes us out of the running." He released her, and she held out the keys to him.

"You were top of the leader board." She rounded toward the passenger door. "Something to be proud of."

"Ridge is running next. Zeus has this. He'll make the final rounds for sure."

"Would Ridge mind if we just took off for my babka's?" She popped the door and waited for him to get the hatch closed and get to his side. "Or should we wait to congratulate him?"

"Ridge and I talked about it while we were waiting for our round. No guarantee we'd make finals." He got in and slid behind the steering wheel, reaching down to adjust the seat back. "I told Ridge we wanted to get on the road as soon as we were done with the competition. He and I have said our goodbyes."

"Okay. Well, let's get the RV and get going then."

The drive was in silence.

When they got to the campsite, she reached her hand out to still Ryder. "Why don't we put the windows down and let Voodoo rest in the car. With Ridge still at the competition, we're here all alone." She used her sexy, come hither voice.

He squinted at her, trying to read what was happening.

She opened the door to give herself maneuvering space, reached down and unlaced her boots, then pulled them off. Her socks, her shirt, were next, and finally, she wriggled out of her pants. She searched each piece for additional listening devices. Planting only one meant you only got one shot; typically, when possible, more than one resource was optimal. An operator had to try to hedge their bets. The old adage was, "One is none, and two is one."

Ryder sat on the driver's side, watching her with curiosity and little else.

She'd admit it that hurt her ego a bit.

Well, he wasn't salivating and leering—so not a horndog.

Sabrin immodestly slid her hand around the inside of her underwear, then her bra. Tada! Bug number two.

The crew from last night had been right next to her through most of today's dog trials. They'd tried to make conversation, which she had mostly rebuffed. It had been loud with the cheering and whistles, so she didn't think it had come off as rude. She'd noticed that they'd tried to take advantage of the crowds bumping and buffeting. She thought they might be trying to plant a wire on her.

When she went to the field potty, she gave herself a once-over and found the comms in her back pocket. It was middle of the road when it came to technology. Cheap enough that they wouldn't mind if they never got it back—not top of the line in terms of stealth. This told her that they didn't think much of her spying chops. They didn't think she'd find it in time for her to protect her op. She bet that they believed she'd say something quietly to one of the Iniquus men that would blow her cover—done deal. A confrontation would be next on the menu—that or maybe the trumped-up charges Bob had referenced. Hiding drugs in her car, a call to the cops, that scenario could drag Ryder and her from the playing field.

America was told to butt out.

Sabrin was almost a hundred percent sure that the

Slovakian government had sent these guys to ensure that the US couldn't disregard that request. She'd run her thoughts by Ryder once she thought they were clear to speak freely.

She held up the comms she'd found in her bra. This one had been placed since she'd gone to the bathroom. What if she came back and changed her clothes? If her pants were in the wash pile, they'd hear nothing. The benefit of sliding it into her bra was that she'd probably keep the same foundation garments on all day.

These guys were smart enough, skilled enough to be problematic.

Ryder was following her lead and searched his clothes. He found nothing. Now he was down to his boxer briefs, sliding his hands around the inside, clearing…that area.

Sabrin focused very hard on Ryder's beard.

When she was a small child, one of her children's books was about a man with a beard that trailed over his potbelly down to touch the tops of his boots. A bird built her nest in his bushy beard and laid her eggs there. The man was very careful not to disturb the nest as he went about his day. The bird would fly around, trying to find where the man had gone so she could settle in and sleep. His beard kept the eggs warm. When the eggs had hatched, the mother flew back and forth, finding worms for her babies to eat. His beard was full of worms and hungry baby birds. Sabrin tried to imagine that was the case here. A beard full of worms, hiding a bird's nest. This effectively kept her mind from the salacious places it wanted to go as he pulled his hand from his boxers.

Her body was signaling, *I'm ready for some playtime. Let's do this!*

Those horny hormones could screw with her rational mind.

Be sensible. Be professional, she admonished herself.

What needed to happen now was that they get away from the comms and talk this through.

Sabrin climbed from the car and walked around to stand in the front. She looked over her shoulder and wiggled her hips.

Luckily, the bra and panty set she'd chosen this morning was as covering as a bikini she'd wear to a beach.

Ryder got out of the car.

She tossed a laugh over her shoulder and ran toward the trees. The trunks' height and the canopy's thickness would prevent radio waves from picking up their communications and would thwart anyone watching with long-range lenses.

Acorns and sticks pressed painfully into the soles of her bare feet. She stumbled forward, thinking about someone with a camera on them.

This scene needed to play out correctly.

Their walking into the woods in their underwear would look very suspicious. The surveillance team would know she'd found the wires.

Sabrin looked back over her shoulder to find Ryder laughing and jogging along behind her, not truly trying to catch her. There was no way in this world that if Ryder Kelly wanted to outpace her, he couldn't do that with ease.

Running was his job, not hers.

The second time she looked back, he held his hands out as if to catch her, his fingers wiggling like he was back on the playground in elementary school.

She pictured what this would look like from a distance. It was good. And as that thought crossed her mind, she tripped. Stretching her hands toward the ground to catch herself, she felt Ryder's arm slide around her hips, still tumbling, he wrapped his body around hers, and they rolled.

Ryder's shoulder hit, his back, his other shoulder, then Sabrin was under him. "Are you okay? Did I hurt you?" He was on his elbows, brushing the hair from her face, planting a kiss on her forehead.

Did *he* hurt her? Heck, he'd wrapped around her like bubble wrap. She hadn't felt a thing. Ryder, on the other hand, had taken the full brunt of them crashing down.

She sucked in a breath and exhaled the word, "Good."

"I assume you were running and playing a part. What's happening? Who planted the surveillance? How would they have targeted you? Why would they have targeted you?" he asked. His eyes searched hers.

She'd thought that Ryder had chocolate brown eyes, but that wasn't quite right. With him so close and looking at her like this, she could see the irises had flecks of gold and green. They were warm and intelligent. Intense.

Hooboy, was she glad that they played on the same team. Going up against someone like Ryder would be a daunting task and not something she would normally do in her job.

You couldn't pay her enough.

She wasn't foolhardy enough.

But they'd paired her with him. And that meant she was on the kind of mission that required the capacity of Ryder Kelly. With him by her side, was she up to the task?

Sabrin's legs bent on either side of Ryder, her thighs resting against his hips. She could feel him growing harder. It was normal, she reminded herself. His mind wasn't there, just his body. It was what male bodies did when they lay between a woman's thighs. "Uhm. We need to reconfigure." Her voice was much deeper and sounded much more sultry than she would have chosen.

"Yes, excuse me." He rolled again. It was like she was caught up in a wave; she just let him move and adjust.

They ended up with his back pressed against a tree trunk. She was leaned back against his chest, looking girlfriend-like. He combed his fingers through her hair and picked the leaves from the strands. "This isn't the way I imagined today going," she said.

He chuckled. "Agreed."

"We need a new plan." She didn't know what to do with her arms or hands. At least he'd put her on the outside of his thigh, so she didn't have Ryder's dick in her back. It was just there under her left elbow, though. So, she pulled her knees up and wrapped her arms around them, keeping her hands safely away from Ryder's body.

It was the kind of body that belonged on calendars filled with ripped guys, usually firefighters, and, of course, romance novel covers. The kind of body she'd always thought of as only found in one's imagination.

And yet, here it was, under her left elbow.

Twenty-six people with their lives on the line.

Sabrin conjured pictures of missions-past where things had gone badly. That instantly extinguished the flame that had flickered under her simmering libido.

"First, what needs to happen for Voodoo?" she asked.

"With those men seeing us as the couple," she stopped to put that into air quotes, "it's too late in the game to switch out to Ridge as my partner. I don't know that a K9 is required for our task. Perhaps we should wait for Ridge to come back, so he can take over Voodoo's care and get him home. I'm not clear about the trajectory of this situation until we hear from Honey."

"Voodoo's fine. That was a trick I taught him."

She spun toward him, suddenly ticked as hell that he'd played her emotions that way.

Sabrin's job required acting. Sleight of hand. Smoke and mirrors. Razzmatazz. How could she *possibly* be mad at Ryder for doing a good job at subterfuge?

Still, her face crumpled as she took an emotional hit of relief. Hell, she'd just spent the night spooning with the dog; of course, she was invested in his wellbeing.

"Hey." Ryder's voice was warm and held the hint of laughter.

She swatted at him as she blinked away the tears that laced her lashes.

"Hey, now." He cradled his hand behind her head and drew her into his arms. "I'm sorry. Okay? I'm sorry."

This was too intimate. And kind. She was messing up. God, she needed to get herself back into her professional mode. They were actors. This was a play. She sat up, winked at him, and said, "Got yah. I can do tricks, too." *Liar.*

Sabrin settled back in Ryder's arms. And to cover the move, said, "I'm sure they have eyes on us. But back here—"

"In our skivvies."

"—they shouldn't be able to hear us."

"Agreed. There's sunlight hitting a lens my four o'clock."

Sabrin forced herself not to search for it.

"Best guess, what's happening here?" Ryder asked. The dynamic shifted back to where it should be. A puzzle to be solved. "Who planted comms on you? I'm assuming it had something to do with our visitors last night and their close attention today."

The sweat forming under her arms was from the anxiety that she felt buzzing her system. Obviously, her antiperspirant wasn't up to its task.

Those guys.

She'd spent the morning with their encounter on repeat in her brain while trying to ignore their attention at the competition.

"Last night, the leader of the four spoke to me in Slovak."

"Okay."

"They addressed *me*, the female in the circle, and not you."

He wiggled around, sitting up straighter against the tree trunk. "Okay."

"We're in Czechia. They speak Czech here."

He stilled. She could feel his muscles tightening.

"A man doesn't come to another man's house—or in this case, two men's camp—and not address them at least to find out if they knew a simple greeting."

"So they were focused on you and knew you spoke Slovak. Do you speak Czech?"

"Yes. Well, a quick language lesson. Slovak is the official language of Slovakia. It's a West Slavik language and so closely related to Czech, Polish, and the Sorbian language of eastern Germany. You remember that the Czech Republic and the Slovak Republic used to be Czechoslovakia, and they separated in the Velvet Divorce." She paused. "Too much information?"

"No, I'm following. So it's like a romance language. I was trained to speak French as part of my tours in Africa. I can bungle my way through in Spanish and Italian."

"Right. And in Czech, it's a bit simpler because the Czech language has two forms, the colloquial and the literary. Slovak is close to literary Czech. That is to say, people who speak Slovak can pretty much understand Czech. But that isn't true vice versa. People who grew up after the split of Czechoslovakia in Czechia, many don't understand Slovak as easily. And I guess that's part of my point here."

"Point being, the languages were close enough that there's no way they were from Czechia. Because someone who spoke Czech would assume someone from Slovakia would understand their native language. And there's no way they didn't know you spoke the language because otherwise when they came into our camp, they would have looked Ridge or me in the eye when they first spoke, and they did not."

"Bingo."

"They had you marked. Huh. That's interesting. You have a read on why?"

"I have a theory. I'm a dual citizen like I assume you are after listening to Bob discuss your passports last night. I'm Slovakian and American. This time, coming into the country, I traveled on my Slovakian passport since I wasn't here on official business, and it's just easier. I come here to Bratislava frequently to work out of the American Embassy. When I do, I travel on my American papers. That might have given customs a heads up. But I had no idea at the time I left the US that I'd be asked to step into a professional role. For me, it was a completely innocent decision about the ease of moving through customs."

"Okay."

"I was calculating time frames." She bit at her cuticle. "My plane out of DC would have taken off a few hours after the US government was told to stand down."

"Commercial flight?"

"Yes. And I bought my tickets a month ago. But the Slovakian government wouldn't necessarily know that. Or know that yet. Or be able to access those records as it was a flight to London and a transfer to Wizz Air UK. I probably popped up a handful of red flags when I arrived. More so when I headed over the border right away and hooked up with Iniquus. Your security group is world-renowned for resolving kidnap and ransom cases. The Slovakian government wants the US to stand down—no mucking around in their business. One read on this situation is that they think Uncle Sam is pulling a fast one."

"When did State contact you and ask you to step in?" Ryder asked.

State never contacted her. "I got a call from my office when I was on a layover in London."

"So that was a clean communication. The Slovakian intelligence didn't pick up the phone call over their telephone surveillance. They might have flagged you at the airport and sent you up the food chain. How would they follow you here?"

"Easily. They have computerized gait identification at the airport in Bratislava. They pick out the time frame for my passing through customs. They send that through their AI system. The computer tracks me through the airport to the car rental. The car rental has a tracker on their cars through the GPS system. I didn't come straight here. I stopped to buy some appropriate clothing and supplies on the way. If they take us into custody and ask what that was about, you should tell them that you finally convinced me that—since you were so close, and I was here—you should meet my family. And you suggested we do some camping and hiking to see some of my beautiful country. I had agreed when I was in London. If that's the case, you should know my layover in London was from 5:00 a.m. local time to 6:30 a.m. local time. A two-hour flight plus one-hour time change, I arrived in Bratislava at 9:45 a.m. yesterday morning."

"All right. Got it. I called you at 7:00 a.m. my time, 6:00 yours, right before trials. It's not on your phone, though."

"I have a program that clears the phone's history. I can say it's part of my job's protocol if asked."

"So the car—"

"If they tracked me here, they'll track me back into Slovakia. I need to return the car as soon as possible. I don't know what they might have put on it or in it for surveillance."

"You think these guys are spooks for the Slovak Republic?"

"I can almost guarantee it. I had some other scenarios in my head…"

"But that was before the trackers."

"Exactly. I searched for the tracker the first time out

of habit. The one in my bra happened later in the day. I didn't feel either of them being planted on me. It speaks to their skill level."

"Since we're heading for your family's home, it's going to be hard to shake a tail." He paused for a long moment. "Any idea what you want to do about it?"

Chapter 8

Sabrin

Voodoo panted on the seat next to Sabrin as she drove.

Sabrin thought that was a pretty big vote of confidence from Ryder.

Up ahead, the RV—or Winnebago, as Ryder called it—led the way.

Other than not wanting to move Voodoo from car to RV in front of prying eyes, Sabrin didn't know why Ryder had made this choice for his dog.

Voodoo sat in her passenger seat with his quick release doggie seat belt on. He had spent the first half hour with his head out the window, mouth open, tongue dangling, looking thoroughly content.

Now that he'd had his fill of wind in the face, he had curled into the seat, one paw extended, resting on her thigh. Something about that touched Sabrin's heart. She didn't know much about dogs. Her mother was a cat lady. And Sabrin was never in one place long enough to have a pet of her own. Sabrin had read an article about dogs that said they had a sixth sense about people and could "smell a bad guy."

Sabrin felt like she had been assessed by Voodoo and accepted.

More than accepted, welcomed.

When Sabrin woke up that morning, after one of the best nights of sleep of her life, she found herself hugging Voodoo with Ryder standing there, coffee mugs in hand, looking bemused.

He'd called Voodoo down from her berth to go get some exercise in before the contest. How Voodoo had gotten himself up there with her in the first place, she had no clue.

Sabrin looked down at Voodoo. "You're stealthy. I'm glad you use your powers for good."

This morning, Sabrin had reached for the mug Ryder extended to her with a smile. But Voodoo's leaving was a loss—the warmth.

Remembering the scene, Sabrin reached out to scratch his ears. "Thank you, Voodoo."

Sabrin had always thought that she'd like a dog. Not a tactical dog. Not even a working dog, like a hunting dog. She imagined one that would curl up on the floor and sleep, maybe play some ball, or go with her for her morning exercise.

Yeah, this tactical dog world was *intense*.

The only things she knew about tactical K9s was what she'd overheard at the competition. The top performers at the contest would cost the dealers eight to ten thousand dollars, unfinished.

Sabrin thought all the dogs looked "finished" until she saw Voodoo and Zeus perform in the trials. Even she could spot the differences. The Cerberus K9s were polished; their rough edges honed.

To be honest, some of those dogs scared the daylights out of Sabrin. They were *ferocious*.

At the takedown task, where the K9s sailed through the air and bit into the protective suits of the "bad guys," Sabrin realized that some of the handlers had shock collars around their dogs' necks. The dogs were so into the bite that they couldn't be called off by voice command alone. Sabrin understood not wanting to put a hand near those jaws. The handlers would need a zap or three…or six. Zeus and Voodoo had looked disappointed and reluctant to release, but still, a command in a stern voice, and they released, ran back to their handler, and sat, ready for the next directive.

Zeus and Voodoo had garnered a lot of attention. The men had talked about them with lust in their voices. Sabrin wondered if that was why the operators put their dogs in the RVs last night when the four riffraff showed up. She guessed there was always the chance that someone wanted to steal the dogs.

Even with the bugs planted on her, that was still a possibility. How do you steal a tactical K9 from a security firm if not tactically? It could well be that Sabrin wasn't targeted by the Slovakian government when she flew in. She could have just as easily been targeted when she was waggling her hot pink Voodoo water bottle at Ryder yesterday. They could have put her on a "potential acquaintance" list and recognized her as belonging with the Cerberus team that night when they'd shown up at the fire circle.

If those men did try to take the dogs—well, how would that work if they succeeded? Voodoo and Zeus were champions, well known in the K9 tactical world. Ryder had told her last night that Iniquus was invited to be part of this competition. The Cerberus K9 stable trained different kinds of K9s—from search and rescue to security, to mission support, where the dogs jump out of the plane with their handlers and parachute into the fray.

Voodoo and Zeus were cross-trained for those kinds of jobs.

Iniquus Cerberus K9 set a high bar. They gave the competition gravitas, and every handler there wanted to watch the Cerberus operators work their dogs.

Neither Ridge nor Ryder had said that to her. Sabrin had overheard it from some guy from the US talking to his counterpart. They were looking for K9s to train for special forces. Mainly, they said they needed a nose and a bite. Sabrin would guess that meant that the K9s were trained to find a scent and to eat the bad guy.

The guy was bragging to his buddy that he could efficiently make his way through all of the dogs that were available for sale and cull out the ones he wanted in ten minutes flat, where it took most guys hours of hanging out with the dog to make the decision.

"Yeah?" his friend had said. "How do you do that?"

"Simple, I put on the bite suit and go hide in the bushes. They release the dog to come get me, right? Instead of the normal way of waving my padding at the dog to get them to aim for that part of me, I flick my hand out and bop them on the nose."

"What?" the guy had asked, stepping back, looking as incredulous as Sabrin had felt.

First of all, it seemed a dangerous thing to do. Sabrin had been startled by just how fast these dogs could move. How nothing seemed to be missed by them, even while the K9 was focused on a task. And second of all, hit the dog on the nose? That was awful. She couldn't imagine someone hitting Voodoo on the nose.

"No, not your nose, sweet boy." She rubbed her thumb between his eyes and over his head the way he seemed to like.

"When I hit their nose, it sets them back on their heels," the guy said. "They aren't expecting it. If they come after me angrier than ever, that's good. If they give me a little space while they try to figure out what's going on—as long as their posture is aggressive, growling and showing their teeth—I'll still consider them. But time and time again, I've seen them back up and give up. I need a killing machine."

"Bonk them on the nose," she whispered under her breath, filing that away as a possible tactical response as a coin toss in a dog attack. It might work to freak a K9 out. It might also power his aggression. She sent a side-eye to Voodoo. He was a killing machine.

Hard to imagine that as they rode peacefully together.

Still, she shouldn't forget it.

As the thought crossed her mind, fear washed over her. Cold and fizzy, it started at the top of her head and dowsed her whole body. Her hands shook on the steering wheel. She was in the car with a killing machine. It had seemed like the right call at the time...

Ryder made that call.

There had been eyes on them…

Well, Ryder had said that he'd seen sunlight glint off a lens. They might have been from binoculars or from a camera lens. She hadn't seen it. Sabrin wasn't sure she'd know what she was looking at, even if she had seen it. Fieldwork in an actual field wasn't what she did.

She schmoozed. She developed relationships. She listened. And she interpreted—languages, motivations, cultural norms.

Why had they sent her to find the short straw and partner with him in the field?

Sure she'd had training. But it was hypothetical training. Fights on the mat. Dummy sparring. She'd never done anything like chase after hostages on the heels of an operator. Her clandestine work was more about sitting near the right people at a dinner table and overhearing their conversations. Yes, if things turned bad, she had the skills to survive—to fight, to drive, to slide into the shadows.

But somehow… Yeah, she'd have to think about why exactly she'd been given this set of orders.

At any rate, here she was, heading to her grandparents' house when the whole family would be there for Babka's birthday, a man in tow. She did an eye roll.

Not just a man but the short straw. And his killer dog.

Ryder said Voodoo should stay with her for the drive, so she'd continued to look the part of significant other.

She had the feeling, though, that Voodoo was here in case something happened, and she needed to be protected. After all, he'd made her practice releasing Voodoo's seat belt three times before they left the farm.

If something did go down, Voodoo would have to figure it out on his own.

Sabrin had zero idea how to command Voodoo outside of a few words that seemed useless here in the car. "Hang on a tick" or just "tick" seemed to mean "wait." And "dunny" was what Ryder said when he was taking Voodoo to go potty.

She was in charge with zero idea if Voodoo would listen to her if she needed him to.

What would happen if something happened?

Like if Ryder crashed his RV…

Or, those four goons swung out of their tree and chased her car to dognap Voodoo?

She blew out a long breath.

"We're in this together, okay, buddy?" she whispered. Needing a distraction, Sabrin clicked on the radio.

Sabrin wanted to get a feel for what was going on in the area—local news, weather. She'd just found a station when Ryder's left turn signal blinked on, and he turned onto a side road.

Originally, she thought they'd need to switch out his RV in case any spyware was planted there, too. But Ryder and Ridge both had cameras and alarms on their roofs, guarding their vehicles, 360. Ryder had checked the tapes and alarm settings on his computer, and it was all clear.

Ryder said that anyone who knew the security field would assume they'd cover those bases as protocol.

Apparently, the person who planted comms on Sabrin expected her to be the chain's weak link.

Down the road a mile, Ryder turned again. This time into a picnic spot by the river.

She rolled in next to him. "What's up."

"Incoming," he said, pulling the folding table and two chairs from the RV. "Can you do the chairs?"

"Yeah, sure." She put the car in park and got out, leaving Voodoo belted where he was as she went to help.

Ryder searched the overhead tree canopy and found a place that was least impacted by the leaves and their satellite connection. "This should do, hey?"

"What's incoming?"

"Honey wants to talk to us."

Honey. Oh good!

Ryder disappeared into the RV and came back with his tactical field computer.

"Ryder, what would happen if a stranger hit Voodoo on the nose?"

"Hit him?" Ryder pulled his chin back as if the idea were preposterous. "He'd rip their jugular out, I'd guess." He popped the top of the computer open. "I wouldn't advise it. Why do you ask?"

"A tactic I overheard."

Ryder let out a half-laugh and shook his head.

She set a chair next to Ryder and opened the other, angling hers, so the sun wasn't in her eyes. "On the drive, I was thinking about those four guys."

"Yeah?"

"What if they have nothing to do with following me out of Slovakia?"

He stopped and looked at her. "How would you explain the wires?"

"Yeah…" She sat in one of the chairs and looked into the woods, thinking. "Most folks there were in the military. Or security. You all work with planting bugs on people."

"On occasion. You said they were middling quality when it came to listening in. Disposable."

"But not cheap."

"What other explanation did you come up with?"

"The dogs."

He stalled.

"And I think you should talk about that possibility with Ridge. He's going to be out at the campsite all by himself. Well, with Zeus."

"How do you mean exactly?" He opened the top on the computer and pulled up an antenna.

"There are some things that bother me about the men being at the competition. Sure, they could keep eyes on me, check out my story. Does that require four?"

He quirked his head toward her, then focused back on booting up.

"Four is actually problematic unless I was in an urban setting, and they were passing me off from one to the other, so I wouldn't suspect I was being followed."

"Okay. I agree. Four, especially grouped, isn't a good tactic."

She moved to her car and reached through the open window for her water bottle. "Back soon, Voodoo. Good boy." Turning to face Ryder as he tapped at the keyboard, she said, "Perhaps it was at the fire circle. I mean, it balanced things, right? Two men, two dogs against four men. Then there was me. I don't count. What would I do under such circumstances?"

He peered back to her, then sat down. "Dunno. What would you do under such circumstances?"

"I'm not you, that's for sure. And he had the gun. So there's that." She was supposed to be State; an embassy worker wouldn't need tactical skills.

"And spoke to you in Slovak." He pulled off his ball

cap and put it right back on, adjusting the bill to send a shadow over his face.

"He might have overheard me speaking in Slovak when I was watching you at the semifinals."

"You were stuck on the number four, though."

"I know how my office likes to pinch a penny. I was going over the costs of the clothes I bought and the camping equipment. I hope they'll reimburse me for them because I need them for this situation. I didn't pack with hiking in mind. Fingers crossed. That stuff isn't cheap."

"Keep going."

"The tickets to spectate cost a hundred and fifty US dollars per day. For four, that was six hundred yesterday, six hundred dollars today. Lodging expenses, food, wages, transportation…"

She could see his mind puzzling through the information.

He nodded. "I hear what you're saying. It's a lot of money just to surveille you. It would have made more sense for them to keep an eye on the vehicles, at least until you came back over the border. You have to return it to the airport, I'd imagine. You're not just going to disappear. One person, maybe two—four, at this stage, seems excessive, we agree. And to show their hand by stopping by for a talk also makes that scenario difficult to understand. They could have stayed lost in the crowd. Had they not shown up at the camp, would you have looked for bugs?"

"Doubtful." She paused. "There are other explanations. I might have been a surprise ingredient to an unfolding scenario." She raised her brows. "If this isn't the Slovakian government—if this was a group of men scoping out K9s for their own reasons, possibly nefarious reasons. Dognapping reasons?"

Ryder rolled his lips in and looked down at his boots. "Dognapping? While we wait for Honey, let's talk about that as a scenario." Ryder focused on her car, where Voodoo sat, looking back at them.

"I was thinking about a case that I had a hand in between Slovakia and the US," Sabrin said. "It involved Iniquus."

Ryder's gaze rested on her. "You did translations for this?"

Among other things. "Yes. It was the first time I had anything to do with Iniquus. My role was very small, and it was performed in Slovakia. When the USSR fell, the Russian Mafia didn't go away. They have families across the USSR affiliated map. Now, these families maintain that old network with Russian oligarchs at the helm. Okay?"

She waited for Ryder's nod, indicating he was following her.

"In Slovakia, one of the main crime families is the Zoric family. They have several family groups working in the United States."

Ryder nodded his recognition of the family name.

"The case was complex with different tentacles to it. The aspect that I'm thinking of was that the Zorics love art. And there's a certain game they like to play in getting things without paying for them. There's plenty of money. They could easily pay. It's the sport."

"Okay."

"In this case, the family members had picked out various American paintings that they would like to have in their private collections. Only family and business associates are allowed at their estates. Stolen paintings could be displayed in their homes without repercussions. So long story short, a group of Zorics, living in Washington, DC, stole the paintings for their Slovakian relatives. These stolen paintings were then divided between several of the Zoric women and brought here to Slovakia. In return for their efforts, these women were given students from Moldova and Slovenia to escort back to the United States."

"Girls you mean. For prostitution."

Sabrin's lips pulled down at the corners. "Yes."

Ryder leaned forward; his intensity told Sabrin how repugnant this was to him. "You stopped them, didn't you?"

"No, I saw the paintings come into Slovakia. But they were fakes. The FBI had switched them in baggage in the US, part of a sting—I wasn't given the particulars. I watched everyone—the women and the students—get on the plane from Bratislava to DC. *That* was my job. And the authorities arrested the traffickers as they disembarked the plane at Dulles. The children were taken into protection until their stories could be sorted." That's not an assignment someone from the State Department would do. But there it was. He'd either notice or not.

His brows drew together. "And this goes back to the dogs…"

"If someone like the Zoric family coveted a dog, they'd want the very best. And because they have estates to guard, the dogs would disappear, and no one would find them. Add to that, Iniquus is the Zorics' enemy. Taking your prize-winning dogs from you would delight them to no end."

Ryder's body shifted. It was as if he were expanding, growing bigger in front of her eyes. His body was primed for combat, though his face stayed neutral. If she wasn't trained to be observant, she might have missed the aggression building in Ryder's system.

"I'm confused by the men," she said. "I don't know what that was all about. None of it makes clear sense. I am simply concerned that Ridge will be sleeping on his own with Zeus. And these men—who could be plain-Jane dognappers—will know that's the case. If they meant to snatch a dog to bring into a private home to work as a guard dog… I heard the handlers talking, and they say that a dog trained like Zeus is, makes him worth more than a luxury car."

"That's true."

"So that's a second possible explanation for the men. I have a third… And just because I've thought of three, that number is meaningless. Honestly, the reason there was a comms in my pocket might have nothing to do with those men. The men might just be a bunch of men who caught my attention. But the bugs on my person means this isn't paranoia. Someone wanted to hear what I was saying or what was being said around me. I guess all of this babbling boils down to, I've come up with three scenarios, but please don't let that limit the field of possibilities." She took a deep breath and exhaled.

Ryder sent her a slow smile that made his eyes twinkle. "Okay. Number three, I'm listening."

She gathered her hair into a ponytail, swirling the length around her finger, then letting her hands rest on the top of her head while she shifted gears from one scenario to the next. "Iniquus's Strike Force and the

FBI brought down the ring leading to the Zoric family arrests. I believe it was nineteen Slovakians in the end arrested in the Virginia–DC area and imprisoned. Even though this was eighteen months ago, the trials are about to get going. Not unusual but relevant timing-wise. You are, right now, on the border of Zoric turf. You're about to go over that border. The Republic of Slovakia is a wonderful place. They are determined to fit into the new world order as a member of the EU. But every country has crime. And every country has crime families. Families don't like it when you come into their homes uninvited. Not to, you know, put bad luck on our efforts here, but Iniquus has enemies. Wealthy, positioned, angry enemies. You should be aware."

Chapter 9

Sabrin

Ryder had gone to the car to get Voodoo out now that the sun was climbing higher in the sky and the temperatures with it. He was attaching Voodoo's lead when—

"Ryder." The screen was black, but they could hear a male voice over the computer.

Sabrin asked, "Is that Honey?"

"Yes, ma'am," the voice replied.

"This is Sabrin speaking. I'm going to walk away until Ryder signals me, so you can have some privacy." She turned. "Ryder, I'll wait in my car."

"Thanks." Ryder sat, then lifted off the seat to move closer to the table. "G'day, mate," Sabrin heard as she climbed into the driver's seat, shut the door, turned on the engine, and rolled up the windows. She wanted to set an example of how this should play out in case she got a future call from her work and needed Ryder to extend the same courtesy to her.

Voodoo lay next to Ryder, but he faced toward her car.

Sabrin felt like she was under his protection. "I would be heartbroken if anything had happened to you, and you'd been hurt in the competition. You're a pretty special dog," she whispered.

Checking her phone, and finding she had no bars, even if they were closer to Bratislava, Sabrin turned it to airplane mode. Once she reached the city, she could call the office. Some lunch would be good, she thought as her stomach growled. "I really wish I knew what was going on." She scanned the tree line, muttering under her breath, "I'm starting to see devils in the shadows."

Reaching for the car's radio, Sabrin scrolled through the channels in search of international news to see if anyone was reporting on the missing bus and the twenty-six researchers who up and vanished. She stopped when she heard the word *hostage*.

"The United States rescued an American hostage in Nigeria, in the early morning hours, sources confirmed," the announcer said.

Darn. Not her case.

"Secretary of State issued a separate statement."

The voice changed to that of the secretary. "The United States is committed to the safe return of all American citizens taken against their will."

Sabrin scraped her teeth over her upper lip as she listened. The secretary was signaling. He was making a political move. She wondered if he should have kept his mouth shut at this stage of the game.

The secretary continued. "Some of our most skillful warriors delivered on our commitment to protect our citizens, no matter *where* they are in the world." Again with the posturing. The Slovakian government would be reading that for what it was.

Still, *warriors* was an interesting vocabulary choice. Typically, on land, Delta Force took up the task of hostage rescue. Honey had honed his tradecraft as a Delta. If the secretary had called them "soldiers," Sabrin would have assumed Deltas. Though, Green Berets were in the area, too, training allied forces. On water, it was normally SEALs who went in, but that could change up like it did for Osama bin Laden. If that were the case, though, the secretary would have said *military.* He said, *warriors.*

Words were specific and calculated in the diplomatic world.

The radio announcer was explaining: "Philip Warrenton is now safely in the care of our embassy. The State Department will follow through with next steps. ABC News broke the story of the operation that occurred in Northern Nigeria. The rescue operation was developed and carried out with the cooperation of the Nigerian authorities. A ransom had been demanded. Warrenton was in the country as a missionary. He and his family lived in the village where he worked on providing solar electricity and wells for access to clean water. His family didn't have the resources to pay the ransom, and it is against US policy to negotiate with kidnappers. The rescue team deployed as fears grew that, under such circumstances, Warrenton would be sold to one of the terrorist organizations, like ISIS, as a propaganda and recruitment tool, which often includes publicly distributed videos of a beheading."

Warrenton's situation was not the same as the researchers'. Sabrin thought as the news moved on to talk about the negotiations over environmental policies that would be happening at the EU Council. Sabrin drummed her fingers on the steering wheel. The researchers had the university insurance policies that offered a pot of gold.

But the Cerberus operations leader, Bob, had said there had been no demands yet. That happened in kidnapping events. Often, the bad guys would sit on the hostage for a day or two to amp fears. But that was typically the case for an individual or a family.

Twenty-five academicians?

Something wasn't reading right about this situation.

And with the Slovakian government asking everyone to step down, that would make it difficult, if not impossible, for Honey to do his negotiation magic.

When Sabrin turned her gaze toward Ryder, he signaled her over.

Iniquus was her asset. She needed to work her asset to the best of her ability without a single misstep that would endanger life and limb of the hostages. Or anyone fighting on the good guy team.

She sat down next to Ryder, saw the camera light was green, and smiled at the blank screen. So Honey could see her, but she couldn't see him? Interesting. "Did you have a good flight?" she asked.

"Yes, thank you. I'm settling in here."

"Good. Where were you coming in from?"

"Panther Force finished up a mission in West Africa."

That *might* well explain the Secretary of State using the term *warriors*. "Ah, I heard about a situation that was just resolved there. If that was you, well done. Everyone come out healthy?" If she was right, who paid for that? It couldn't have been cheap. Perhaps a corporation stepped up, having decided that allowing the kidnapping of a missionary to fly might mean emboldening criminals to reach out and snatch their corporation's workers. Not only did that increase the cost of business, but it narrowed the field of people willing to work in risky geopolitical areas.

"Healthy, yes. Thank you, ma'am."

"Is Panther Force in Slovakia?"

"No, ma'am, we've divided and staged outside of the country, each at a different border crossing to be quick getting eyes on a situation. For diplomatic reasons, we're keeping our footprint in-country as small and invisible as we can. Only you and Ryder are in the interior. Bringing everyone across the border is something we're going to try to avoid. If you all find the hostages, we'll come up with a plan based on your intel."

"All right. Since I'll be working within your group, can you tell me your chain of command? How does this work, Panther Force and Ryder?"

Ryder let Honey answer.

"While Cerberus works as a K9 response force for training and deployment to natural disasters, they typically will attach to an operational team, as Ryder is doing now. I'm the negotiator in the pecking order. It doesn't look like negotiation is going to have a place in this situation. And so, I take on the mantle of ground command. I'll be directing Ryder's actions, and you're welcome to join him or not, depending on what your superior tells you."

"All right." Sabrin adjusted herself in the chair.

"However, when you're with Ryder, you'll have support from our TOC—tactical operations center—at our Iniquus campus in DC. That will be provided by Nutsbe."

"Operations, Nutsbe," she practiced. "Negotiator, Honey. Ground, Ryder. Got it."

"Ground could expand. We have six boots other than Ryder and me. We'll see how things roll out. Okay. Your turn, Sabrin. What role are you playing here?" His voice was warmly encouraging.

"Me? Uhm, I'm a loaner like Ryder is. They asked me to tag along and see if I can be any help. I'll keep up with Ryder as best I can." That sounded innocuous like she was a low-level paper pusher who happened to be around. She could be that. She looked soft. There were people in the field with their head always on a swivel and their gaze always searching for the thing that didn't fit—the odd can in the road, the doll in an alley, covering a bomb that got you vaporized. She didn't have that. She looked a little harried. Maybe a little tired, or so she'd been told. It worked for her.

"State has never sent anyone to attach with Iniquus and be helpful before." Honey's voice was a deep, resonant bass, a little hypnotic. It was the kind of voice that made you feel like you could confide—a tool in the negotiator's toolbox.

"Yeah." Sabrin scrubbed her palms on her thighs. "It's a first for me. I'll try to be a positive on the team."

"Tell me how this is different from other cases we've run." Not giving up. Push. Push. Gentle push. An open-ended question. The kind of question that bubbled up unexpected information.

Luckily, her training meant she knew when she

was being manipulated. Sabrin opened her eyes wider, pressed her lips flat, and shook her head.

Honey said nothing. Just let her sit and wiggle in the silence. A trick that worked especially well on women.

She knew she needed to play the game. "I would be speculating," she finally offered. "And I don't want to plant seeds."

"Please," Honey said, invitingly.

"I see a few possibilities. One is that State understands you'll be here, doing what you do, and there's nothing they can do about it. I may be here to keep tabs on you as I provide you with what help I can. Here are the things about my background that might be helpful—an understanding of the geography, the politics, the traditions. State may think that my language skills, my connections in the country—it's a small country, comparatively, one can drive across it in a day—may be of help. I might just give you a better cover, so you don't make the US government look weak and unable to keep Iniquus in line."

"Ryder told me there's a family, the Zorics, that has family members in the American courts, about a dozen Slovakian citizens. How does that play into the political emotions?"

"The Slovak Republic is feeling bruised. That FBI sting put their country in the news in an unflattering way at an inopportune time. They've asked that the Zoric family members be tried here in Slovakia, and if found guilty, that they are imprisoned here." She took a breath. She could feel Honey thinking. "It's like the black sheep of the family. They can bring shame to the family, but in the end, they're still family. I read the cases, what wasn't redacted. I shared a bit with Ryder."

"We discussed that. Sabrin, what do you think would happen politically in Slovakia and the EU—since four other nations had citizens on that bus—if Slovakia fails to save them. Then, it comes to light that US help was offered and rejected?"

Sabrin leaned closer to the camera so Honey could read her eyes. "I'm sure each country wants to be involved in protecting their citizens. Slovakia *is* capable. They have their own special forces. You should be aware as you—we—head forward, we are walking on a path we've been warned not to take. There is always the possibility we could interrupt and even screw up their operations. Surely, we here at this table aren't so arrogant to think the American way is the only way, or that no others could elicit a positive outcome."

"Agreed," Honey said.

Sabrin felt deflated by the conversation. "Do you have anything at all to work with other than that the bus is gone?"

"I do. It's the way the university discovered there was a problem and called us in, to begin with. Many universities share information through onion routers over the Darknet and have since the inception of computer networking. The person—and we don't know which of our four principals did this—was able to press Dictate. The computer produced a document that was autosaved in a shared file. A lab tech opened the file as part of their daily task of data entry, read the dictation, realized the significance, and called university security."

"Well done, them," she said. "This captured what was happening on the bus? And you have a copy of it?"

"Yes, and like many times when you're dictating,

some of the words don't make sense. We have a program that deciphers that. I'll put it in the cloud for you."

"I'd rather you keep the cleaned version. That would mess me up. I want the version as it was received by the lab tech if you please."

"All right. I'll send that as soon as we get off here."

Ryder sat quietly, listening. But it was active listening. His mind was obviously whirring.

"Did you share this with the Slovakian government?" Sabrin asked.

"No," was Honey's decisive reply.

She scratched the side of her face. "How long has the research team been gone now?"

"The timeline: It's been sixty-four hours Central European Standard Time since anyone last spoke to someone inside of the hostage group. But they were in the Tantras Mountains, the connection might have been difficult. The shared file was created approximately forty-seven hours ago, but it took eight hours for it to be delivered, opened, and the call for help made to Iniquus."

"Twenty-six people," Sabrin said softly. "Twenty-six is a lot. A lot to manage as they go to the bathroom. A lot to manage in terms of food and water. Shelter. Illness. The captors are responsible if anything bad happens to any of these people. If anything bad happens to the people, the hostage-takers will be less likely to keep anyone alive."

"We're well into the yellow zone," Honey agreed. "After seventy-two hours, we budge up to red. Sufficient water being the most pressing survival concern outside of violence."

"I'm assuming that without getting a ransom request," Sabrin said, "each hour of each day that passes, their situation grows more deadly because we don't know the goal."

"Exactly," Honey said.

Sabrin turned to search out Ryder's gaze. "This is going to be a tight rope. A fine line to keep the bigger picture politics safe as well as the researchers. With twenty-six lives on the line, we can't make any mistakes."

Chapter 10

Sabrin

Sabrin grabbed her shopping bag by the black cord handles and gave the rental car one last check to make sure she'd left nothing behind. She stopped at the kiosk to drop off her keys before taking the elevator to the main airport terminal, where she hoped to shake any eyes that might be keeping track of her whereabouts.

Her suitcase and camping gear had been loaded into Ryder's RV—along with Voodoo—after they'd finished speaking with Honey at the roadside stop. She and Ryder had decided to part ways in the hopes that if someone put a tracker on Sabrin's car, she could slip that noose.

Sabrin gave Ryder an address where they could meet for lunch.

It was 1:30, and she was starving.

Back in the US, Sabrin's freezer was filled by a food delivery service that sent prepared meals composed of flash-frozen fruits and vegetables. That and whey protein powder constituted most of her diet. She was *meh* about food when she was in DC. And eating like that worked with her crazy schedule and often impromptu calls to head overseas—nothing to rot in her fridge.

Now, when Sabrin arrived in Slovakia, *that* was a different story. As soon as she landed, it was like she was a medieval peasant home from a strenuous day in the fields, needing the calories that were served up as potatoes and salty cheese. She couldn't get enough. The food here was earthy and sublime. It tasted like tradition and shared endeavors. Family. And, yes, she'd say it, it tasted like love.

It was a good thing she wasn't here for long periods of time. It would require much more strenuous workouts to deal with the excess calories that she'd gobble down. Sure, her job demanded that she was fit. But when she was recruited into the intelligence community, it wasn't for her innate athleticism. Sabrin would put in the work necessary to do her job, but not a single step or arm curl more.

Today, though, she salivated at the thought of salted fried potatoes and cheese.

Her stomach grumbled at Sabrin to hurry up and get to the restaurant already.

Sabrin saw a group of people heading her way and dipped behind a large potted plant. Reaching up under her skirt, she tugged down the leggings, she'd rolled up and hidden under the pleated fabric. Plucking off her flip flops—thongs, Ryder called them—she pulled a pair of ballet flats from her bag. Before she slid her feet in, Sabrin took a moment to drop a pebble into one of them. Painfully stepping on the stone would change her gait enough—without her having to give it extra focus—that the airport security's AI computer system wouldn't recognize her.

Unzipping the skirt, Sabrin let it drop to the ground, stepping out of it while she yanked the elastic band from her ponytail. She shook her hair to add volume as she bent. She gathered up the skirt, putting it into the bag while retrieving a cotton over-sized sweater. As the travel group reached her spot on the corridor, Sabrin tugged the sweater over her head.

She crumpled the bag, shoved it into the waste bin, and joined the group progressing up the corridor.

It was a clothing change that was practiced at The Farm repeatedly until she could smoothly make changes in mere seconds. There, at the CIA training grounds outside of Williamsburg, Virginia, Sabrin learned the secret was to wear layers. It was also imperative to have a repertoire of characters in one's arsenal. When she changed, it wasn't just clothing; it was a change in *appearance*. She also had to change her attitude. Sabrin had walked into the airport as a woman running through a to-do list; she left as an exhausted traveler with a cramped limp.

Head down, hair in her face, she moved with the group all the way out the sliding glass doors and toward the tram.

On and off.

On and off.

Into a cab, she leaned forward and gave the gal

the address for the restaurant where she'd be meeting Ryder and Voodoo.

A little overdone? Sabrin wondered as she sat back on the seat and watched the city buzz by. It was always useful to practice. It was good to keep one's skills fresh.

If anyone was following Ryder, then her exit gymnastics was ineffectual.

And sure, she was going to her Babka's house tonight, so if anyone who might possibly be following her knew anything at all about her, this was her performing theatrics for no reason other than maintaining muscle memory.

But there was always the possibility that she might shake someone and buy Ryder, Voodoo, and her a bit of space to work.

Looking out the side window, a smile slid across Sabrin's face as she spotted Ryder and Voodoo walking up the block.

A text pinged her phone: 9:00 a.m. Embassy.

At their hotel, where they'd stay that night, the bellhop opened the door with an unexpected flourish. *Tada!*

Sabrin sent him a smile and a nod as she passed through the entry, Ryder's hand on the small of her back. It wasn't a room but a suite, and it was…romantic. A bottle of champagne stood ready in an ice bucket on the table, fresh flowers and candles were arranged on the bedside table—chocolates on the pillows.

"This is lovely, thank you," she said to the bellhop. Her gaze caught on Ryder then slid away as he directed the placement of their bags.

"Sabrin, what's the tip rate here?" Ryder asked.

"A Euro a bag," she said as he pulled the coins from his pocket.

When the door shut behind the bellhop, she watched Ryder take in the room, lift then drop his brow. Yeah, he realized it, too. This place was set for seduction.

It smelled of roses and something warmer and more carnal. She couldn't place it.

There was only the king-size bed in this part of the suite. The people downstairs had said there were two beds when she'd asked. Now that she was here, Sabrin assumed they thought she was asking about the second bed for Voodoo. Sabrin walked into the adjoining room, lifted the cushion on the couch, and was relieved to see it was a fold-out.

A welcome letter rested on the table written in Slovak, French, and English. Sabrin read the hotel's offer of congratulations and best wishes for their future happiness, along with an explanation of how to signal the staff that the newlywed couple was not to be disturbed, to Ryder. He chuckled as he unleashed Voodoo.

Yup, they'd gotten the bridal suite.

No wonder the woman at reception had touched her heart and wished Sabrin good luck in Slovak.

To keep their name off the registration and their credit card numbers from out of the computer systems, Iniquus had arranged the room in a hotel that allowed dogs. While they were signing in, the manager had had to turn away a family. The hotel was full. It made sense that they got last available and that the bridal suite wasn't done purposefully by Iniquus.

It shouldn't be a problem, Sabrin told herself. They'd only be here the one night. It was clean. Looked comfortable. The rest was just…seasoning on her "I hadn't planned on this" burger.

"Maybe take the champagne to your grandmother tonight?" Ryder asked, lifting the bottle and wrapping it in a plastic bag meant for dry cleaning services and placing the bottle back in the ice to keep it cold while protecting the label from becoming mushy.

"She'd like that." Sabrin hefted her suitcase onto the folding luggage rack and unzipped it.

As Voodoo leaped onto the bed and lay down where he could look out the window, Ryder stepped around the luggage. One for him, one for Voodoo, and one with office equipment, including a printer, so Sabrin could take a look at what was said to the hostages as the attacker—attackers?—got on the bus.

Ryder pulled out the printer first thing and was setting everything up. "While you work, I thought Voodoo and I could get out of your hair, give you some peace to focus unless I can be helpful?"

"Alone is very helpful, thank you." She pulled her dress for the party out of her bag and gave it a shake.

"I saw a park up the road. I thought I'd take Voodoo for a run then to wear him out a bit with some Frisbee." He leaned down to plug in the machine, then reached for his computer.

She nodded.

"Better for when we go to the party tonight. When he's got too much energy, Voodoo can get himself some bright ideas and get himself into mischief."

That thought tickled a smile onto her face. "And what kind of dog mischief does Voodoo like to get into?"

"He enjoys a good buffet, for example. And he enjoys unrolling toilet paper. And retrieving balls from the tops of bookshelves." He sat at the desk, tapping at the computer, while Sabrin pulled out an ironing board to work on her traditional white dress with hand embroidery that was worn to parties like this.

"Did you bring only Iniquus uniforms and outdoor clothing?" she asked, knowing that either would seem unusual for such an occasion. Not rude, just odd.

He tapped a key, and the printer whirred. "I have dress slacks, is that what I should wear?"

"Yes, good." Ryder Kelly in dress slacks… Sabrin tried to silence the "yum" that hummed through her body.

She slid the dress onto the board as the iron heated. "Ryder, can you call the guy who's doing your operations support? What's his name again, Nutsbe?"

"Nutsbe."

"Is that a last name, call sign?"

"Yeah, call sign, his last name's Crushed." His hand hovered as the pages came out—five of them.

She stalled for a minute, processing, then snorted. "Nutsbe Crushed? His mother must be horrified."

"One would imagine. What do you need from him?" His gaze slid down the page then he brought them over to her.

Yes, this was precisely what she was expecting—no paragraph indentation. No punctuation. Just stream of consciousness. "I was wondering if there was any way to tell or any way to find out what dictation software was used for this, because this readout is a mess, as I expected it to be. I have theories…"

Ryder pulled out his phone and said, "Out of curiosity, why would it matter?" as he texted.

"Computers don't speak a language. They predict from a graph of knowns." She set the papers on her suitcase.

Ryder sat on the bed next to Voodoo. "I'm listening."

"Yeah, okay, so you're texting." She lifted her hand toward his phone. "When you do, there's a predictive algorithm to help you. The software has no idea how to speak English. What happens is that there is a table of possibilities." She licked her finger and tested the iron. "That table is refined as you teach it what kinds of words and phrases you often use based on probability."

"Okay. By the way, I was texting Nutsbe with your question. We'll see if he can't figure the answer," Ryder said.

"When you set up your phone," she waggled her finger toward it as Ryder slid his cell phone into the thigh pocket of his tactical pants, "you set the software to your primary language. Suppose you wanted to dictate in a different language. In that case, you'd have to tell the computer system, or it can't figure out what the heck is going on in terms of vocabulary, spelling choices based on the grammatically predicted next word. *'La chaise'* is French for 'the chair,' which sounds like 'latches' in English. In a French program, knowing that 'la' indicates a feminine noun will follow, masculine nouns wouldn't show up in the possibilities table in the prediction pool."

Ryder leaned back with his hands laced behind his head, making his chest look just that much more...*more*. "Is that document reading like gibberish? Like the program thought it was taking dictation in English, but it was someone speaking from a different language?"

Sabrin refocused on her dress, so she didn't scorch

the fabric. "I'll need to sit down and study it. That's why I'd like to know what dictation program was used. There is a program that you train, for example. The machine learns an individual's syntax choices and accent. When I speak, I have a little New Jersey from my childhood, though most of that has burned away since I haven't been there in a decade. Still, there are a few words here and there that have a stronger accent for me. I have a little bit of a mixed international accent, sometimes pronouncing things correctly in the native language—like *hors d'oeuvre* or *Paris*—rather than in an American English accent. Sometimes people can hear a pronounced Slovakian accent in my speech. It depends on how much I've been drinking, how tired I am, whom I've been speaking with, what language I'm thinking in. It all has an impact." She stopped speaking while she turned the dress. "You, on the other hand, you know you have an Australian accent though our English grammar is the same. So the program listens. Little by little, your program knows your personal language."

"I get it. If this was dictated into such a program, then the computer would be guessing words based on the prediction of the individual instead of the prediction of a less refined algorithm."

Ryder patted his pants leg when his phone buzzed. He tugged out his cell phone and looked at the screen.

"Yes. And that will make a difference when I decide if what the person was saying was recorded correctly or if these are just words that make sense algorithmically."

"The text is from Nutsbe. 'Good question. I called the lab. It's a Word document.'"

She pulled the freshly pressed dress from the board

and reached for a hanger. "Do you want to press your pants while the iron's hot?"

Ryder stood. "That's a lovely dress. A work of art. Is it hand embroidered? Did you do the work?"

"My aunts." She placed it in the closet and gave it a last brush with her hand. "Not many men I know use the word 'embroider' in a sentence."

"I have sisters."

"How many?" She moved to take up the place on the bed that Ryder had just vacated.

"Eleven."

She blinked at him. "You're kidding."

"I am not." He pulled a pair of dress shoes from his luggage and set them in the closet. "Eleven sisters, one brother. We are a baker's dozen of kids."

"Are any of those siblings half or step?"

"We never think in those terms." He pulled out a pair of charcoal gray dress slacks and a tailored blue shirt. "We're a blended family with normal family dynamics, but one thing I can say is that there is no hierarchy. A sibling is a sibling is a sibling."

"Lovely."

"It can be." He sent her a grin. "It can also be bedlam."

Chapter 11

Ryder

Once they were dressed and ready, Sabrin and Ryder headed toward the birthday party. Sabrin had the bridal champagne in one hand. She held a gift for her Babka in the other—a small golden box. Ryder had the gift basket tucked into the crook of his arm and Voodoo's lead in his hand, leaving one hand free in case quick reflexes were needed.

While he and Sabrin walked together, now there was more space between them. Not a gulf of space, but before, when they had walked companionably, their arms brushed every once in a while. Now there was more air. Yeah, he noticed. *Come on, mate, it's not bloody well that much farther away.* Why was this bothering him?

Ryder glanced over the basket down to his dog. Voodoo seemed to know they were headed for a party; he was prancing along in good spirits.

Something… The energy between Ryder and Sabrin had *seriously* shifted.

It wasn't that they were bunking in the bridal suite, Ryder thought. Though, the romantic setup could have been awkward—*more awkward.* They were already two strangers thrown into an intimate relationship—*seemingly* intimate. But Sabrin had let that roll off her shoulders and got to work on the cryptic pages…

Something. Things *felt* different between them, a wariness, a bracing of her muscles that hadn't been there before.

Was this bothering him personally? Or professionally?

An interesting question. A weird sensation at the pit of his stomach.

Ryder couldn't remember experiencing this feeling before. It reminded him vaguely of a terrible day out on the station, growing up. He must have been seven—maybe eight years old when he realized he was lost with no landmarks 360 degrees around him—just dirt and sky. Ryder was usually good about directions based on the sun. But it was high noon, and he was hungry and not willing to wait for time to pass, the sun to move, and the right tack to show itself. He'd tried to find his way back to the big house, walking until his legs turned to rubber. Finally, Ryder had seen success through the blur of midday heat, only to discover when he got there, it had been a mirage.

Yeah, that hollow feeling of loss and disappointment in the pit of his stomach.

More, there was that same underlying vibration of

threat when he'd realized he didn't know how to get home again.

Wasn't that an odd memory to pull up?

He didn't like it.

Leaving this evening, he and Sabrin had walked out of the hotel's side door and taken a taxi rather than the Winnebago, which made sense. They'd gone to a mall where they got out of the car, walked through to another door, and taken a different cab. And again, in a third cab, which let them out at a church.

Now, they were walking up an alleyway in a neighborhood. Silently. Stiffly.

Possibly angrily?

Sabrin had said she wanted to keep her family safe and away from her work life. But she had known this was their destination. She could have said no all along. She hadn't said no, and she hadn't seemed particularly bothered that this was the set up before they reached the hotel.

Ryder checked "destination" off the list of possibilities for the change in temperature between them.

He backed up in his mind to when things were still okay. He'd left to go for a run with Voodoo. Sabrin had her head down, focused on the pages that he'd printed off for her. He was out on the run for about an hour, giving Sabrin space and quiet to do her work. She'd said that was a good plan, had thanked him.

Everything was okay then.

Ryder had stopped into a florist's shop and picked up the basket on the way back to the hotel. He chose the kinds of things that his gran would like—a blooming plant, a box of fine chocolates, some other gourmet snacks, cookies…he'd seen a little beanie kangaroo and thought that might be funny, coming from an Australian. He hadn't wanted to show up to Sabrin's babka's empty-handed.

When he got back to their room, Sabrin had been staring at the wall, muttering.

He'd set the gift down and taken Voodoo into the bathroom where Voodoo could safely eat.

That all seemed fine.

She was still in her little thinking bubble, and he'd tried not to be distracting. Then, he'd asked if she needed to be in the bathroom to get ready first. His sisters always got ticked when they went in to put on their makeup, and the mirror was fogged, or the steam frizzed their hair.

But Sabrin had wagged her hand at him and focused back on the paper. Not upset. Not annoyed, someone absorbed in their work.

So he'd gone on and gotten ready. He shaved his beard, showered off his jogging sweat, dressed in the clothes Sabrin had said were appropriate, and exited the bathroom, bending over his suitcase to get Voodoo's chew toy that was a special reward for sitting nicely at an event. He'd said, "Bathrooms all clear. It's six thirty."

Still good.

Sabrin took her dress in to change. When she emerged, her silky brown hair, so dark it was almost black, had been braided up and looped into a crown on her head. She'd added flowers and multicolored, streaming ribbons on the sides. Her blue eyes were so bright they were electric. She looked like a figure out of a children's book. She looked…perfect.

Heart-stoppingly beautiful.

This was a problem.

He knew it would be from the time he'd seen her smile when she drove up to Ridge and him on the road, heading toward their camp—that he found himself attracted to her.

And he'd been thinking about her in the shower, so when she saw him through the front window on the Winnebago, his junk wasn't exactly in neutral position. Though he wasn't sporting full-blown wood, thank god.

Seeing her dressed in her traditional style, Ryder had grinned, ready to offer a compliment.

BOOM, that's when the energy had changed.

She'd stood there blinking at him. Blank faced and blinking. After a moment, the muscles around her eyes and mouth tensed as she'd pressed her lips together.

"Am I late?" He'd searched for a reason why he felt so warmly toward her, and yet he was getting this sudden blast of arctic freeze.

"No. It's just…" She took a step back and brought her hands together, rubbing her palms. "You shaved your beard." She'd exhaled. "You. Shaved. Your. Beard." She seemed to give herself a shake, and she turned to get her shoes out of her bag.

Something though…definitely odd. "I'm sorry?"

"Nothing."

Definitely something. Ryder had eleven sisters. *Eleven.* So he had that perspective as part of his early warning system of the female sort. This was what Ryder had come to term "iceberg communication." He got the tip—a word, maybe two of women's shorthand. Underneath that word was a whole lot of thought. A whole lot of processing. And it all synthesized down to the conclusion that sharing those thoughts wouldn't get the desired outcome, so here you go—a word to tell you to move on.

The reason Ryder labeled these instances as iceberg communication was that he had no idea what lay beneath the waters. How treacherous. Or even how to navigate around her dismissive, "nothing."

Ryder could read that as passive-aggressive, or, more likely, it was a personal thought, and this was a professional setting.

Ryder jostled the basket in his arm to look over the top and check on Voodoo, who seemed intent on a shadowy spot up ahead in the alley.

You. Shaved. Your. Beard. Maybe she was disappointed about his beard?

His mind slid back to analyze that moment in the hotel room. After their exchange, Sabrin moved toward the gift basket and fingered the kangaroo's ears. Her mind was working so hard that Ryder thought she'd forgotten to breathe.

"I don't have to take it," he'd said, pointing at the basket. "Or you could maybe choose which elements?"

She turned back to him. "It's thoughtful. Babka will be very pleased. Thank you."

And that was pretty much it, from then until now, except for a few directives to him and to the cabby, she'd been silent and brooding.

Someone clicked on their back-porch light, suddenly illuminating the alley.

Sabrin turned to him, her brows drawn together.

"Is something bothering you?" Direct approach.

"I was just thinking… You shaved your beard."

Back to the beard. He stroked a hand over his jaw

and chin. "I was feeling a bit feral. I'm better spiffed up for company, hey? Did you prefer the beard?"

"Uhm, professionally, I thought it might be a better disguise."

"Which would be true, but that was last year's trend. This year, it's clean-shaven or a three-day stubble. I was sticking out as different with the beard."

"Oh. I...haven't kept up with that trend." She started walking again. "Have you ever been to Slovakia before?"

"It's my first time in this part of the world."

"Couple of things. My name is Sabrin Harris, no middle name. Middle names aren't part of our naming ways here. My last name is Harris, as my mom married an American. My mother's family name is Novák. That's the male version of the name. So the men will be Mr. Novák, formally. To show gender, we add 'ová' to a woman's last name, so the women here will almost all be formally Mrs. Nováková."

"That's interesting."

"While you're here, they will offer you *Borovička*. Listen to the sounds, *Borovička*."

"Borovička," he parroted. "What's that?"

"Slovakia's national drink. It's flavored with juniper berries, so similar to gin. You will accept the glass." She stalled and pressed her fingers into his arm to stop him from walking on. "But you won't drink it. I know you're ex-special forces, and I know their reputation for fight hard-live hard, and that means drinking like a fish—no judgment. Here, as a population, they drink more than almost anywhere else in the world. My ninety-year-old grandmother can drink you under the table. If my cousins think they have a mark, they will put you in the hospital with alcohol poisoning. I just don't have time for that."

"Neither do I. Ever." He grinned, hoping to take some of the grimness from her face. When she looked at him like this, he thought about his elementary teachers or fussy librarians. It really was a different side of her than he'd seen before.

"Here we are." She approached the back gate at a tall fence.

Ryder could just peep over. The back garden was laced with strands of tiny white lights, live music floated through the air, and it smelled of meat on the grill.

Sabrin stretched her eyes wide for emphasis. "Brace yourself for the adoration that is about to hit you like a rogue wave."

She flipped the latch, and the door swung wide. With hands held over her head—the bridal suite congratulatory champagne in one hand, the little gold box in the other—Sabrin called out a greeting in Slovak.

The people in the garden launched at her, arms outstretched, smiles on their faces. Even without understanding a word, Ryder could tell they were cooing loving things at her, welcoming her home.

Suddenly, there was silence.

All eyes turned on him.

Blushing hotly, Sabrin took a step back until she was standing next to him. In English, she spoke slowly, saying, "My family, we have an extra guest this evening. This is my *friend* Ryder Kelly. He's from Australia and was in Czechia with his dog. This is Voodoo with him, there. Voodoo was competing in a dog challenge and was in second place until he hurt his paw. I invited

Ryder to come home with me, so he could see how Slo-vakians celebrate their babka's birthday."

In unison, they looked from her to him, to her, then him, and this last time, the tide turned, swelled, and surrounded him. He was clapped on the back and cheek kissed, hugged, and welcomed.

Sabrin had done a valiant job of putting plenty of daylight between them and any thoughts that they had a committed relationship that would bring him to their door. Still, Ryder got the distinct impression that her family had concluded Sabrin was bringing Ryder home to meet the family in advance of an announcement of their betrothal.

Ryder saw them peeking at her hand; he'd guessed to see if she wore an engagement ring.

He had figured there might be a misunderstanding, but he'd assumed Sabrin could define the situation. He'd been wrong. And while he didn't fully understand the dynamic, he realized that there was a cost that Sa-brin would pay for using this evening to cement her cover for this op.

She was right. They needed this in place. The fam-ily needed to interpret their relationship as important, if not permanent. Sacrifices had to be made—even deeply personal ones—so he and Sabrin could do their part, trying to help those twenty-six desperate hostages.

Chapter 12

Sabrin

Her aunts were in the corner of the garden planning her wedding, Sabrin was pretty sure.

Sabrin loved her family. Loved their warmth and that they were very ready to embrace Ryder into their fold as her supposed future husband. And here, Sabrin didn't even know his real name, surely not Ryder.

Their being here was a lie that she would never be able to explain to her family.

When Sabrin got home to America, she'd write to her grandmother that things hadn't worked out in her relationship with Ryder. Maybe she'd have better luck with the next guy.

Even thinking about writing that letter saying her phony relationship was over felt sad to her.

Bereft.

Huh, wasn't that a funny feeling?

"Why are you like this?" Babka asked. "Sour face. You know men like their women to be sweet."

Sabrin's dedko laughed and said he preferred his women salty. Babka chuckled, leaning in for a kiss. They'd been married just shy of seventy-two years. Their relationship was everything Sabrin wanted for herself; the two were still head over heels in love. It was time; Sabrin needed to focus in and try to find her life's partner.

Love certainly hadn't just magically shown up in her life. She'd need to make a more concerted effort.

No more guys who were "living their best life" and "in it for the fun," where anything heavy or real sent them whistling off in the other direction. She needed someone who would roll with her if she was tumbling, just like Ryder had done in the woods.

But Ryder wasn't "the guy." Of that, Sabrin was sure. He wore his player energy like a superhero's cloak.

Turning her gaze toward Ryder, Sabrin found one of her great aunts measuring Ryder's bicep with both of her bony hands, cackling. She gave Sabrin a nod and a thumbs up.

Ryder was enduring it all with good grace. This was his job. He wasn't really enjoying Aunt Olga's approbation.

Sabrin smiled and gave a little wave, accepting Aunt Olga's compliment: Yeah, she reeled in a fine one. If only it was true. That she had found *her* guy and was introducing him to the family as the two of them started toward their happily-ever-after.

Yes, everyone thought Ryder would probably be a

family member soon. The longer the night went on, the more uncomfortable that made her feel. While her family was genuine, she was using them.

Dedko smacked Sabrin's knee. "Get your man. I want to see how he dances."

Her cousins stood in a half-circle with their instruments, playing the old songs that Babka loved. The stone patio was dappled with dancers. The men did fancy footwork; the women spun to make their dresses billow out like upside-down tulips.

Sabrin caught Ryder's gaze; it held. Her aunt Olga pushed Ryder toward Sabrin with a, "Go. Be nice boy. Sabrin wants for dancing."

Boy? Yeah, Sabrin had seen the man naked. *Definitely* not a boy.

To her surprise, Ryder didn't demur. He signaled Voodoo to stay in his place and handed him the chew toy that had been in and out of Ryder's pocket as needed throughout the night.

It was like Ryder was the dad, and Voodoo was the lethal toddler.

Ryder smiled as he made his way over to her, extending his hand. "May I have the pleasure?"

She sent him a tentative smile with a little bit of a grimace that asked, "Do you know what you're getting yourself into?"

On the edge of the patio, Ryder watched the men for a moment, then tugged her hand, moving them into the group of dancers. It wasn't astonishing that Ryder had such command of his body and could mimic what the men were doing. He had to have muscle control and coordination to be in the Australian Commandos. What caught Sabrin was his grace and comfort dancing in front of people. Most men she knew needed a drink or three before they'd hit the dance floor. And Ryder, as she'd asked, wasn't drinking tonight, simply carrying his glass around with him.

Soon, Sabrin had spun herself silly. As the bow drew the last note across the strings, Sabrin laughingly stumbled into Ryder, and he caught her in his arms.

Babka took advantage of the moment. She picked up a spoon and dinged the base of her champagne flute.

The whole family turned to Sabrin and Ryder. "Kiss, kiss, kiss, kiss," they chanted in heavily accented English. Sabrin turned and looked up at him, a mixture of "please do this for me" and "oh crap."

Ryder sent her grandmother one of his grins—mischievous and fun-loving—then sent her bicep-squeezing aunt Olga a broad wink, which was received by her family with cheers and foot-stomping.

He reached for Sabrin's hand and twirled her out, spun her back into his arms, and dropped her into a dip. His lips found hers, warm and soft. Without the prickle of his whiskers, all she felt was pleasure. They held long enough to satisfy the onlookers, then he lifted her back to standing and spun her wide again so she could curtsy, and he could bow to their applause.

That kiss wasn't enough.

Sabrin wanted more.

More of the kiss. More of being swept into his arms. *More*.

She blinked at that thought, then thrust it away from her. She wanted more, but not from Ryder. He was not the settling down kind. Finding someone like her grandfather—someone to love and create a family with—was what Sabrin really wanted. She wanted babies. And stability.

Actually, what she really wanted was to find and protect the twenty-six hostages.

As the clapping came to a stop and the music started up again, Ryder drew her across the yard to Voodoo. Sabrin's cousin's baby looked like she was toddling toward the dog. While Ryder had promised Sabrin that Voodoo loved children, she was glad that Ryder would be right there to prevent any possible tragedies.

Sabrin's uncle waggled a stern finger at her. Pointing at Voodoo, he said. *"Pes, ktorý šteká, nehryzie."*

"What's that?" Ryder asked.

"It translates to, 'Dog that barks, does not bite.' He means that you've brought a dangerous dog to the party. He doesn't bark." She stalled and said it again, her voice trailing off, "Dog that barks, does not bite. A barking dog rarely bites. It's an idiom." She stared at the ground, her body rocking back and forth, her lips muttering through words she'd read from the pages earlier in the evening.

Maybe.

Sabrin turned to her uncle and told him in Slovak, "This dog is too well trained to go to someone's home and bark."

He nodded and reached for Voodoo. Ryder stopped him. "Sabrin, can you explain not to pet Voodoo?"

"Idioms." *Yes, maybe. That may be it!* Sabrin's hand gripped Ryder's arm. "Time to go," she said, excitement lacing her words.

"What?" Ryder asked.

Sabrin turned and lifted her arm. "Everyone, it was so good to see you." She touched her free hand to her heart. "I love you so much! Ryder and I need to go." Her words were colored with excitement and urgency.

Her goodbye was met with a lot of sly looks and elbow bumps. Great, her family all thought Ryder's kiss had made her horny, and she needed to get him to the hotel and rip his clothes off.

To be clear, those thoughts weren't far from the surface, but that *wasn't* the thing here.

Ryder lifted his hand, too. "Wonderful to meet you all. Thank you for having me."

He gathered Voodoo's lead, put his hand on the small of her back, boyfriend-style, and headed them out the back gate.

They were a block down the road when she looked around to make sure they were alone. "I think I've figured out part of the puzzle of who took the researchers hostage. At least I have a way to figure it out."

Chapter 13

Ryder

Sabrin had been in her head from the time they left the party until she unlocked the door of their hotel room. Ryder was learning that was a space she liked to inhabit.

The quiet didn't bother him. He kind of liked it—the easy silence that rested between them. Though, it did make him curious about what she was wrestling with.

He didn't press her to share.

It had been interesting being with Sabrin these last two days. When she spoke, she pulled from a depth of knowledge, and that was both intriguing and sexy as hell. Ryder was starting to understand the hot librarian memes. A head full of books and body built for sin.

Watch it, bloke, this is a professional relationship; no knuckle-dragging allowed.

But, Ryder acknowledged, there was a big difference between Sabrin and the women he'd dated. Ryder had gravitated toward women who were a lot more extroverted—their energy more smiley and bouncier.

Fun. They'd been fun.

He'd enjoyed their company.

But they came in succession.

After a while, the women all seemed to blend together. In his line of work, that had made sense to him. He was only home for brief periods of time between deployments, not enough to develop strong relationships. Just enough time to enjoy the affections of women who represented the opposite of his work world.

He hadn't been open to something deep or abiding. He wanted colorful, happy vacations from the dust and misery. He'd have a few weeks with his boots on Australian soil, then he'd be back mucking about in blood and suffering.

A serial monogamist just like his dad…

Though, his dad kept trying to break that habit by marrying the women he dated. Those vows didn't seem to have the sticking power they should.

That's where Ryder thought he and his dad differed. While his dad lacked self-discipline and a code where you determined your goal, and you stuck with it, those were Ryder's strengths. They had to be, or he couldn't have succeeded as a commando.

Yeah, Ryder thought, it wasn't really that he was a serial monogamist because of his genetics or his dad's role modeling. It was that Ryder hadn't found the person that he wanted to vow his life to—the relationship that would inspire him to persevere through all of life's challenges.

Shiny and colorful was easier, for sure. But Ryder felt he'd grown past that and was looking forward to the challenge of a possible forever relationship. He just had to find her.

This year, two of his mates on the Cerberus team found love—the lasting kind.

Tripwire and Dani—she was an Army veterinarian, and they fit hand in glove with their love of K9s.

Ridge and Harper—she was an artist with a brain that was hardwired for science. Just crazy smart, and brave as hell.

Dani and Harper shared two traits that Ryder observed: One, they were as passionate about their jobs as his Cerberus brothers were about theirs. Two, they brought depth to their relationships—intelligence.

Ryder wanted that for himself. He was ready. Finding someone though—

Sabrin cut into Ryder's thoughts. "My family really liked you." She didn't look happy about it.

"I really liked your family." He softly shut the door behind him and threw the latch. "That's going to have ramifications for you, isn't it?" He turned.

"I'll deal," she said as she walked farther into the room.

The scent of seduction wafted around him as he followed Sabrin in. Something the hotel staff had sprayed to set the right mood for a honeymoon suite. Ryder would like to get the name of it to have on hand at home; it was doing a bloody good job on his system. Well, that and Sabrin with her hair braids and her pretty ribbons, and the taste of her kiss still on his lips.

He surreptitiously rearranged his hard-on and untucked his shirt. *Keep yourself in check, bloke.*

Reaching down to unclasp Voodoo's lead, Ryder said. "Tell me what needs to happen now. Back at the party, you seemed to stop on the dog barking idiom, and that's where we left off."

"Would Voodoo like a last walk before we go to sleep? His panting is distracting, and I need to think."

Voodoo heard the word "walk" and dashed over to sit expectantly by the door, tail thumping the carpeting.

"Apparently, he would." Was she trying to get rid of Ryder, so she could contact someone in private? If he was a bloody shithead, he could leave a comms open.

Yeah, he was going to be that piece of shite. This wasn't a tea party. These were lives on the line. Iniquus needed to be standing on solid ground. "Let me use the dunny, then I'll get out of your hair. Do you want to ring me when you're ready for me to come back?" He grabbed up his Dopp kit.

"No, no, just…a half hour? Forty-five minutes?"

"Will do," he said, shutting the door. After using the loo, he rustled through his kit for the little box that held his comms, small magnetic devices that he dropped into his ear canal. He used his phone to turn them on. One went in his ear, the other he palmed.

Before heading out, he placed the second bud near the lamp, slid his phone into his back pocket, grabbed up Voodoo's lead, and said, "Call me if you need anything."

Down the elevator, out the door, crossing the street, he heard nothing from the room. As Ryder turned the corner, a toilet flushed, telling him the comms were on, working, and fairly sensitive to surrounding sounds. He'd definitely hear if Sabrin was having a conversation with anyone.

Ryder dialed Honey over an encrypted line. "Ryder here. Are you available?"

"Roger that. I was hoping you'd reach out. Are you alone?"

"Yep, Sabrin had an ah-ha moment at the party. She wanted to go back to the room to work on it and asked for some privacy."

"Huh."

"Yeah, my thoughts, mate. I left an earbud operating. So far, I haven't heard anything. You can access it if you want to record. It's on the normal channel."

"Doing that now…" There was a long pause. "The computers picking up airflow and rustling but little else. She's in the room, though… She's not on her computer. There aren't any keystroke noises," Honey said. "Could be texting."

"She could be anything." Ryder paused, then crossed the road, head on a swivel. He didn't feel eyes on him, but habits were habits.

"How was the birthday party?" Honey asked. "Did that seem legit?"

"Yeah. Older neighbors stopped by. Babies. Young kids… Why?"

"We've done a little digging on Sabrin."

"Listening."

"First, no ransom ask has come through that we're aware of. State said they'd be notified if there was, and they'd provide all intelligence to us. They've been radio silent. Either the Slovakian government isn't sharing—which would be foolhardy because America would politically retaliate—or nothing new has come through."

"Sabrin got a text that she needs to stop off at the American Embassy in the morning. Maybe the State

Department wants to tell her something in person so as not to get caught by the spooks."

"Anything they could hand us would be more than we have now. I'm working with summoning charms and pixie dust."

"Yeah, I hear yah. Other from the inside of a demonic trance, has anyone spoken to witnesses?" Ryder asked.

"Nothing. It's as if someone snapped their fingers and the bus disappeared into thin air. That's hard to do. Twenty-six people leave a trail. It's tricky to move a group that big with no one seeing them, especially by a single person. A single perp was the assumption I drew from the dictated file the university handed over. I'm looking at a printout of the conversation after the Iniquus computers tried to make sense of it. And there's no sense to be had. It's not very useful to our case. To me, anyway. Not so far. I'll keep going over it. The dictation program wasn't great."

"It's a Word file," Ryder said.

"Yeah, Nutsbe said Sabrin had asked which dictation software was used. Astute. And interesting. I told Nutsbe that when I get back, I'd like to meet with a linguistics programmer, sit down and get a thorough understanding of those concepts. I don't have Sabrin's linguistics background."

"You said you were digging into her, though."

"I got curious as to why State sent her. She might not be fully sharing who she is and why. She's not with State. *That* we know."

"And no one thought we'd look?"

"On paper, she's got a good cover. She's been traveling on diplomatic credentials for a while and working out of the embassy."

"So...what is she about then, hey?"

"We've found only one connection that might make sense."

"Does this have to do with the Zoric family?" Ryder asked. If Sabrin led a cloaked life, that meant she swam in the depths with some genuinely evil people; she didn't just dip her feet in from the shoreline. Thinking of her working for an intelligence agency—the CIA or NSA perhaps—and their inherent dangers sent an odd tingle of cold up Ryder's spine. He picked up his pace to burn off the energy that was pumping through his blood.

Sabrin's voice came through Ryder's comms unit. She spoke clearly and slowly, "Find Carl's hi ya Trom so."

"Did you get that?" Ryder asked Honey.

"Copy. I'll focus on it later, see if the computer can't figure it out. Sabrin told you about the Zorics?"

"She said she was the person who watched the Zoric women—wouldn't they be Zoricova women?"

"Normally, yes, but the family adheres to American name traditions when they come to the United States."

"Okay, so Sabrin said she watched the women on an art scam that the FBI was involved in."

"What were the circumstances that led to that conversation?"

"When I told you that Ridge and Zeus needed to get to a safe location at the competition, it was because she was making the point that those four men that turned up at our camp I was telling you about—"

"Yeah—"

"Might have been there to steal the dogs. And Sabrin talked about how sometimes people of power like to take things just for the thrill of taking them. That's when she gave the example that the Zoric family stole some art, not because they couldn't afford to buy it but because it was a thrill for them."

"If Sabrin was the one watching the Zoric women board the plane with the students, then she was involved in the first steps that led to that takedown of the entire branch of the Zoric family in Washington. Sabrin would know it was Iniquus that found the evidence to have them charged with a laundry list of crimes," Honey said. "It was in the news here in the States when this happened, about eighteen months ago. You were just then getting signed on with Iniquus and getting moved to the United States."

"Who was on that case?"

"Strike Force. And that also involved Steve Finley, FBI terror. Speaking of Finley, because he speaks Slovak and focuses on crimes connected to Slovakian citizens and ex-USSR countries, Nutsbe gave him a call and asked if he had backstory on Sabrin. Finley didn't know anything about Sabrin's workload. But the two of them had met one time when she had some connection to the Sausage-Link King."

"Fat bastard or serial killer who grinds up his enemies?" Ryder asked, turning his head toward the sound of a can rolling in the breeze.

"Can't say, maybe both. The Sausage-Link King is an oligarch with ties to the Zoric family. Two years ago, six Russian GRU officers were charged in the US in connection with implementing worldwide malware and what they're calling 'disruptive actions in cyberspace.'"

"This is getting interesting."

"Yeah, well, they caused about a billion, that's 'B' billion US dollars of losses," Honey said.

"Who were they targeting?"

"The 2018 Winter Olympics and the French election are two of the bigger victims."

Ryder let out a low whistle.

"It was a retaliation and destabilization effort, according to Finley. The Russians were pissed that when they used Novichok, the weapons-grade nerve agent, on foreign soil that there were consequences in terms of the European sanctions. That and the Sausage-Link King had a family member, his nephew, who was on the list of athletes who were banned from the Pyeongchang Winter Olympics for doping."

"I can imagine his family was disappointed. At least that makes sense as to why the Olympics was on the target list. So what did the malware do?"

"Among other things, it caused widespread blackouts across Ukraine, including hospitals. And this wasn't an isolated event. This started in November of 2015 and went on through fall 2019. This week, the US just sent paperwork to Moscow asking that the men involved, including the Sausage-Link King, be sent to Washington for trial."

"But that's Russia."

"A Russian oligarch with close business ties to the Slovakian Zorics. What is it called when the two organisms help each other survive? My wife, Meg, would have the term on the tip of her tongue."

"Parasitic?"

"That's one sucking the life energy out of—*mutualism*, that's the word I'm looking for. It's the 'you scratch my back, and I'll scratch yours' brand of international crime."

"Mutualism… Are we considering something about the Sausage-Link King and computer attacks to be the reason that Sabrin has been sent in? How did that go down anyway, her joining Ridge and me?"

"The call came in saying to tread softly and oh, hey, we have a helper we're sending to you. Where would you like the package delivered? We'd already concluded that we'd pull one of the Cerberus teams from the competition."

"Short straw."

"'Room to grow,' is how I like to frame that for you. My guess is that Sabrin works for one of the intelligence alphabets, and she was sent in for one of these reasons: to keep an eye on Iniquus, to *stop* something from happening, or to be first on scene if we were successful. Honestly, we're clueless as to what's going on over there." Honey paused. "Yeah, all we've got are some panicked American families. A distraught university. At this point, it's throwing darts at the board to see if anything sticks. Did Sabrin seem dexterous with computers? Technology?" Honey asked.

"I've only ever seen her text on her phone. She hasn't asked about our technology capabilities. She was allowing me to lead on encrypted channels, what have you. She seems uninterested. Sabrin maintains that her job's translation. We both know that can mean bloody well anything. We've got some traveling to do tomorrow. It'll give me time to get her talking, see if anything useful comes up. Like, 'I'm a white hat computer-hacking genius.' We need to be careful there with the whole idea of the Sausage-Link King. Sometimes things look like they align when really it's clutter."

"A true story," Honey said on a sigh.

"Look, Sabrin asked for a half hour. I'm heading back to the room. Bridal suite, mind you."

"Ha!"

"I'm going to assume Nutsbe made those arrangements because that was the only suite available, and he wanted Sabrin to have some privacy."

"Romantic, though? Heart-shaped jacuzzi tub? Red velvet padded headboard with handcuff rings?"

"Both, but tastefully done." Ryder signaled Voodoo, and they turned around to retrace their steps. "Hopefully, Sabrin's come up with something that she wants to share. Grain of salt, she could be running us in the wrong direction, perhaps to give some*thing* or some*one* space. That could be her role here, operational malware if you will."

Chapter 14

Sabrin

While Ryder was gone, Sabrin changed from her dress into a pair of yoga pants and a t-shirt that would be modest enough to sleep in and comfortable enough to hang out in their rooms. She'd just chuck the bra later.

The bridal suite had an interesting setup. There was a wall between the bed area with the desk and the area that had the fold-out sofa and eating table. The wide opening would have easily fit a pair of French doors, and yet there were none.

So there wasn't the privacy that Nutsbe might have imagined for them.

It was fine. Heck, she'd slept on the bunk in Ryder's RV, hovering over top of him all night.

And sure, she'd been uncomfortable, wanting to relieve some sexual tension on her own, but that would have been so wrong on so many levels. So many…

She made her way into the bathroom and looked at herself in the mirror. "You need to watch your step," she said aloud as she reached up to unwind her updo. "You are about to get yourself into the world of hurt." She combed her hair out and spun it into a bun at the nape of her neck. This wasn't a vacation. "I *will* do whatever it takes." She and Ryder were on a team, after all, with the goal of saving lives. "*Whatever* is asked of me on this mission, I'll do it." Even if it meant blending her personal and professional life.

She pulled out a disposable cloth provided by the hotel and started to remove her makeup. "And yes, that includes dealing with Ryder Kelly. Distractions can turn deadly." She could set her attraction to him aside, both for the sake of this operation and for her own well-being.

Everything she did had ramifications.

She stared at her face in the mirror. "*I* can be deadly." That's a hell of a thought. Sabrin threw the cloth in the trash. But yes, her actions or her inactions could, in fact, save lives or get people killed, even if it was in an arm's length kind of way.

When she heard the door to the suite softly open, Sabrin stopped her mirror pep-talk.

She waited for a moment, so she wasn't bursting through the bathroom door into Ryder.

Keeping physical distance between them was probably a good idea…there had been a lot of kissing since she'd met him yesterday afternoon.

When Sabrin came out of the bathroom, Ryder was picking something up by the lamp and sliding it into his pocket. He pulled out his phone, drew his finger across the screen, and tapped, then looked up at her with the strangest look in his eyes.

"Is everything okay?" she asked.

"I bloody well hope so." He crossed his arms over his chest, tipping his head back, looking down at her with veiled eyes.

She advanced toward him, but Voodoo stopped her, rubbing against her legs. Sitting at her feet, Voodoo looked up as if asking for a scratch.

Sabrin obliged. "What's happening?"

Ryder stared at his dog. "The hell if I know." He scrubbed a hand over his thick brown hair. "About the only thing I know for certain is that I always trust my dog."

"Wow, is that cryptic."

Ryder's gaze landed on her phone over next to the flower arrangement, then back to her. He pointed at it with a question in his eyes.

"No, I haven't heard anything new," she said.

He planted his hands on his hips. "I'm going to splash some water on my face. I'll be right back." He moved into the bathroom. It took a couple of minutes before she heard the water turn on. With no flush of the toilet, Sabrin wondered what he might be up to in there. Maybe he needed a mirror pep-talk, too.

Wouldn't that be something if Ryder was feeling for her what she was for him? That would bode badly.

Twenty-six people's lives.

Twenty-six.

I have zero time for hormones, and I have zero appetite for getting rolled up by another player out for a good time.

"Did you have any success while I was gone?" he called to her through the bathroom door.

"I believe so. I'd like to talk to you and Honey at the same time if that's possible."

The bathroom door opened, and yeah, there was definitely the energy of confusion around Ryder.

"Did something happen while you were out?" she asked.

"Like what?" he asked.

She shook her head. "I don't know." She sat down on the bed, leaning back with her weight braced on her hands. "So... I'm ready for you whenever you want to do this."

He blinked at her.

"I don't know how to contact Honey..."

"Oh, right." Ryder shook his head as if clearing a thought and moved to the desk, positioned across from the foot of the bed where their computers lay. He booted up and tapped on the keyboard, then tugged the chair over and sat down.

After a moment, she heard, "Honey here."

"You're on an open communication with Ryder and Sabrin. We're in the hotel room."

"Roger."

"Per the other thing we were talking about the last time the two of us spoke," Ryder said. "There was a recent communication. Did you pick it up?"

"Roger. Good luck to you, man." He chuckled. "You should sleep tight, knowing that's the situation."

Sabrin frowned at Ryder. She wondered when the two men had last talked. Maybe when Ryder was waiting for her to return her rental car to the airport. It was probably about another case Ryder was working on.

This was, after all, sprung on all of them yesterday.

"Per Sabrin and the hostage situation," Ryder continued. "I went for a walk to give Sabrin some time to contemplate. She thinks she's landed on something and asked that I reach out to you. She doesn't have a way to communicate except through me. With your permission, I'd like to give her Nutsbe's direct line."

"Roger. Sabrin, I'm sorry for overlooking that. And good evening to you."

"Good evening." Sabrin put on her most professional voice. "I'd like to get right to this if it would be all right."

"Yes, ma'am."

"I have some notes." She turned to Ryder. "I printed off copies for you and me, so we could refer to them. Can you send a copy to Honey?" She pointed to her open computer, then got up to retrieve the two pages she'd printed in preparation and handed one to Ryder.

Ryder pulled out his phone and took a picture. "Encrypted end to end." He reminded her.

She moved to the top of the bed and sat down with her legs crisscrossed in front of her, using the second pillow to support her back.

"Okay," she said, looking over her work, "you have the page in front of you, Honey?"

"Yes, ma'am," Honey replied.

"I was talking to Ryder before about computer systems not speaking a language but filling in letters based on algorithms within the AI systems. The words that are speech to text aren't dependable or clear in any document produced that way. In this case, there are three problems with the text. One, the inherent limitations of the software. Two, that the person seems to be speaking English as a second language. That's the assumption that I was working under."

"Learning from you," Honey said. "How did you come to that second conclusion?"

"Many countries have excellent language programs. Their students speak near-native English, especially those who steep themselves in American culture and read a lot of our books that have modern syntax, idioms, and relationship perspectives. To address your question as to why I think he's speaking English—albeit good English—as a second language, I'll answer in a moment. Why would this man be in Slovakia, speaking in English? I believe he's doing so because there were five nationalities on the bus, and English is typically the common language in such cases, especially amongst academicians."

"You said three problems," Ryder reminded her.

She pressed her lips together. "I've come to the conclusion that the third issue with understanding what's going on, during the time frame documented in the pages you sent me, Honey, is that the person is bat shit crazy."

Silence filled the room.

"And that makes the situation that much more deadly." As she said that, adrenaline dumped through her body. She was truly terrified for the hostages.

Ryder leaned his forearms onto his thighs. He held the page that Sabrin had handed him out in front of him, but he was focused on her.

Voodoo jumped onto the bed and walked in circles until he'd found his spot. Curling up beside Sabrin, Voodoo rested his head on her knee.

Sabrin bent and kissed him, grateful he was there.

"Okay," Sabrin said, "let's begin." She picked up her page. "I was focused on this sentence here that I copied at the top. Do you see where I highlighted 'aunty loving' in yellow? It must be something else. It reads, 'If we all understood that aunty loving isn't just for humans, it's for all things the air and the water, the soil, the bees and yes the birds, too. We're all equal.' I focused on that last sentence, 'We're all equal.'" She stopped and scratched her forehead. "Without knowing the accent used, it's hard to say what that might be. However, there's a set of...principles, I guess, is the best way to explain—that is a way of life in Scandinavian countries—Norway, Denmark, and Sweden— called *Janteloven*. It translates to 'Jante's Laws,' though they aren't laws, more like the ten commandments of being a good citizen. A list of ideals that people are to live up to. Basically, they're a means toward having an egalitarian society. No one is better than the other. The J in *Janteloven* is silent, possibly sounding like aunty loving."

"If we all understood that *Janteloven* isn't just for humans..." Honey replaced 'aunty loving' for the new term. "That makes sense."

"If this person is bringing up *Janteloven* in a stream of conscious diatribe, as this seems to be, then I imagine he is either from a Scandinavian country or grew up there. It might narrow things down a bit. Not much. This person is plainly crazy. There's not just delusional thinking that we often find under such circumstances, but he seems to be describing auditory hallucinations about the trees speaking to him and directing him to take action. It was the trees that were telling this guy that *Janteloven* applied to them, too. Humans weren't valued greater than other aspects of nature."

Ryder lifted his chin. "When we were at the party, you said, 'idioms,' and seemed like something had become clearer for you. That's what you've got listed here."

"Yes. That's right. When I first attempted this as a linguistic puzzle, the language seemed so outlandish that I worked under the assumption that these phrases were put together through the algorithm's mistakes. But at the party, I started thinking about idioms. I wanted to look over the words with the idea that they weren't AI mistakes but actual idioms. Having already concluded that this man was from a Scandinavian country, I tried looking for idioms that showed up in those cultures. Can you take a moment to read through this? Then I'll go over my thoughts."

Sabrin was quiet, giving the men a moment to read through:

☐ *"If we all understood that aunty loving isn't just for humans, it's for all things the air and the water, the soil, the bees, and yes the birds, too."*

☐ *"I got blood on my tooth from the trees."*

Blood on my tooth = to become inspired by—to feel driven to do something.

☐ *"There, I stood with my beard in the post box, receiving my award for my research when, in fact, it was the trees that deserved all of the praise."*

Beard in the post box = cheated your way into a situation(ish). Award for my research might be a clue. He does research. The people who were taken were researchers, connected???

☐ *"Now comes the time, I speak directly from my liver. There are owls in the moss. I can't figure it out. Perhaps it's how dare yah? Perhaps she recognizes a boy living free. Let's live in Carl's hi yah Tom, so."*

Speak from the liver = tell one's truth. Owls in the moss = something's not right.

☐ *"We must not swallow some camels. We must act. I'm acting. I hope you will all forgive me. But I'm following the direction of the trees. They spoke to me clearly. And everything they say is turning out right the way they said it would. You're here, aren't you?"*

Swallow some camels = ignore something to keep the peace.

"Okay?" she asked after a moment.

"Yes," the men said in unison.

"One thing we know is that we're looking for a man. It's a 'he' because he calls himself a boy."

"Right," Honey said.

She paused again. "Can you focus on the part about the owls?"

"I'm looking at that now," Honey said.

"These idioms are Norwegian. When my uncle talked

about dogs being all bark no bite, I thought, that's an idiom used all over the world. Some idioms, though, are specific to a country." The paper lay on the bed in front of her, and she was talking animatedly with her hands.

"These are odd, right?" she continued. "We might say, 'I'm speaking from my heart' instead of 'I'm speaking from my liver,' but we don't have anything like *'owls in the moss.'* These are specific to Norway. And this guy uses a lot of them. More than one would think reasonable even over five pages of dictation."

"And you think that has significance?" Ryder asked.

"I would conjecture that he probably grew up—or was living for an extended time—in a small town, a place that was kind of cut off. I would also speculate that he is *at least* forty years old because he doesn't have a pattern of speech that was developed once the Internet encroached on our way of expressing ourselves."

"Interesting," Honey said.

"Staying with that same section with the owls." She put on a finger on that passage. "The computer heard, 'Perhaps it's how dare yah.' What could this be in Norway? 'How dar yah' has to be a force, a person, an entity… There's a mythical being called the Huldra. The Huldra is a seductress that's akin to a Greek siren. She has long golden hair and lives in the mountains of Norway. She rewards men who can satisfy her sexual appetite." Unbidden, Sabrin's lashes flicked up as she sought out Ryder's eyes.

When she caught his gaze, a blush rose up her cheeks. Sabrin swallowed and shifted her eyes back down to the page. "The Huldra kills the men who fail to bring her to orgasm. Either way," Sabrin gave a little shrug, "once the Huldra chooses a man to seduce, he's never seen again."

"That's *terrifying*," Ryder said with a grin.

Sabrin couldn't imagine Ryder ever failing to bring a woman to orgasm.

She cleared her throat. "Again in that section on owls. '…free. Let's live in Carl's hi yah Tom, so.' In Norway, they live by the concept of *friluftsliv*. This translates to mean open-air living. Norwegians spend a lot of their free time out in nature, hiking, camping, no matter the weather, no matter how cold. *Friluftsliv* is a tradition of making time outdoors part of daily life. Let's stipulate for the time being that 'Perhaps she'— refers to Huldra—'recognizes a boy living free. Let's live…' becomes, 'Perhaps she recognizes a boy living friluftsliv'—in the open air, enjoying nature."

"Yup," Honey said. "That fits."

"Then that last bit, 'in Carl's hi yah Tom, so,' could well be referring to the place where he was living. Tromso is fairly easy for me to hear when I read that aloud. When I used voice command in Google maps on my phone, saying, 'Find Carl's hi ya Tromso—'"

"Ah!" both men said together as if that one aspect, in particular, had been a puzzle for them.

She paused, waiting for them to fill her in.

"Sorry," Ryder said. "Please continue."

"When I used voice commanded on my phone, saying, 'Find Carl's hi ya Tromso,' it found a small island just off the coast of Norway called, Karlsøya, Tromso."

Neither Honey nor Ryder said a word.

She pushed herself into the pillows, rubbing her

hands, moist with perspiration, on her thighs. "Or this is gibberish, and none of this is correct."

"No, I think you're on to something," Honey said. "I didn't respond because I was sending a message to Nutsbe back at HQ to see what resources Iniquus has in the Tromso Norway area. We need someone native to the region to get onto the island and talk to the locals. Ideally, tonight."

"Full-summer," Ryder said. "Plenty of daylight that far north. The sun doesn't go down but for about an hour. That should help them out."

Sabrin frowned. "The more time I spend with these pages, the more afraid I grow for the hostages." She picked up the paper and waggled it at Ryder. "These thoughts are disorganized." She put the page down. "Even if some of this makes sense and some I'm still trying to reason out, this guy is exhibiting delusion and hallucination. I would be thinking in terms of schizophrenic traits. But then, if he were schizophrenic, he couldn't do this on his own. Disorganized thoughts lead to disorganized behaviors. I see two viable possibilities. One, this man is the front of a group. Which is terrible but *might* mean the hostages are still alive."

Again, the room filled with a dense silence.

"And two?" Ryder asked, his muscles visibly braced.

"There's always the possibility that a madman was out and randomly came across the bus. He boarded. He started talking crazy talk. An American researcher had the computer open and pressed Dictate. Luckily, it automatically saves as a group file shared back with their university, and we know how it unwound on our end once the file was opened and read. On the bus, though, the madman could have sat down in the driver's seat, put the engine into gear, and driven them off a cliff. That scenario would explain why we can't find the bus, and there are no witnesses to any of this."

"Twenty-six people." Ryder put his hands on his head, arching back to look up at the ceiling. "Bloody hell."

Chapter 15

Sabrin

Sabrin sat at the table, finishing up a second cup of coffee. She was a little blurry today. Last night she'd tossed and turned in and out of nightmares until Voodoo had come and jumped on the bed, curling up against her stomach like he'd done in the RV when she was having trouble sleeping.

Voodoo was aptly named. He was magic. She'd wrapped her arm around him and fell into a deep sleep, feeling safe from whatever monsters wanted to raise their nasty heads.

Last night, she'd dreamt again about being trapped underwater by the king of frogs. Such a weird, strange dream, the sticky kind. The kind that hovered in the consciousness even once she was awake.

Lots of watery dreams. The Huldra...that one made

all sense to her. But even Huldra quieted down once Voodoo got in bed with Sabrin. "I want to take you home with me so we can cuddle every night," she'd mumbled groggily and had gotten a rough tongue lick across her cheek as a response.

These last two nightmare-filled nights were unusual for Sabrin. Normally, she slept like the dead.

This morning, Ryder had softly whistled for Voodoo. "Sabrin, stay asleep. I'm going to go exercise Voodoo."

She'd fluttered her lashes open just enough to peek at the clock. 5:00. "More power to you," she groaned as she punched her pillow and rolled over.

Ryder chuckled. As he was going out the door, she heard, "I'm starting to think you like our Sabrin better than you do me, mate. My feelings are hurt." Then the door quietly clicked into place.

"*Our* Sabrin…" She fell back asleep with those words playing in her head and stayed asleep for another two hours. When she finally pried herself out of bed to take a shower, she saw that Ryder had made a pot of coffee earlier, she assumed for her. "Bless you," she said as she poured herself a cup.

After ordering breakfast for the two of them, Sabrin took her coffee into the bathroom with her while she took a shower and got dressed for the day—a suit and heels, her hair neatly pinned in a chignon, her makeup subtle and professional, pearl earrings.

When the breakfast arrived, it filled the room with thick savory scents, making her stomach rumble and thankfully masking that scent of seduction that housekeeping had sprayed that somehow wasn't dissipating. She wondered if the hotel had it available for sale in the gift shop. It wouldn't hurt to have this on hand when she went home. It had a strong effect on her libido. Or maybe it was just sleeping in the same room as Ryder.

This morning, Sabrin had chosen typical Slovakian breakfast foods, hoping that was okay with Ryder—she'd chosen the heavier foods from the menu, not knowing how their day would turn out. In Sabrin's experience, it was always better to get in a hardy breakfast. Sometimes meals later in the day never happened. Get while the getting was good.

Ryder and Voodoo were just coming back when the waiter rolled the service out, having arranged their food on the table. Thick peasant-style bread, butter and honey, cheese, ham, boiled eggs, roasted vegetables, cut fruit, and a bowl of yogurt to mix it into.

"This looks amazing," Ryder said. "I'm just going to take Voodoo into the bathroom to get him fed."

While he was in there, a text dropped into Sabrin's phone. "Hey," she called to him. "I told you I need to run by the embassy on our way out of town."

"Yeah."

"They want me there by nine to sign some papers."

"That's doable. It's not far from here, right?"

"At that time of day, twenty minutes. We just need to eat, check out, and go."

"I'm getting Voodoo's tucker together, then I'll come join you. That looks delicious. Thank you for ordering."

Sabrin wasn't sure why Ryder fed Voodoo in the bathroom. She surmised it had something to do with the carpeting. Sabrin's phone pinged; she read the text. "Hey, what's your real name?" she called out.

He poked his head around the corner.

She waggled her phone. "It's for the security gate.

They won't let you in unless your ID matches your name on their list. If you want to keep it secret—if you're Homer Eugene Kelly, and you don't want anyone to know—I'd understand, but you'll have to wait outside. Cover-wise, it's probably better if you're with me."

"Tristan Patrick Kelly."

"Tristan… Patrick… Kelly and K9 Voodoo," she said as she typed that in. "How did you become Ryder Kelly? It has a romantic ring to it. Sort of cowboy against the prairie sky…"

"Sit tight." Tristan gave Voodoo his command, then louder for Sabrin's ears, said, "In Afghanistan, we couldn't get vehicles to the places we needed to be, so I suggested we take horses in. I was the only one with experience." There was the plinking of kibble into Voodoo's meal bowl. "It was on me to buy local livestock and then teach my mates how to ride a horse. It was…a process." He laughed.

"And they spelled it with a y?"

"That was part of the schtick. There was a whole lot of whys going on. Why are we doing this? Why did you come up with this? Why can't I straighten my legs out anymore?"

"Ha, sounds like a good time was had by all. I'm going to dig in if that's okay."

"Yeah, please start. I'll be there, just a moment." There was a clatter as he put the food bowl on the tile floor. "Tuck in," he commanded, then shut the door behind him.

Sabrin spread butter on a thick slice of bread. "How did you learn? Riding, that is." She took a bite. So good. So, so, so good. A little moan slipped out despite her best efforts to keep it contained.

When she opened her lashes, Ryder was sitting at the table, a look of endearment, maybe a little laughter in his eyes.

"Try," she said, using the back of her hand to push the basket closer to him.

He picked up a slab of bread. "I grew up out on a station—what the Yanks call a ranch—working livestock. I lived on the back of a horse."

"Do you miss it? Being in Washington, DC, that's sort of going to extremes in changing lifestyles."

"There are things that I miss. My family." He took a bite. "Wow, you're not kidding. This is tasty." He wiped his mouth with his napkin. "I miss the beauty of a sunrise over the expanse of nothingness—never-ending skies. Nights lit with a view of the Milky Way. It had its romance. It pulls at my heart. But it's not a good lifestyle fit for me. I'm comfortable where I am."

Her phone pinged. Sabrin read it, then lifted the screen for Ryder to see: You're on the list at the gate. Make sure K9 Voodoo stays on lead and under the control of his handler.

"Speaking of texts," Ryder said. "Honey says they have someone over on Karlsøya island, checking to see if they can't track down any information on who might have been talking on the bus. He said it's tiny and the population very small. Everyone should know everyone there. Narrowing down to a specific individual, if done correctly, shouldn't be hard."

"Unless the locals circle the wagons." She paused. "That's an American-centric idiom that references pioneers heading from the East Coast to settle on the West Coast in the nineteenth century. They used Conestoga wagons to bring their supplies to their new homes, and at night, they'd create a circle with them as a defense against wildlife and attacks."

"Interesting. I'd heard people use it before and got the gist of what they were saying. I just didn't know why they said it," Ryder said.

Sabrin's body tensed, and she blew out a breath. "Man, I hope that's not a wild goose chase out to Karl-søya. Nothing I said to Honey last night was concrete. It was all speculation."

Ryder took a sip of coffee. "If Honey didn't think it was actionable, he would have said so."

Working with Iniquus for the first time, Sabrin wanted to make a good impression.

Who was she kidding? She wanted to make a good impression on Ryder. She needed to cut that out. It wasn't just unprofessional; egos got in the way of good decision making.

There was a knock at their door.

"Mmm," she said, putting her fork down. "That's got to be the bellhop. I told them 8:15." She pulled her napkin from her lap as she moved to stand up.

"I've got it." Ryder sauntered over to check through the peephole, then swung the door wide for the bellhop.

"Mr. Kelly?"

Ryder nodded and pointed to their bags that were sitting out ready. "If you want to start down, we'll follow in just a moment."

Chapter 16

Sabrin

Sabrin was glad Ryder was not only driving the RV but was using his phone's GPS to get them to the embassy.

She needed to think.

Each time she was in a meeting with Honey and Ryder, she could feel the questions hanging in the air. "Who are you, and what the heck are you doing on our mission?"

She felt like she'd proven herself to be a valuable team member with her linguistic skills, but the next time they had a meeting, she needed to clarify her role.

That thought amused her. Sabrin didn't have clue one about her role. She hoped to gain some insight today at the embassy, something beyond the fact that she could speak the language, and she gave Ryder cover.

Ryder needed cover, too. Big time. Did he even know?

And more important, could she even ask Ryder about it? That was something else she needed to talk to Green about.

She wondered why her superior, John Green, had summoned her to the embassy this morning with the text.

In Sabrin's job, she was told to go perform a finite action. Rarely was a bigger picture painted for her, letting her know how her puzzle piece fit in with the others to make a connected whole. It occurred to her that Ryder's job was the same or had been back when he was a Commando for the Australian military.

She'd mentioned to Ryder that she'd watched the Zoric women and the students board a plane. That had been her mission. Sabrin only learned the broader story by reading an American newspaper account about how instrumental Iniquus had been in stopping the Zorics and getting the bad guys jailed and awaiting trial.

The trial was about to start in the Northern Virginia court system.

Iniquus was a Zoric enemy, and she, Sabrin, was consorting with that enemy on Slovakian soil.

That thought made her sweat.

As Sabrin scratched her forehead, she felt Ryder turn to look at her before redirecting his focus back at the street he was navigating.

Sabrin hadn't looked up. She didn't want to engage in conversation. She needed to *think*.

What she thought was that Ryder shaved. His. Beard.

Personally, and selfishly, Sabrin had preferred him wearing it because it took the edge off her desire for him. Which was a distraction that was growing harder to deal with. The hormones made her brain fuzzy. And now, she had to contend with those hormones. She was turning into a walking storm of desire, and she wasn't sure what to do about it. This level of horny had never happened to Sabrin before.

It was distracting, and she was *pissed* he'd shaved the beard.

But more than that, his shaving his beard was damned dangerous, and she needed to bring it up with Green today while she was at the embassy.

With his beard shaven, Sabrin had recognized Ryder Kelly immediately from intel videos.

He was a goddamned hero.

Balls of steel.

I'm proud to be on a team with him, but if the Zorics see his face, they'll recognize him too.

Late November last year, her friend Anna, who was with the Asymmetric Warfare Group, told John Green that ISIS had a new weapon developed by a bomb maker. Sabrin worked on the translations that Anna was able to get hold of. From this, Sabrin knew the case had loose ties to the Zorics, but the lines of connection were never drawn for her. What she did know was that the bomb developer was Saudi.

The terrorists depended on the Zorics for key contacts to get the right players to the table to make the attack happen. The Zorics had facilitated funding, which had been siphoned down from Russia and an oligarch nicknamed the Sausage-Link King.

While there had been shoe bombers and underwear bombers, few people looked askance when a woman dressed in business attire walked up the jetway to her

plane with a laptop computer bomb in her briefcase—
undetectable by airport security.

Undetectable.

The window for retrieving that technology was
sliver thin. They'd had to reach out to boots that were
already on the ground in the area. The CIA had found
out Iniquus Strike Force was in Northern Syria after
saving a hostage there. And Sabrin knew they had a
dog team that had followed them over to lend a hand
but had arrived after the hostage had been rescued.

For certain, *that* handler was Ryder. Sabrin had
seen the photos of him, and as soon as that beard was
gone, *whew!* she had felt the fear of knowing that while
Iniquus was the Zoric's enemy, they would like nothing better than to have this man's head on a platter.

Had Voodoo been with Ryder?

The Iniquus team drove their Jeeps to the meeting
house of an ISIS cell mapped by Angel Sobado and
John Grey. Both CIA operators were off-grid and unable to affect the mission.

Which turned out to be fortuitous.

The K9 on the Strike Force team had ended up being
the crucial ingredient.

The goal at that ISIS house was to hear every word
that was said about the terrorists' plans. They ended
up sending the K9 in. He wore a camera collar with
night vision and a radio, just like Ryder had used to
direct Voodoo through the tunnels at the competition.

Was that really just two days ago?

Carrying the listening bug in his mouth, leaping
onto the roof, climbing through the open windows, the
K9 had followed his handler's directives and dropped
the listening apparatus, then returned to get another.

That meant the handler had to have been right there in the yard of the ISIS compound.

Silently, the K9 laid the technology throughout the sleeping household.

A hero dog.

A ghost in the night.

Sabrin's body trembled as a shiver raced through her system.

That task was an incredible feat.

Sabrin, on the other hand, had been holed up with Green and others watching this unfold on the screen in the command room.

At first, Strike Force reported that they were afraid the listening devices had been damaged in the K9s mouth, chewed and broken. But they were wrong. As the household awoke and breakfast was served, ISIS troop members began to discuss the process of transforming the laptop into a weapon that couldn't be detected at airports. The bombs, they assured their leader, would explode into fireballs in the sky.

That intelligence was acted upon.

The skies continued to be safe.

Was that Voodoo? She'd never know. That case was highly classified, so she couldn't ask or even hint at her guess.

What were the implications of this particular man working with her here and now?

This felt dodgy to her. Things were too…too… Yeah, they were lining up too closely to her job here in Slovakia, instead of being a one-off event that she was helping to resolve.

It made her think in terms of conspiracy theories. Once again, Sabrin was considering that there was someone on that research team now held hostage—possibly one of the Americans, possibly not—but someone that was playing a role in the Zoric terror plans.

There were lots of people working for State in Slovakia. Any one of them would have been an okay choice for a mission to keep Iniquus away from a jackpot and protect diplomatic ties.

There were even plenty of people, CIA, FBI, that could have given Ryder tactical support if he needed more than a cover, and the US government wanted Iniquus to be successful.

Heck, the thought that Iniquus needed anyone outside of their organization to be successful seemed odd.

She was chosen.

For. A. Reason.

More information would sure be helpful here.

The intelligence community loved to play their games.

Was Iniquus playing chess, too?

Did they know more about this hostage situation than they were sharing? Was that why they gave her the short straw as if it were chance? If Ridge had come in second, would Iniquus have changed their minds, feinted—like Ryder had done with Voodoo's fake injury? How would she know the difference?

She wouldn't have known the difference.

It had taken Ryder shaving that beard of his, taking off the mirrored sunglasses and the ball cap with the brim casting shadows over his features.

It did seem to her that they were either extremely good at acting, or she was indeed a surprise to Ridge and Ryder when she showed up at their camp.

Danger. Danger. Danger.

Sabrin whipped her head toward Ryder as he reached over and cinched her safety belt tighter.

His eyes never left the road.

With hands comfortably on the wheel, Ryder's whole body had the feel of a radar scope, searching for information, pings on the instrument panel.

Sabrin searched for a reason for this dynamic shift, and then she saw it: Up ahead of them, two men were in the black sedan. Both were men who had stopped at Ryder's camp that first night.

"You see them?" He didn't wait for her to answer. "Two more in the yellow one behind us. They just sandwiched us in."

Sabrin looked around at where Voodoo was strapped to the passenger seat that served as one of the dinette seats, his K9 safety belt in place. "Voodoo, lie down." She tried to remember what Ryder had said to get Voodoo to do that. "Hit the mats, mate," she tried.

It was the first time she'd tried to command him.

Voodoo looked at her, confused. Sabrin tried a hand signal she'd seen Ryder use, and Voodoo lay down.

"Good boy. That's a good, good boy." That felt safer to Sabrin.

"I'm going to get away from them as soon as we reach that intersection," Ryder said smoothly. "Be ready. Three. Two. Here we go." With his feet playing both the gas and brake pedals, Ryder spun the wheel, and they turned one-eighty.

Sabrin was tossed about on her seat as she gripped the armrest.

"Still coming. Here we go, three. Two." He slammed on the brakes and threw them into reverse, backing into an alley.

Mere seconds later, the men in the yellow sedan whizzed by. No way they had time to even block them into this alley with the press of traffic. Sabrin knew that one bad guy car could wait at the crossroads and the other could simply circle the block and come up behind them, boxing them in.

She didn't want to be caught in this alley with no escape.

Surely, Ryder knew what he was doing. He obviously had some mad driving skills under his belt— even in this behemoth of an escape vehicle. Maybe from driving trucks in the war zone…

"Guns," Sabrin said. "Both of them."

"Roger." It was an everyday voice. No stress at all.

Meanwhile, Sabrin was sweating it out beside him, thinking that her stiletto pumps were a poor choice for today if they ended up having to get away on foot.

Ryder powered them backward up that alley, trying to get to the roadway before the yellow car could circle. How he could see to maneuver the RV like this, she had no idea.

"Sabrin, call the embassy, remind them we're in a bleeding Winnebago, and tell them we're coming in hot. We need the gates open and everyone out of our way. We'll stop for ID once we're inside. Do it now."

It was good that Ryder had tacked on the "Do it now." It helped spur her brain into action. She searched for her purse, but it had been flung somewhere in the cabin. She reached over and felt Ryder's thigh, found his phone there, and pulled it from the pocket. "Code?"

"The shape of a delta."

"Delta, got it."

Ryder spun the RV again. "Bleeding hell," he muttered as they lurched out of the alley. "There's the other set."

They wove in and out of the oncoming traffic, trying to get space and time between them and the black car.

"Emergency," Sabrin called into the phone when the receptionist answered. "Sabrin Harris. Tristan Kelly and I have a morning appointment with John Green. John Green. John Green," she repeated as if it was a magic incantation that would unlock the key to their safety. "We're coming in hot, two cars in pursuit. Individuals are armed. Request an open gate."

Sabrin's head was snapping back and forth from Ryder's maneuvers. *Can you get whiplash like this?*

"Hang tight." Ryder slammed on the brakes. They came to a sudden and heart quivering stop. Then he pressed down on the gas again, and they rocketed—as much as a top-heavy, cumbersome as all get out RV could be rocketed—up the street.

Behind her, the screech of tires and the bang of a car plowing into the rear of the other. Ryder grinned. "That works almost every time the driver lacks balls."

Ryder had balls of steel.

Chapter 17

Sabrin

"God, I hope I didn't pee myself," Sabrin muttered as they *bump bumped* over the grating and came to a stop.

Guns in hands, the guards jogged toward their vehicle.

Of course, they had their weapons drawn. Ryder had roared through the checkpoint like their tail was on fire. Since the two cars trying to stop them had crashed, Sabrin assumed Ryder was just having fun at that point. Why the heck was he grinning like he was stepping off the roller coaster at the fair, ready to go again?

The gate clanged shut behind them.

Sabrin tapped Ryder's phone to pull up his photo gallery. She stared down at the screen.

"What have you got there?" he asked. Ryder kept

one hand on the steering wheel while pressing the auto-down button on his window, then placed his other hand on the steering wheel.

Keeping both hands easily seen by the guards meant no one got an itchy trigger finger.

Sabrin held Ryder's cell phone up for him, so he could see. "I thought I got their picture for identification, but all I captured was a shadowy face and the pistol. Piece of crap Russian *Makarov*."

There was a tap-tap on her window, and she pressed the button to roll it down.

"*Makarov*, huh?" Ryder said. "Russian arms are part of linguistics training?"

"My dad's military with a collection of guns." She turned toward the guard at her window. "Sabrin Harris, here to see John Green. My ID is in my purse, and that got tossed somewhere while we were being chased."

"Yes, ma'am. I'll need to see that ID."

"I'll vouch for them," John Green called out. Sauntering toward their RV, Green sported well-tailored pants on his tennis player's body. His thick hair had turned prematurely gray, giving him a suave, metro air. A man as comfortable in opera houses and taste-testing on weekend vineyard tours as he was sliding silently through the alleys and drainpipes doing whatever was needed to keep America safe. But no one would guess the last part, and Sabrin felt sure that it had been a while since he had done that kind of intelligence gathering.

Green stopped short. With his hands on his hips, he took in the length and height of their vehicle. "This is what you were driving while being chased by someone with a gun pointed at you?"

"Go big or go home," Sabrin said, popping her door open. "It was actually four someones with four guns in two cars. Ryder got them to crash into each other. Had that disabled their vehicles, it would have been a great way to identify them. But I watched in the side mirror as the two cars hobbled away."

"No horrific injuries? More's the pity." Green's voice frequently held that dry, almost British satiric humor to it. "We'll need to sort your transportation. Change of plans, no more camping for you." Green lifted his chin. "You're Ryder Kelly?" Green looked through the passenger window at Ryder, sitting there, cool as a cucumber.

"Sir," Ryder said.

"Leave the keys in the RV. We'll get things loaded into an alternate vehicle and get this returned to the rental place."

Ryder didn't answer.

"Unless, of course, you're enjoying high-speed chases through the streets of Bratislava. Hard to look for hostages when you're causing a stir." Green paused as that thought settled low in Sabrin's gut.

Green had no authority over Ryder.

But if Green thought their antics were angering the Slovakian government, he could pull Sabrin from the case. Sabrin wasn't ready to leave the mission. She felt herself mentally setting her claws into the fabric of the case and clinging on.

"The local police aren't going to like your driving technique, even if a gun was pointed your way. We need to get rid of the RV. Period." Without waiting for a response, Green turned, gesturing with a scoop of his arm that they should follow, then walked away.

Ryder moved through the RV. He handed Sabrin her purse that he'd found as he got Voodoo out of his safety belt and onto a lead.

The three of them clambered out.

Side by side, now on the blacktop, Ryder tipped his head to look over her shoulder at Sabrin's butt. He ducked his head and whispered, "No pee."

That made her laugh, breaking the hold that stress had had on her throat from the unexpected way of arriving at her workplace.

Ryder touched her elbow, and they followed behind Green as he went through a side door into the embassy.

Voodoo seemed completely unfazed by the car chase and trotted next to Ryder, looking around with interest, being a good boy. Sabrin wished she were the one holding the lead.

"It's kind of funny," Sabrin said, loud enough that her superior could hear. "That I'm working with Mr. Kelly and Mr. Green. Kelly Green. And on top of that, I met up the other day with Ridge and Ryder. Ridge Ryder." Sabrin knew the layout of the embassy well; she had guessed where Green was leading them. "Fun with names and sounds…" she muttered to herself as they took the carpeted stairs to the third floor.

Green reached around and handed her a Russian language newspaper he'd been carrying folded under his arm. "I thought you'd find this interesting."

She opened the front page and read the headline. *The well-beloved oligarch known as the Sausage-Link King was killed yesterday evening at his home in an apparent attempted robbery.*

She blinked at it.

After a moment, Sabrin locked eyes with Green. "Wow. That's a surprising turn of events."

"You'll find the circumstances unusual. It's got nothing to do with anything you're working on now. I just thought you'd be…fascinated." He turned and started back up the stairs. "And to know that our onward investigation and litigation will no longer include trying to get him brought to the US."

Normally, Sabrin would be too curious to wait to read the article. But her plate was full. She'd save this for later. "I can keep this?"

"It's all yours. I'm done reading it," Green said.

She opened her purse and stuck the folded newspaper inside, feeling Ryder's curiosity flowing through his fingers now resting on the small of her back as he guided her, boyfriend-style, up the stairs.

Petrov Armanov, AKA the Sausage-Link King, was dead. There were twenty-six hostages who were still *potentially* alive, Sabrin thought as they reached the top of the stairs. *Priorities.*

Up on the third floor, there was an office that had revolving users. Whoever was in town working with the diplomatic staff could use it. Secure and soundproof, that's where they were heading now.

The staff Sabrin knew greeted her as they passed by on the sweeping, opulent staircase. They looked at Voodoo curiously and then up to the man holding Voodoo's lead. More than one woman raised their brows at Ryder and fanned their faces for Sabrin's benefit.

Yeah, Ryder was drool-worthy.

And yeah, she was sure he was excellent at the sweaty tumble between the sheets that was obviously filling the women's imaginations.

Too bad Sabrin had already decided she wasn't playing anymore. Those kinds of fun and done relationships were distracting her from her goal.

Sabrin was determined to find her happily-ever-after—not in the Disney princess vein, but like her grandparents had.

Honestly, Ryder's sex appeal was problematic. Sabrin was having trouble controlling her systems. And she needed to be focused on the hostages.

The hostages.

Why was *she* the one assigned to help find the hostages?

Sabrin was determined to get some answers from Green.

One thing seemed clear to her, someone on that bus was critical to national security. Sabrin just didn't know who. Or why. But now, she thought she might have an inkling.

If she was right, given what she'd been working on with the Sausage-Link King attacks—and what Ryder had done for the coalition forces in Syria, then this was about terror and not about a crazy guy talking to trees. She needed to be thinking along those lines.

She wished she had a gun.

Green had told her no weapons. Period. She was a tourist.

And now Ryder had no safety beard.

Not only was that beard helpful in keeping him disguised, but it was also the device she had used to keep herself emotionally—and physically—distant from a man that she had a definite lust for.

Stop. It's not just lust. I'm not that smarmy. I genuinely like the guy.

Yeah, her attraction to Ryder was more than physical. It was also intellectual and emotional.

But it was transient.

And that was the thing Sabrin needed to guard herself against. Ryder just didn't seem like a guy who was interested in white picket fences.

"Mr. Kelly, would you excuse us for a moment?" Green pointed to a sofa in an alcove outside of the office space.

Ryder caught Sabrin's gaze. She sensed that he was checking her temperature, making sure she thought everything was okay before he responded. With a hand resting comfortably on Voodoo's head, he said, "Sabrin, I think I'll go outside with Voodoo and see what arrangements are being made for the Winnebago. There's some equipment there I'd rather not have touched."

She nodded.

"You'll call me if you need me?" He seemed hesitant to leave her.

"Yes, thank you." She offered up an "it's fine; I'm fine" smile.

He looked her boss in the eye. "Green." Then walked off.

Green opened the office door with a chuckle. "Larger than life."

"Yeah. You attached me to a superhero. When I met Ryder at the K9 competition, he had a thick beard." She made her way into the office and aimed for the guest chair farthest from the door. "He shaved for Babka's party, then I recognized him from that Syrian mission last December. That was him, wasn't it? And Voodoo?" She swept her hand across the back of her pencil skirt and sat.

To her surprise, Green took the chair next to hers rather than sitting behind the desk.

"That's right," he said. "And I can tell you're lining cases up in your head, looking for connections. You're thinking I was signaling you with the article about the Sausage-Link King, and you're primed to think about terror attacks because of the role Ryder and Iniquus's Strike Force played last winter in Syria. On this, there aren't any connections. Everything is as it seems. I will repeat for you your involvement with the case. Iniquus is here fulfilling a contractual obligation with the insurance company to get the four American university researchers home safe and sound. We don't want Iniquus pissing off the Slovakians, ever, but especially right now with the Zoric trials starting Monday. Your job is to make damned sure that while Iniquus pulls rabbits out of magical hats, they don't piss off the Slovakians. Meanwhile, you're to help them to the best of your *linguistic* abilities."

"Yes, sir."

"What have you got so far?" Green asked.

"We have a theory that Honey is testing. If it's accurate, it will lead to the name of the man who took the hostages." She watched Green's eyes.

There was a flicker of excitement. "Well done."

Sabrin didn't like the feel of that flash she'd seen. It had a *greediness* to it. It felt like more than hope about getting the hostages back, but rather, getting them closer to the *real* concern.

He obviously wasn't going to use today's meeting for a big reveal.

One thing that Sabrin didn't like about the intelligence world was that missions were more significant than human life. It was a bigger picture thing. Risk one soul to save many. Fortunately, as a linguist, Sabrin wasn't involved in implementing those hard decisions. That task was on others who better fit those responsibilities—like Ridge and Ryder had in their days rolling out as special operators.

Another thing that Sabrin hated about this job was the chess-playing, where she was the pawn. Okay, rook, maybe. But she was someone who was confined in what moves she could make and was still considered disposable in the grand picture. The implications of what she did on the job weren't readily apparent to her. It was for the kingmakers to understand how she affected the strategy playing across the board.

Sabrin shifted toward the edge of her chair. "Green, why did you call me in?"

Chapter 18

Ryder

"I'm in the embassy parking lot," Ryder told Sabrin over the phone. "I'm the bloke with the crazy-ass K9."

"Voodoo?" Her voice sounded offended for Voodoo. "He's the sweetest dog that ever lived."

"You haven't seen him when he wants to snack on squirrel."

"I'm heading down the stairs now."

"Okay, but when you get near me, and in the car, we're going to be on silence."

"What?" She gripped the handrail to help her balance on her stilettos. "How long is this silence going to last because the place we're heading is two hours away."

"Not long. Ten minutes. Silence, though."

"I'm almost to you."

As Ryder hung up, Honey was ringing into Ryder's phone. "Are you at the embassy?"

"Outside, Sabrin is talking to her handler. I'm giving her some space."

"Green? You know his role here is handler?"

"Had that vibe." Ryder's gaze scanned the tree-lined road, looking for any curious eyes that might be focused on him.

Voodoo was calmly watching a butterfly flitting around the weeds.

"When you texted me Green's name, I recognized it. He's CIA Head of Station. Good guy. That he's having a private chat with Sabrin makes me think she might also be CIA. They often run under embassy titles. Undoubtedly, the CIA has a lot of translators on their payroll." There was a pause where Ryder could hear Honey drumming his fingers on a metal surface. "That feels right to me. Does it feel right to you?"

"Not really. Sabrin seems too soft for that lifestyle. Intense blue eyes, but they have that doe-like quality. Her emotions are too… I don't know, the word that comes to me is 'available,' whereas most spooks I've met have ice in their veins. Poker faces." Ryder bladed a hand on his hip. "Yeah, that's a stretch to imagine. There's no fight in her. I couldn't imagine her drawing a weapon or making it through The Farm."

"Ridge says she's fit."

"Sure. Sabrin exercised yesterday and today, but is she go-to-the-mat fit? Nah, I can't see it."

"We checked for a military background," Honey said, "and that's a no."

"All right." Ryder reached his hand farther down

Voodoo's lead as a German shepherd started his perimeter patrol of the embassy. Voodoo didn't look interested; he had his butterfly friend. "I'm not sure where this speculation is going to get us, but NSA is a possibility…her background you were telling me about with Sausage-Link King would make that make sense. Another agency might be running her through the CIA with Green…"

"That still doesn't explain why they'd want her to attach to us," Honey said. "Other than they saw an opportunity to lend us a resource, so they could be actively involved in the situation without causing diplomatic fallout. And it certainly doesn't explain that odd conversation she was having in the bathroom when you got in last night. Glad to see you're still walking amongst the living this morning."

"Voodoo was vigilant. Yeah, weird that. Her phone wasn't in the bathroom with her. I went in and did a search of the loo and didn't find anything that looked remotely like a comms device. The comms could be on her person. If she's CIA or NSA, probably, I'll never find bugs without equipment."

Honey said, "I can't see how I could get equipment like that to you or how you'd deploy it when she's joined at your hip."

"How about the hostages on the bus? Are you running them down as individuals to see if there was a target that isn't apparent?" He spotted Sabrin coming around the guard station. "Yup. Yup. Good. Thank you for contacting me. I'll get back to you later. Goodbye."

Sabrin raised her hand in a hello wave, quick-stepping across the pavement.

As Ryder slipped his phone back in the tactical pocket on his thigh, he found himself grinning.

When she reached him, she slid her hand into his, rose up on her toes, and kissed his cheek. "Thank you for waiting." She tipped her head to the side, her eyes filled with affection, a little smile on her lips. "And coming with me this morning. Let's get me changed, and we can get going on our adventure. I thought we could stop on our way to the Tantras at a little village for lunch. I think you'll love it."

It was smooth and natural and not at all for him.

Maybe there were eyes on them, maybe not. But you never tip your hand. Once you assumed a role in public, you had to stick to it. Sabrin seemed so natural. Sincere.

Training.

Ryder needed to make sure he didn't fall under that spell. Like a mythological Huldra of Norway, Sabrin could be tempting him toward a bad end.

Though, if she were a Huldra, it would be fun making sure he satisfied her sexual appetite.

Way out of line, mate.

Ryder flicked his wrist up for Voodoo, and Voodoo lifted his paw in the air, whining on cue. Ryder took a knee as he massaged along Voodoo's leg, getting a tongue bath for the effort.

When Ryder stood, Sabrin looked up at him, true concern shining in her eyes.

"He'll be okay. He can rest on the road." He tugged her hand and got them moving to the embassy-provided sedan. Just as he'd asked, she was silent as he unlocked the car door.

After loading Voodoo in and snapping him into the safety belt, Ryder drove them two blocks down to a parking garage then circled around to the top. There in the corner, he parked next to another car. He held up a "wait here" finger and got out.

So far, Sabrin was playing along. This next part might be telling. She climbed out of the sedan and rounded the back of the car.

Ryder felt along the top of the front tire to find a set of car keys, just as Iniquus had instructed the rental company to do. He popped the hatch. Then worked on loading the luggage from the embassy provided car to this SUV that Nutsbe had produced, seemingly out of thin air. A rental in someone else's name.

As he lifted her case into the back of the SUV, Sabrin put her hand on his arm. "Can I have a quick second to change? I'm about done with these heels and hose."

"No worries." As she pulled jeans and tennis shoes from her case, Ryder got Voodoo.

Sabrin simply opened the front and back doors to their new SUV and stood between them, stripping down.

As she unbuttoned her blouse, Ryder turned his back. He remembered how it felt to have her lying in his arms in the woods, dressed in only her bra and panties. It had been an all-out battle not to stroke his hands over her satin skin.

His dick had been rock hard then. It was rock hard now.

This was going to be one hell of an uncomfortable mission. He untucked his shirt, calling out, "You have a lot of looks. You're like a chameleon."

"What does that mean?"

"It's uncanny how different you become—not just clothes but attitude. At the campsite, you looked… friendly, kind of a girl-next-door vibe."

"Uh-huh."

Dashing into the woods in next to nothing, she'd been an erotic nymph, but he'd keep that observation to himself. "At the party, you looked like you fit into the family. Domestic in a grown-up Heidi kind of way."

She laughed.

"At the embassy this morning, the way you scowled at your boss, you looked like a bloody badass shark going into court. Not just clothes, it's like the whole of you shifts. If I didn't know better, I'd say you were a spook."

"Yeah, that's me. 007 was taken as a designation." Her words were light. "I'm double-oh-nine and a half. By the way, don't play with the lipstick in my purse. It's a bomb."

"So what was in the newspaper that bloke Green handed you?"

"Craziest thing. Totally unexpected," Sabrin said as she bumped into the door. "Hang on."

He could see her in the reflection of the sedan's window, jumping into her jeans. There was a bang and an "oof" that tugged his lips into an amused smile.

"You can turn around now. I'm covered."

When he did turn around, she was buttoning up her cardigan that was serving as a shirt. It clung seductively to her curves, showing off the roundness of her breasts.

"There's a guy in Russia." Sabrin sat on the seat to pull on her socks. "An oligarch nicknamed the Sausage-Link King."

"Yeah?" Ryder tensed. *Here it is. This is what Honey and Nutsbe had found out about her background.*

"He's dead." She tugged on a tennis shoe and pulled the bow into a triple knot.

"Dead how? Novichok? A fourth story window? Beat the shit out of himself when he tripped over his shoelaces?"

"No…" She reached down to the blacktop for her other shoe. "Kind of a horrible image, really." She stopped while she pulled that on. "He was murdered with a blowgun. The kind you lift to your lips and blow out a poison-tipped dart." She peeked up at him.

"Get out." He moved his hands to his hips. "A blowgun?"

"He was in the hot tub with his partner when two masked assailants burst through the doors," she said as she tied her second shoe.

"Someone had to have survived if they were able to report that in the paper."

"His girlfriend crawled out of the hot tub and jumped through a window." She bent to gather her earlier outfit and took a moment to fold the suit. "First story window, cuts, and bruises, but she's fine."

"Did she say what the masked guys wanted?"

"Robbery gone bad. The woman said that two men burst through the doors and demanded money. The King asked, 'What are you going to do, shoot me with that thing?' Then he was laughing so hard he started choking. And the guy let the dart fly, hitting the King right in the heart. He gasped and passed out. That's when the girlfriend's limbic systems said, I'm outta here."

"No doubt. But they left the guy in the hot tub? That

water's like, what? A hundred and four? If he was left floating in there…"

"I know." Sabrin's body tremored. When she stood, Sabrin looked a little green around the gills. "The visual is pretty upsetting."

Yeah, she didn't seem like good double-oh-nine and a half material. The puzzle pieces just weren't coming together.

She put her hand to her heart. "His family…" She shook her head with a frown.

Nope, way too tender to be a spy.

"And the blowgun?" Ryder slammed the backdoor shut, so she could get to the cargo area to put her things away in her case. "That seems a rather unlikely way for one to meet their demise, hey? I mean, it would be like if I killed someone with a boomerang."

She laid her things in neatly, then zipped her bag closed. "It would narrow down the suspects for sure. That's not a talent shared by a wide population. Just as an aside, do you know how to kill someone with a boomerang?" She walked to the front of the car to sit in the front passenger seat and pulled the door shut as Ryder rounded to his side of the vehicle.

"You're probably picturing the kind of boomerang that you throw out," Ryder said, punching the engine button. "And it comes back to you. That boomerang is a sport, sort of like going out and throwing a ball with your friends, only you can do it by yourself because it comes back to you. And that, I'd be glad to show you how to do when we're both back at Iniquus."

"Fun! I'd love that." She smiled at him. A genuine, pretty smile. "Thank you."

"It's a date then." He regretted that choice of words. They seemed to throw cold water on what had been warm banter.

With belts in place, Ryder backed out of the parking space and headed them down the ramp.

"We switched cars because you don't want us tracked?" Sabrin asked, reaching around to pet Voodoo. "He always seems unhappy in his seat belt."

"He does. But that's the way it goes. Safety first. About the car, I'm more concerned with someone listening in. I imagine that we'll be talking about things other than the case as we drive along. If I share personal information or views, I'd rather that not go into an AI system somewhere, so people have information to manipulate me in the future."

"Yeah. Good. I'm glad you were able to get hold of this so quickly."

"Not all that quickly. You were in there for a while."

"I was trying to get Green to tell me what's going on with this case, why I'm involved. He's insisting that it's exactly as it seems. I'm here to give you cover and translate." She made a face saying she wasn't convinced.

Ryder wasn't convinced either, but at least they were both in the dark. He was fairly certain she wasn't lying to him.

"So you can't kill with a boomerang?" Sabrin got them back on track. "That's disappointing. I kind of liked that image in my head."

"There's a weapon called the kylie, a throwing stick, that'll do the job of killing. You don't see it coming, and if you see it coming, your body isn't going to get you out of the way in time. Dangerous. But once you throw it, you don't want to miss, or you've just tossed a lethal weapon to your adversary." Ryder clicked on the turn signal. "I'm heading us north. There's a park outside of the city. Honey wants to chat with us."

"Okay." Sabrin adjusted her seat back a bit and stretched out her legs.

"John Green is CIA, isn't he?" Yeah, just go for it, Ryder decided.

"Head of Station."

"And he handed you the paper, telling you about the death of the Sausage-Link King..."

"The United States was bringing charges against him, and I was one of the translators on the case. But I guess I'm done with that now. Which is fine with me. I mean, I'm just translating between the US and Russia. I'm not in the crosshairs of any of that. Still—" She shuddered. "Fatalities like you'd mentioned, Novichok and fourth-story windows, aren't a fate I want to tempt."

"Are those kinds of things possible for you?" Ryder held his breath, clicking on his right turn blinker and slowing for the turn. He was careful not to look her in the eye and challenge her. He exhaled slowly. "Tell me the truth, scale of one to ten, how dangerous is your job?"

"I don't know. What's a five on your scale?"

"Dentists."

"Dentists?" She laughed.

Good. Sabrin thought this was chatter.

"I'd think dentists would be a one, maybe a two," she said. "Though, now that I'm thinking about it, if someone bites you or breathes a virus on you, that could bring you down."

"Plus self-medicating anesthesia and suicide. On an industry list, it's actually pretty high. But in the case of my scale, ten would be Alaskan Coast Guard in a storm, nuclear operations technicians—"

"With a major earthquake rattling the cooling tanks—"

"Spying…" He pulled to a stop at the stoplight and turned to her.

"Ah, I see where you're going. I never think of my job as dangerous. I mean, most accidents happen at home, so just being away from my own bathtub makes me safer. I'm probably closer to the dentist than a coast guard on your scale. But then again, here I am with you. It's a first. This case is the only reason I'd budge myself toward the dangerous job of dentistry."

His eyes were unblinking as he searched hers for a clue that she was lying to him. There were none. If anything, he read laughter there, like she was wondering how he could be so far from the mark. "Translators don't know how to dodge tails." He pointed out. "You do."

A beep-beep from behind him told Ryder the light had turned green and got him heading down the street again.

"True. But to become a translator with the kinds of clearance I need to have, I had to go through the training like people who have field jobs. We all have training beyond our job titles because embassies are inherently marks for terror. Less so for, say, the receptionist. But I know things." She put finger quotes around the word "things."

"And I guess if someone wanted to know what I do, there might be some inherent risk. To them and to me." She sniffed. "Speaking of risk, what does Honey want to talk about? Did he get anything from Norway?"

"Dunno. He said to call him once we get someplace for lunch." He glanced down at the SUV's dash clock. 10:32. "Honey should have an update for us then."

Chapter 19

Sabrin

"Here." She pointed at the little restaurant tucked in a row of ancient storefronts as they drove past. "That little place there, that's where we should get lunch." She turned to Ryder. "It's famous." She clasped her hands and held them to her chest. "So, so good."

"All right." Ryder scanned the roadside. "Tell me if you see a parking spot."

"Try over there." Sabrin leaned forward and pointed down the side street. "Near the park. Because of Voodoo, why don't I just run in and get us something for a picnic? Then we can play tourist. Oh, look." She smiled. "A band's playing."

"Why would that be?" Ryder asked. "Holiday of some sort?"

"We're a couple of blocks away from a UNESCO World Heritage Site. If I remember correctly, there are about fifty buildings in a cluster, traditional log houses that've been here since basically the dawn of man." She wiggled her fingers in the air, talking with her hands. "They're painted with traditional designs. It's charming. I'm betting that the tourist board hires the band to dress in their traditional clothing and play, so tourists post enticing things on their social media sites."

Ryder turned onto the street parallel to the restaurant, driving along the outside of the park. "Did you come here with your folks when you were growing up?"

"My mom, yes. Not dad. Dad was in the Navy— submariner. He was gone, mostly." She pointed at a car pulling out of a spot.

"That's rough."

"I missed him, and there were parts that were hard on my mom. But Mom said she liked it because she got the best of both worlds, living her life the way she wanted to, and a loving relationship on her own terms."

Ryder pulled past the empty space and put on his blinker to back into the spot. "That was good for your mum, what about for you?" Ryder put his hand on the back of her seat to swivel and see behind him. And for a brief flash, Sabrin imagined curling herself into his arms.

She shifted around on her seat as that thought tingled through her system.

The power he had over her body without even touching her was a very new sensation to Sabrin.

Focus elsewhere. Now.

"My dad's this amazing guy. He'd take textbooks

with him onto the sub and study during his off time. He's like an encyclopedia. He has this vast wealth of knowledge. Talking to him is always interesting. When he was on leave, he was solely focused on mom and me. It was like…huh, well, like Ramadan." She paused. "I'm not Muslim, so I'm hesitant with this metaphor, but I have friends who follow the Muslim faith, and during Ramadan, they fast for a month. They don't eat or drink from sunup to sundown." She released her safety belt and tipped the cover up on the visor mirror to make sure she was presentable. She looked like the stereotype of a librarian with her bun and cardigan. Pulling the pins from her chignon, she stuck them in her mouth, then fluffed her hair as it fell past her shoulders. "Not even water," she said past the bobby pins. "Nothing. In the morning," she dumped the bobby pins into the cup holder until she could get them put away properly, "my friends get up and eat and hydrate, absorbing what they could, knowing that they'd be consciously and willingly deprived." She turned to Ryder. "Yeah, it was a choice for Dad to be away from us. But when he was with us, he'd gorge himself on time with Mom and me. And vice versa. We'd fill to satiation. He'd leave. We'd grow uncomfortable, needing him, and he'd return. It was like that. Feast and famine."

Ryder's gaze traced over her face. He reached out to move a wisp of hair that had fallen across her cheek. "You look lovely."

"Thank you." She self-consciously snapped the mirror shut. She sent him a smile.

"Do you want me to walk you to the restaurant, or shall I stay here and throw the Frisbee?"

Voodoo gave a "Woohoo! Let's do it!" bark.

"Ha! I think it would be hard making Voodoo wait patiently outside now that he's heard the word Frisbee."

Voodoo barked again, then lay down, whining to get out and go!

"Should I just choose for you, or do you have a preference?" she asked.

"It's probably best if you do the choosing," Ryder said. "I want to take the opportunity to experience local foods, and you know best." He climbed from the SUV, rounding to the cargo area, and got Voodoo's Frisbee from his bag.

Sabrin swiveled in her seat, watching as Ryder tucked the toy into the back waistband of his pants.

He leaned into the back seat to unclasp Voodoo's safety belt, which wasn't the easiest thing to do with Voodoo squirming with excitement. "So that's your dad's story," Ryder said. "Submariner. What about your mum?"

"I was a well-loved child from a stable home—two committed, caring parents. I didn't know any kids like me growing up. Mom didn't want to live a Navy base lifestyle." Sabrin reached for her purse. Normally, she'd never wear one of these backpack-style bags so fashionable right now in Slovakia, but she'd put her ID and credit card in a front pocket and mostly had the purse as a bit of subterfuge. No one in the intelligence or security fields would choose a bag so easily pickpocketed.

"Mom was a social worker," Sabrin said, "working with a Catholic charity to help acclimate refugees. English lessons, helping them navigate rental contracts, making sure they had food, clothing, beginning household items. That's actually how I learned to love languages."

When Sabrin got out, she slammed her door shut.

Voodoo rounded the vehicle to check on her, deemed her safe, and went back to Ryder.

"Yeah?" Ryder leaned against the vehicle like he was settling in for a long talk.

Sabrin moved onto the sidewalk. "When I was little, I'd go to work with Mom and play with the refugee kids. Mom said it was helpful to the children to have me there. I thought it was fun." She shrugged. "But as I got older, that didn't work out anymore. I saw the experience differently. I didn't like that there were all these kids whom I enjoyed, but the friendships were brief as the families moved around to new opportunities. Then I was sad." Interesting to hear myself say that, Sabrin thought. It sounded a lot like her romantic relationships. And now she'd matured out of the transient being okay. "I wanted *my* friends. BFFs."

"Do you have best friends forever?" He made a little heart with his fingers over his chest and grinned.

"Eleven sisters. You know the lingo. Well, I became a preteen and became disruptive. Mom decided I was old enough that I should go 'home' in the summers. Now, home meant here to Slovakia in Mom's mind. She wanted me to get to know my extended family. To get a broader use of the language. For my babka to teach me how to make her best dishes. Family is very important. Keeping close."

Voodoo stomped his impatience that this conversation was going on during his Frisbee time, but Ryder signaled him to sit quietly.

"And that means time and focus," Ryder said.

"Exactly. I was used to drinking deeply and quickly from the relationship well. My father and all. That's what I did. I spent summers here, and I absorbed. And as an adult, I found a job that brings me back and forth between my two homes Slovakia and America. It's wonderful."

Ryder's grin had slid from his face. He was looking at her thoughtfully. "You planned this trip months ago."

"It's my vacation. I needed to take off from work and come on my own dime, so I wasn't pulled away from my visit. I needed to be sure to be here on the right day. My babka deserved to know that I did this special for her."

"And that got messed up."

"Best laid plans… I'll explain later. My family will approve of my decisions." Explaining Ryder, on the other hand, that wouldn't be as well received. They had accepted him into the circle. "At any rate," she shifted her purse onto her shoulders, "that's my unusual background that my employer wanted to capture. I was in the US during the school year and then was in Slovakia for the summers. I absorbed the culture, the language, and an understanding of the mindset. There's a difference between, say, someone like my mother who came to the US as an eighteen-year-old."

"Left one life for the other?"

"She wasn't raised in the American mindset. She can only understand it to some extent. Is that like you and Australia?" She took a step closer to him and looked up into the depth of his warm brown eyes. She was enjoying this conversation, and truth be told, she didn't want for them to be going their separate ways, even if she was just going to order some lunch.

"I was born in the US and was moved to Australia when I was four. Now I'm back as a thirty-six-year-old.

Even though I don't have that American mindset, I fit in fine, mostly because of my accent, I think."

She lifted a brow. "Which gets you all the women you want."

He bent his head to the side and scratched at his ear. "Truthfully, you're right. For some reason, Australian accents are an aphrodisiac for many American women." Then he laughed self-consciously.

She shook her head as she started down the sidewalk. See? Transient. A player. Gets whomever he wants, whenever he wants. "I'm going to go get lunch now. Voodoo, you were a very patient boy," she told him. "I'm going to bring you back a treat." She looked at Ryder over her shoulder. "Can he have bones?"

With the food bags beside her, Sabrin sat under a tree near the band, watching Voodoo leap through the air spectacularly.

When Ryder saw her there, he raised a hand then whistled Voodoo back to his side.

They came and settled in next to her.

"Guess who was sitting in a picture window at the pub, beer in hand, watching the street." She pulled a bag from the top of her sack, opening it to show Ryder that it had a raw joint.

He reached for the bag. "Voodoo and food is a bit of a trick," he said. He pulled the bone from the pack, signaled Voodoo it was for him, then flipped it up.

Voodoo snatched it from the air, trotted over to Sabrin, and lined his body up with her outstretched legs as he gnawed on it.

Ryder watched that carefully, some tension in his body, some curiosity, and confusion that Sabrin didn't understand. "Keep your fingers away from his mouth," he said.

"Well, duh." Sabrin had seen how Voodoo could take down a two-hundred-pound man with the power of his jaws. She wasn't a moron.

"Someone in the window?" Ryder asked. "Just the one? Did he see you?"

"One. And no. I saw him and swung into the alley to walk around back. A black sedan that looks like it was in a recent wreck was parked behind the pub."

Ryder rubbed a hand over his chin. "It would be fun to get him in a corner and have a little talk."

"Except you don't speak the language."

"Would you be willing to stand there and translate while I pummel him?" He accepted a cardboard food box and utensil package from her.

Beat the guy into telling them what his freaking problem was? It wasn't what they were going to do. They were going to stay off his radar. *"Tsah."* She gave him a sarcastic half-laugh and focused on getting her cutlery from its plastic wrapping.

"How do you think he got into the right town to find us?" Ryder took a bite and closed his eyes as he savored the aromatic spices. "Good god," he said.

"I know, right? I thought you'd like that one." She looked over her shoulder in the direction she'd come from. The coast was clear. "If we're playing the tourist card, the guy being there makes sense." She spread her napkin across her lap. "This is straight up the highway from Bratislava. They may have four roads staked out and each man charged with watching for us then calling in his fellow thugs. You can't get into this village without coming up that main road. It looks like we beat him in, and that was our saving grace."

"It's like Tweedle Dee and Tweedle Dum, isn't it?"

"I have a theory."

He grinned at her. "Is this theory number four?" He jabbed his fork toward his food. "This is amazing. No wonder you like to live between Slovakia and the US." Then scooped up another bite.

"Yeah. It's funny. I miss here when I'm home in DC. I miss home when I'm here." She twisted the top from a bottle of sparkling cider. Then held a bottle out to Ryder. "I can't seem to find my settling place."

"Thanks. So go on…your theory?"

"What if the Slovakian government is piggybacking?"

"I'd need more—"

She held out her box to him. "I thought we could share, that way you can taste all of these dishes. Is that okay?"

"Yeah, good. Thank you." He took a bite of her stew. "Go on about piggybacking. If we're sharing, the longer you talk, the more for me."

"Eat all you want. My stomach is still ishy from this morning's bumper cars." She settled her back against the trunk of the tree.

Finished with his bone, Voodoo crawled over and rested his head on her knee.

Sabrin bent to kiss him, then stroked her hand over his head and back. "You said that people in the security field would know that you would secure your RVs with technology." She took a bite and chewed thoughtfully. "If it were me, I'd try to figure out a way that my being there at your camp, next to your RV, would be seen on video as non-threatening. Or threatening but in a way that was a feint. Like someone starts a fight, and the other person quietly sits beside the RV and plants trackers and audio bugs."

Ryder lifted his gaze and scanned the area. Something had shifted in his demeanor.

"The configuration you made at the camp made that nearly impossible. But they were rude by ignoring you and addressing me."

"Trying to seduce you from my bed to theirs."

"Seemingly." She circled her fork in the air. "They wanted me to translate. Perhaps they were trying to pick a fight."

"Huh. Keep going." He shoveled up another bite.

"The university talked to the US Embassy here in Bratislava, and the embassy reached out to the Slovakian president's office. The Slovakian president told the embassy, America, to stand down, right?" She paused. "As soon as the university knew about the missing researchers, that immediately triggered the security contracts. Everyone would know it was the case that the insurance would pay a private business to get involved. The Slovakian military and their equivalent to the secret service had K9s in that competition. You know that, right?"

Ryder nodded.

"The Slovakian government would know you were around."

"We went over this."

"Another angle. What if the Slovakians believed you would be successful in finding the hostages?"

"And they're tracking us to get to the hostages themselves, possibly arrest us on drummed-up charges, and dive in to save the day. Not that I care who ultimately saves the day, as long as the day is saved, and everyone goes home safely. This isn't an ego trip."

Ryder leaned onto one hip and pulled his cell from his thigh pocket. He checked his text message: I have information.

"That's Honey." Ryder texted back where they were, what they were doing, and the presence of one of the thugs.

Honey told them that when they'd gotten down the road, to pull off, and then call in.

Sabrin was full; she handed Ryder her box and leaned back again, cradling her drink and petting Voodoo.

Ryder slid his phone away. "Explain why they'd pull guns on us?"

She shrugged. "Maybe they wanted to threaten you into standing down?" she speculated. "Maybe it was fine that we were here to see my family, but once you were headed toward the embassy, things changed? Maybe they really wanted to capture and pummel us, rather than vice versa, to figure out what we know... Maybe—no, that wouldn't work. Yeah, that was unexpected and doesn't make sense to me. It wasn't a very professional move. They didn't seem trained in car tactics to me, did they to you?"

"They weren't amateurs. But no, they didn't seem to have elite skills. Man, I'd *really* like to get hold of one of them and take away some of this guesswork."

"Again, we can't ask because we're here covertly. Tourists on holiday. Here's another point. The US was told to stand down. Having done that, if the Slovakians now asked for help, it would make the Slovakians seem weak."

"There's a female president. Usually, dick knocking is a man's stupid game."

"Dick knocking?" She snorted and put her wrist under her nose as she laughed, imagining two men using their hard cocks as lightsabers going after each other. "Thanks for the visual. It's both amusing and horrific."

Chapter 20

Ryder

After lunch, Ryder drove outside of town, pulling into a wooded space where they'd have a visual field of the road and privacy for their communication.

The magnet on the bottom of his external satellite antennae dragged the unit from his fingers as Ryder placed it on top of the SUV, then climbed back into the cab to boot up his computer.

As he waited for Honey to connect with them, Ryder's gaze scanned, making sure they were alone.

Verdant green enveloped them. This was a gorgeous country. Actually, being here on vacation with Sabrin, instead of undercover, would be amazing. Maybe someday they could do that. Ryder could fly over and meet up with her while she was working at the American Embassy, and they could relax and enjoy a long weekend.

Ryder realized that he was putting Sabrin into his future plans, feeling excited to see them through. He didn't remember thinking thoughts like that before… feeling this way before. Ryder was used to living in the moment with the women in his life. Enjoying the "now" of a tightly framed picture.

With Sabrin, that wasn't enough.

Ryder wanted to pan out and see farther down the road. And yes, he had realized almost from the beginning that—while Sabrin was his colleague and obviously an effective and respected professional—Ryder thought of her in personal and frequently in intimate terms.

Man, he just wanted her back in his arms like they were when she'd made her sexy half-naked dash into the woods after discovering she'd been bugged, and she'd fallen.

And he'd fallen with her. And it had felt…it felt…

It didn't even have to be more than her lying in his arms—though more than that would be great. Just holding her and talking had felt good to him. Was right. And he wanted that level of intimacy—emotional and physical—back. He wanted the right to touch her as his.

That was a hell of a thought.

His.

He hadn't thought in those terms about any other woman.

Is there any truth in Sabrin's kisses, or is she just doing a job?

And there was Voodoo. Ryder was Voodoo's handler, but he was also Voodoo's dad. And Voodoo seemed to think that Sabrin was mum. When Voodoo had nestled in next to Sabrin, chewing his gift bone, that was a *hell* of a surprise.

The green light on his computer flashed on. "Honey here."

"Ryder here with Sabrin. We're in our vehicle."

"Good?"

"So far. As I texted, Sabrin marked one of the gang of four in the village, watching the street coming into town. I haven't spotted any kind of tail as we left."

"Weather report," Honey said. "There are thunderstorms on the radar. Expect that tonight. You're still heading toward the Tantras?"

"Yes," Sabrin said. "I've mapped out some popular hiking trails that would seem typical for a vacationer to take that are in close proximity to the last known position of the bus."

"I'd appreciate it if you'd text coordinates of the trails to Nutsbe, times on and expected times off the trails. Thank you, Sabrin," Honey said. "Speaking of Nutsbe, he ran diagnostics on GPS and communications in that area. There are a lot of blank spots. With cloud cover disrupting satellite connectivity, and no radio or cell tower signal, that can put you off-grid."

"I'd rather not disappear like the bus," Sabrin said, then cleared her throat and tugged at the bottom of her sweater. "Your asset in Norway… Anything?"

"I have an update for you. But before I cloud your thinking with new information, can you tell me why you're heading toward those hiking trails? Do you have a goal in mind?"

"First, it makes sense with our cover. Second, I'm riffing off the idea that this guy on the dictation is from Norway. Norwegians, remember, embrace living with nature, being outdoors. They don't think of the outdoors the way most people in the West think of it. If it's true that he was referring to *friluftsliv*—outdoor living—in the dictated file, then I ask myself, where would he feel at home? The terrain that most closely approximates the Norwegian topography is the Tantras mountain range. It's rugged, sparsely populated, with few resources. If the hostages are there, it would be hard to find them in modern conventional ways, satellite photos, and witnesses. If they're there, how can one man maintain the health and safety of twenty-six hostages on a bus or outdoors, especially during these storms? The storms are typical of Slovakian July, not Norwegian July. He may not be prepared for them. And, too, here we have long summer days, but in Norway, they have almost no night at all. Would someone with mental health issues have planned for the dark?"

"Keep going," Honey said.

"There's water to be had. But unless it's treated, it can give the hostages a host of health issues, some life-threatening. If he didn't think about food, that can be uncomfortable. But if no one has a health issue like type one diabetes, they can go on for months without food. Maybe the hostages had snacks with them. Bathrooming… Yeah, this weather is the biggest threat. If the hostages get wet, and they're outside in the wind with temperatures in the sixties, that can lead to hypothermia and death. I'll tell you, Honey. This feels like there's a ticking bomb, sped up by the man's mental health situation. Let me boil that down to answer your question. I'm going to the Tantras because I don't know where else makes sense. We're hiking the paths because I don't know what else to suggest."

Ryder's muscles were tight as he sat next to Sabrin. "You said you had news, Honey?"

"I do." Honey's voice shifted from casual to more pointed. "We believe we have a hit on Sabrin's work. Our guy is on the island staying above the pub. Small place, smaller population, the way you suggested Sabrin. Most of the people on the island are away on their summer vacations. July, as I understand it, is a time when most people just go."

"Yes, that's right," Sabrin said. "Some places even shut down their police departments. There's no one in town to protect."

"Our asset was directed to an elderly woman's house. Her son, Ketil Reistad—does that ring a bell?"

"No," Sabrin said.

"Forty-nine-year-old, Caucasian male. In March, Ketil was in the news for showing up at a hydroelectric dam in southern Slovakia and talking about the migration of birds and how our need for electricity was throwing off their flight patterns."

Ryder looked over at Sabrin. Her face was rigid with concentration.

"Ketil's mother said that he was working on his PhD when he was in his early twenties, had been prolific in his research, and had won some impressive accolades. He ended up leaving the university because of his mental health. In the decades since his diagnosis of schizophrenia, Ketil has continued to do his own research. Some of that entails going to the mainland."

Sabrin scratched her forehead. "By himself? So he's high functioning?"

"He has trouble maintaining his personal hygiene and forgets to eat and take his medications. He is incapable of living on his own."

"So he's there on the island, or somewhere else under someone's care?"

"No, he packed his ruck and headed out, leaving a note on the kitchen table saying he was going to save the trees. His mother has been very worried. But she assumed this was just another event like in March. That the authorities would find him, hospitalize him, and contact her like they had before. He left without his medication. That incident made the front page of the papers in Norway last March. Must have been a slow news cycle."

"So his thinking has been organized enough to travel for a cause. Any specific information that could tie these two incidents?" Sabrin asked.

"Our guy, Sven, read Ketil's research notes. Some phrases replicate almost word for word what was said in the dictated file. Ketil wrote in his research notes, for example, about speaking to the trees, and the trees requiring him to take the actions they'd commanded. While Sven told me the gist of it, I obviously can't read it myself as it's written in Norwegian. I have photos of the notes. I put them in a file for you. Maybe they'll give you some more information. If you could, please look them over."

"Yes, of course." Sabrin's hand wrapped her throat.

"According to the mother, Ketil has delusions that make him prone to think in terms of conspiracies. Infrequent hallucinations of being able to speak directly to nature. Before being taken to the hospital in Slovakia in March, Ketil had occasionally talked to birds who encouraged him to speak on their behalf, which is why he had been down on the dam. But since he was there in Slovakia, Ketil's mother thought Ketil had become worse."

"Worse, how?" Ryder asked.

"The trees were talking to him. Instead of infrequently, his mother said he came back with daily tales—mythical figures like the Huldra, the trolls, and even music talked to him. He'd been distraught, visibly agitated."

Sabrin put her chin in her hand. She seemed to turn inward as she listened. Ryder imagined that she was developing a theory for them to work on.

"Huh, give…let me just think for a second," Sabrin asked. The car fell into silence. "You said that he goes for walks on the mainland?" she asked.

"Yes, most days," Honey said. "He has a motorboat that he takes back and forth since he was a teen."

Again there was silence.

"I just don't understand this at all. I'm putting myself in the role of a hostage. There seems to be a man with a mental health problem who captures me on the bus. If this is true, then someone should have escaped by now. The captives should have figured out how to manipulate him." She swallowed hard.

"What was that thought?" Ryder asked.

"I hate to say this out loud. It just seems improbable to me that under these circumstances that they're still alive. And saying that aloud, I don't mean for one second that our foot should come off the gas pedal, every second we aren't getting to them…yeah." She sighed. "But then there's also the conspiracy theory that's forming in my mind."

"Really?" Honey asked.

"I translate for some of the best propagandists and manipulators in the world. And when you said this guy both made the newspaper, and then you said that he was worse…"

Both men sat quietly, letting her brain churn. She'd been right about Norway. Had practically walked them to the guy's door, just looking at a few pages of incoherent words.

"Honey, is this Sven guy still on that island?" she asked. "Could he, and I'm sorry, I don't know how to do this technically." Her brows were pulled together, her eyes blinked robotically as she sifted through whatever was going through her head.

"Yes, he's in place waiting for next instructions. What should I tell him to do?"

"People tend to repetition. They find comfort in routine. I'm wondering if someone knows where he likes to walk. What path he takes daily? Are there trees there? The question I'm asking myself is, why would the trees suddenly be talking to him. And then there's a story—" she waggled a hand by her head "—that's in the back of my mind. I can't quite pull it forward. But let me throw this out there. I'm thinking about stochastic terror…something similar to stochastic terror."

"Interesting. Walk me through that," Honey said.

"All right, so we understand that stochastic terror happens when mass communications are used to rile up lone wolves. Someone says something, hoping that another, unknown person will carry out the violent act for them. So it's statistically predictable that if X is said, then Y will occur. The unpredictable thing would be who does the act. Skillful rhetoric, aimed at a predictable outcome, performed by an unknown person."

"Interesting," Ryder said. "Can you give me a real-world example?"

"Mmmm, a lot of hate crimes over the last few years have risen out of politicians' words. The El Paso shooting was based on a lone wolf's fear that caravans of illegal immigrants were crossing our borders. The call to stop them went up, the lone wolf with a rifle did his best. People died. The violence was predictable. The person to carry it through was the unknown. So could it be…hmm no, that doesn't line up exactly because he'd actually be a target."

"Keep going with that line of thinking," Honey said.

"Imagine this. And it really seems to be… I've studied something that is just out of reach, some strategy. I think pre-Hitler Germany. That they found a willing idiot, who could be manipulated to be their weapon without having any association. So imagine that this guy, Ketil, is in the paper. He has an environmental agenda. He has a mental health issue. He's isolated. Some unknown person tells Ketil what to do in such a way that he would do it."

"Talking trees," Ryder said.

Sabrin nodded. "Exactly. What if the tree spirits he mentioned weren't a figment of his health condition? What if instead, someone was taking advantage of his illness and put communications systems in the trees so that as he walked along, he would hear voices?"

"That's a unique way to develop a dupe," Honey said. "Though, according to the embassy, Ketil's been on the watch list for a very long time, showing up and making the news with environmental agitation."

"Which might have made him the mark," Ryder said. "But why?"

"I've mulled this as a possibility," Sabrin said. "And I have no clue as to an agenda. The only thing I can think is that there's more to this than meets the eye. This is a sleight of hand trick. This will resolve, and they will take Ketil to the mental health facility, a done deal. No one will be looking further."

"If it resolves quickly." Ryder crossed his arms over his chest, a scowl on his face. "If people don't die. But there has to be a bigger get. A reason behind all of this effort."

"The first step—to see if we can't find equipment to prove your theory," Honey said.

Sabrin leaned toward the computer. "Or disprove it."

"Not sure that can happen," Ryder countered. "If this is what happened, then after their guy went kinetic, they might have retrieved the equipment so it couldn't be found."

"Boo." A frown dragged at the corners of her mouth.

"I'm picturing this," Honey said. "The tactic would be easy to do if Ketil had a known path he walked. Just like tracking wildlife, action activated cameras could be placed in the trees. Someone waits for the alarm and watches on a remote computer to make sure it's Ketil, and he's alone on his daily walk. When he's there, they have a native Norwegian speaker tell him stories about Huldra and trolls. The trees become his friends. The voices tell him that they are equal to humans in importance, and he needs to act. He should do *this* thing to act."

"You should take the bus," Sabrin said.

"Be their dupe," Ryder said. "In court, anything

Ketil said would be ignored. He's delusional. How could he tell reality from hallucination?"

"I actually like this as a theory," Honey said. "Mainly because why not? Also, because it means there might be adults in the room—"

"Evil adults," Sabrin clarified.

"At least adults who know that people need to eat and drink and have shelter to stay alive," Ryder said.

In the distance, a boom of thunder rolled slowly across the sky. Sabrin looked out the window to see the storm clouds gathering.

Chapter 21

Sabrin

Honey stopped mid-sentence then said, "Incoming call from the American Embassy in Slovakia. Sit tight. Out." The green light went off on the computer.

Sabrin turned to Ryder. "I'm going to get out for a minute. I need some fresh air to fuel my thoughts."

"Tell the truth, you want to go chat with the trees and gather intelligence," Ryder said.

"You caught me." Sabrin undid her seat belt and popped the door open.

Voodoo stuck his head up and looked around, ready to charge into a new adventure.

"I'll be back," she said. "If Honey calls, give the horn a toot."

Sabrin walked into the trees and looked up into the

branches. "It would be nice if you could talk to us. We could probably use your wisdom." She put her hand on the trunk and felt herself grounding as she breathed in the fresh scent of the old-growth evergreens. They smelled like she imagined how the Earth smelled at the beginning of time.

These trees had survived through lifetimes, generations, through world wars and natural disasters. Strong and sturdy, and for a moment, Sabrin felt how fleeting her life was by comparison. How fragile she was.

She wanted roots, too.

"Sabrin?" Ryder called through the open window.

Sabrin traced her steps back to the car. When the door shut, she said, "Here."

"They've secured three of the hostages," Honey said without preamble. "Ukrainians."

"What can they tell us?" Sabrin leaned forward. She felt perspiration dampening her underarms. Fear ran over her scalp. "Are they okay?"

"They're hospitalized for observation. This is what I've been told. The President of Ukraine got a message that three Ukrainian citizens were being held hostage in Slovakia and that they would be released if and when the president posted on his Facebook page a message that said that everyone should watch the movie Earthlings."

"Is that a real film?" Ryder asked.

"It's a movie about how humans use animals for profit from pets to clothing," Honey said.

"Environmentalist?" Ryder asked.

"Well, animal cruelty," Honey said. "The president followed through immediately. The hostages were released. My understanding is that the president has now taken down that post."

"When?" Sabrin asked. "Where?"

"When, we're not sure of. We think last night during the storms. They were wet and disoriented this morning, hypothermic when they were found on the side of the highway E58 near Zvolen."

"Central Slovakia," Sabrin said. "That's a ways from the Tantras, say a two-hour drive from their last known position. Did the survivors say how they got to Zvolen?"

"There's not much there in terms of helpful detail. They all say a man got on the bus and was talking crazily. He had a gun, and he had zip ties. He instructed the driver to zip tie the researchers' hands to their seats. They were kept there for a day, no food, no water, they had to pee in their pants because their bladders were bursting."

"Oh, god." Sabrin pressed a fist into her chest.

"The next day, the man pulled out a bag and handed out food and bottles of blue drink. Like bottles of blue Kool-Aid is how they made it sound. The next thing these Ukrainian nationals knew, they were in the middle of nowhere on the side of the road, wet and freezing to death. A farmer found them and took them to the hospital."

"This morning?" Ryder asked.

"This morning at sunrise."

"They were taken Monday," Sabrin said. "I joined the case Tuesday. Wednesday we left the competition, and it was Babka's birthday, and so by this morning— Thursday morning—they were delivered someplace to be found. Monday no food or drink. Tuesday, hungry and thirsty to the point of dehydration, they consume what they're given. Obviously, drugged. And they don't remember forty-eightish hours."

"That's how I have it on my timeline," Honey said.

"Are they checking the hostages' blood? Where would Ketil get drugs like that?"

"I was told the embassy would share the medical lab report when it comes in. It might be another clue. It certainly puts me in mind that he's getting help and your theory becomes more plausible."

"Okay, so Ketil arrives at the bus, he must have a car. He could possibly get three people into his car and drive them in the night down to Zvolen, where they're sure to be found and cared for, then he goes back to wherever the rest of the people are. That's horrible."

"That's bad news for the four Yanks," Ryder said.

"How's that?" Sabrin asked.

"America doesn't negotiate with terrorists," Honey reminded her. "1976, there were pro-Palestinian hijackers who took the hundred Israeli hostages. The Israel Defense Force Commandos jumped in and saved most of them. But after that, in an attempt to tamp down on hostages, a good number of Western countries said they'd never negotiate with terrorists. As a matter of policy, we do not."

"I knew we didn't. I didn't know there was a triggering event. But Ukraine did as they were asked. Is that because it was a small ask?"

"I think that the social science has evolved," Honey said. "In countries that will negotiate and pay, there aren't the increased frequency of attacks that were feared, and their people are much more likely to get home alive—Switzerland, Austria, France."

"Okay," Ryder said. "We now know everyone was alive Tuesday. That's something."

"Sabrin, I've contacted our asset in Norway. Sven had already asked Ketil's mother about the route and has it mapped. I put that in the files—with the research notes Sven gathered from Ketil's mom—for you and Ryder, in case it means anything to you in terms of linguistics—word choices, etcetera. Sven is going to take a dog and some equipment and see what he can turn up."

"Carefully," Ryder said. "If this is a thing, and there are cameras that someone's monitoring, it seems to me we don't want them to know that we have any inkling that we're figuring this out. It might mean that live hostages are disappeared."

"Agreed," Honey said. "Sven brought up the same concerns. The dog will give him cover to snoop around when his equipment pings."

"Okay." Sabrin sighed, her body held tight and stiff.

Ryder reached out and rubbed his hand up and down her arm. "With this information, Sabrin, do you still want to go to the Tantras mountains?"

"No, actually, I have another theory. Some things Ketil was saying on the bus makes much more sense if there are other people involved in helping him. Unseen, mind you, so Ketil thinks that magic gifts are being provided by nature. But I need to spend some time with the research notes pages to see if it makes sense with this new information. I think it's best to go stay near the place the Ukrainian survivors were found. If Nutsbe could arrange something there for us."

"I'm sending that message to him now," Honey said.

"Expect a text with your hotel name. Keith and Karen Tucker is what the embassy is calling you?"

"Just to keep our names out of files." Sabrin focused on Ryder. "One of the reasons I took so long at the embassy this morning was that Green was having a credit card made for each of us. If anyone searches the card number, they'll be directed into the CIA computer system so they can track the interest." She opened her purse and handed the Keith card to Ryder.

"Thank you." He slid it into his pocket.

"We shouldn't use them as cover names just for money transactions," Sabrin stipulated. "The embassy asked that I not contact them myself, but to go through you, Honey. No work contact phone calls while I'm on vacation. Hey, Honey, is the embassy asking you to share your information with them? Are they caught up with what we've found?"

"My sense is that they'd rather not know what we're up to. If they know," Honey said, "they'll have to share that with the other countries, and America was asked to stand down."

Sabrin frowned. "Such stupid games when lives are on the line."

Chapter 22

Sabrin

Ryder pulled up to the front door of their new hotel. "I'll run in, get us signed in, and bring back a trolley for the bags."

"Can you handle the suitcases and Voodoo at the same time?" Sabrin asked. "I'd like to drive the car to the hotel we passed up the road and park there. Just in case Tweedle Dee or Tweedle Dum spotted our car."

"You don't want me to do that?" He looked past her up the road. "It's three kilometers from here." He opened his door and climbed out.

Sabrin shut her door behind her and rounded to the driver's side. "I've got this nervous energy." She shook her arms. "And a little car sickness from reading the research notes pages Honey sent while you were driving."

"You pick up something from them?"

"Only if Sven found equipment. If not, I'm back to square one." She handed Ryder her purse. "Could you take this up, please?" She climbed into the driver's side. "I'll jog back and shake some of this energy off me. I'll meet you in the room after you get us signed in. Okay?"

After Ryder loaded their gear onto the trolley and rolled it inside, Sabrin took off on a circuitous route to the other hotel. Head on a swivel, there really wasn't much to see. Everyone was home now, cleaning their dinner dishes, reading bedtime stories to their little ones.

What was happening for the hostages?

Over and over again, she thought about what the Ukrainians were able to tell the authorities. Going twenty-four hours as a conscious fast was one thing. Not knowing if you would ever have food or water again, quite another. She wondered who the first person was who made the decision, "Screw it, I'm just going to pee right here where I'm sitting." Was there a discussion, a collective agreement?

Twenty-six people urinating on a bus.

The smell.

The acidity on the skin.

The dehumanization of it.

The arrival of the food and drink on the second day would have seemed like a miracle.

If Sabrin had thought she'd never eat or drink again and was offered sustenance, Sabrin thought she'd gobble it down without a thought to poisons or medications. Why the guy had chosen blue… Where had he gotten the sack…

Sabrin parked and walked into the lobby of the

other hotel. She went to the ladies' room to urinate, thinking how clean it was, how much this was just an assumption—a way to relieve herself, a sanitary way to do it, never really thinking what a privilege it was to have the facilities. Sabrin washed her hands, taking a moment to look at herself, scowling into the mirror. She put her hands on her stomach and took a few deep breaths; the ferocity in her eyes would call attention to her. She needed to release the stress.

Pushing through the ladies' room door, Sabrin wandered the hotel a bit.

When she left out of a side door, the first fat raindrops splatted onto the sidewalk.

The temperature had dropped sharply. Sabrin's summer cardigan didn't provide her with nearly enough warmth.

Looking up, the sky was painted in bruised shades of green and purple. The wind lifted and floated Sabrin's hair out around her like she was underwater in a pool. The atmosphere had an eerie other-worldly feel to it.

If Ketil was outside in this, it would seem like a page from a folktale playing out. Huldra showing her displeasure that her lover didn't give her the orgasms she craved.

The rain came down in earnest. Ryder would see the downpour and worry. Not because she'd proven herself fragile, but because he'd mind that Sabrin was cold and wet.

The thought that Ryder cared enough to be concerned spread a momentary smile across her cheeks.

Her pace quickened into a jog. Normally running in a cardigan and jeans would catch someone's attention, but not when it was starting to rain. While attention during a mission was something she avoided, here, she wasn't fleeing someone; she was simply trying to get someplace dry.

Lightning cracked like a whip across the sky.

Long fingers of electricity stretched down to scratch the ground.

As thunder bellowed its outrage, shaking the walls of the houses she passed, Sabrin ran full tilt.

The clouds unleashed their burden.

The rain fell with such velocity that Sabrin put her hands over the top of her head to protect her scalp from the painful onslaught.

The heavens were angry.

When Sabrin crashed through the lobby door of her own hotel, she stood there, streaming water just like Ryder had done when he pulled himself out of the pond back at the competition.

What a glorious sight he had been—like one of the slow-motion shots in the movies, there for the sole purpose of titillating the viewer—revving their hormones.

Sabrin's hormones had been revved ever since then.

Turning, she caught her own reflection in the glass doors. She was far more drowned rat than demi-god ascending from the dog pond. She swiped at the mascara that smudged her cheek.

A hotel worker came over with a towel in her hand. Sabrin accepted it gratefully and did her best to dry off enough that she wasn't leaving puddles in her wake as she made her way to the desk to retrieve her room number and key card, then took the elevator, heading up to Mr. and Mrs. Tucker's room.

As soon as the elevator doors slid open, Sabrin heard Voodoo yip.

By the time she got to their room, Ryder had the door open.

His gaze scanned her from head to toe.

Her fists tucked tightly under her chin, her teeth chattering, her body shook.

Ryder reached for her elbows and tugged her into the bathroom.

Bending to adjust the water, he got the shower going. He put his hands on her hips, directing her back to sit on the toilet, then getting on his knees to unlace her shoes. "You're alright," he said. "We just need to get you warmed up, is all."

"Okay," she chattered.

Ryder worked to get the wet laces untangled, then pulled off her shoes and socks. He reached back and felt the water. "You're blue," he said. Scooping her into his arms, Ryder stuck her—clothes and all—into the shower. "I want you to stay there until you're pink again." He shook a stern finger at her, then slid the curtain closed.

Voodoo was making yawny-whining noises. His claws clicked on the bathroom floor as he stomped his paw.

"I know, buddy. I'm taking care of her." Ryder soothed in a calm voice. "Pink," he said louder. Then the door clicked shut.

The water warmed Sabrin. She stood there past the point of turning the required pink and just let the droplets carry her stress down the drain.

She was tired.

Stressed.

Fearful.

Her brain had been running gerbil-like on a wheel of limited information.

But now, she was becoming a prune; it was time to get out. She shut off the faucet, taking a moment to wring out her clothes and hang them from the towel rack to dry before she stepped out of the tub.

Looking around, Sabrin realized she didn't have any clothes to change into.

She wrapped herself in a towel then reached for the doorknob. Did she care that she was prancing out in front of Ryder, mostly naked?

It seemed late in the game for that to be an issue. There was the spectacularly naked Ryder within minutes of meeting each other, then the panty run into the woods the next day.

She opened the door and made her way to her suitcase.

Ryder had the covers thrown back and was lying on the bed in a t-shirt and a pair of running pants. His clothes, wet from lifting her into the tub, lay across the ladderback chair.

"Voodoo, don't look. Sabrin's naked," Ryder said, doing his own looking with a wolfish grin.

"Well, not as naked as you were when we first met," she reminded him as he came to the edge of his bed.

"Granted." He tipped his head. "Seems unequal that you've seen me, and yet…"

"You have to stop doing that." Her voice was playfully sexy. Not how she'd meant to sound. *It's hard to sound professional when you're dressed in just a towel, standing in front of a sinfully sexy guy.*

"You're going to have to be more specific," Ryder said. "What exactly should I stop?"

"Putting out sex-rays."

"What's that?" He chuckled. "X-rays?"

"No." She crossed her arms over her chest, stuck a foot out, and tapped her toes on the ground. "*Sex* rays." She wiggled her fingers in front of her face. "They're zapping my brain and making it hard for me to think."

"That sounds dangerous." His brows drew together. "Possibly painful."

"And frustrating." She laughed at her candor. It felt good to laugh.

He stroked his thumb along his jawline, considering her. "What if I proposed a scientific experiment?"

She raised a brow.

"We take a tumble and see if that relieves the radioactivity?"

"Curiosity satisfied, I would be freeing myself up." She canted her head. "In the interest of cognitive behavioral science, would you be willing to go along with such an experiment?" she asked.

"Yes," he said earnestly. "In the interest of science, I'd be willing to do my part."

She bit her lip. Something had to be done. There was too much at stake to be this distracted. "But what if this makes it worse instead of better?"

"I'm willing to give my *all* to the mission." His eyes were full of warmth and laughter, with…affection. And she wanted it. All of it.

But to be clear, here, Sabrin. He said, "mission."

The mission. A defined period of time. This was physical, not emotional. Under other circumstances, Sabrin could talk herself out of this next step. She was disciplined. She'd made up her mind about what she wanted in life. But in *this* case, her body was growing insistent. She couldn't afford to be sidetracked by her libido, she told herself.

She took a step closer to the bed. "Did you bring a condom?"

Ryder reached out and pinched the bottom of the towel. "Say yes, Mrs. Tucker."

"Yes." Sabrin lifted her arms out to the side.

When Ryder tugged the bottom of the towel, Sabrin immodestly let it slide to the carpet.

"Come here." He held out his arms as he scooted back on the bed. "Let's get you wrapped up and warm. We can't have you turning blue again."

When she crawled into his arms and settled her cheek over his heart, one leg thrown across his thighs, he covered her with the blanket, wrapping his arm around her to hold her to him.

Ryder combed his fingers through the strands of her damp hair. Little kisses dropped onto her head every once in a while.

Sabrin realized he was giving her time—a time to relax and be cared for. Maybe, time to change her mind… She had no desire to change her mind—she just had desire.

Her body softened with Ryder's calm attention.

Being here felt like solace. And kindness. An oasis of goodness when shadows whispered conspiracy theories.

"The weight. I feel *them* sitting on my shoulder." She moved up a bit to tuck herself under his chin.

"I know," he said, combing her hair.

"This storm… The temperature dropped. It's so so cold outside."

"I know." He combed her hair.

She made a fist on Ryder's chest. "I *hate* that those men are chasing us. It's ruining our cover and making this more complicated."

"Yes." His voice was that smooth velvety warmth, that steadiness that couldn't be wrested from Ryder's sublime control. He combed his fingers through her hair.

"I'm heartbroken for the hostages," she whispered, then tipped her head up.

Ryder kissed the tip of her nose, then drew his thumb across her eyelids, wiping away the tears that clung to her lashes.

It was Sabrin who changed the temperature. She lifted her lips to his.

Ryder's kisses were soft. They sent strange sensations through her system, warmth, vibrations, and colors.

In the kisses that she'd delivered over the past few days, as part of staging her character, Sabrin had captured glimpses of these sensations and had thought… there was danger there. Ryder was like a drug in her system.

But now that these were truthful kisses, Sabrin and Ryder, not two people playing mission roles, she could immerse herself in the sensations.

While it was indeed an odd, intoxicating experience, it was more than that.

It was…

She parted her lips to his tongue, and she sank deeper into a place of…*them*.

Ryder held her tight to his body as he turned until

her head rested on the pillow. His weight melted her into a place she'd never explored before.

Her thighs stroked over the soft fabric of his pants as her legs bent on either side of him.

His hands, warm on her skin.

Sabrin reached down to drag his shirt over his head. Her breath ragged as she rode the sensations of his touch, his lips, his tongue—it was disorienting in the newness flavored with the spice of nostalgia.

Ryder shifted to take off his pants. He placed a condom from his pocket on the bedside table.

Sabrin's mind stumbled through her vast stores of words, looking for some way to understand what she was experiencing.

She whispered, *"Fernweh."*

Ryder moved back to his place between her thighs, flipping the covers over them, keeping her warm. *"Fernweh?"* he asked, smoothing her hair from her face, waiting for her explanation.

"It's a German word for *farsickness*. *Fernweh* describes a place that you've never been, and you've always *longed* for."

And it was here.

This was it.

A place she knew existed, but she'd never found her way to before.

It was right here in Ryder's arms.

She gasped at the discovery.

Ryder stared into her eyes, his pupils dilated, making his irises black as night. "Farsickness. Yes. I *know* that feeling. Yearning for a place, *my* place, but not knowing how to get there." He tipped his head back, closing his eyes. When he looked down at her again, his gaze was filled with discovery. *Hunger*. Victory. "I have traveled the world, Sabrin, feeling like a visitor. Right now, for me, it's like I've just opened the door. A sense of relief that I made my way home. And it's curious because it doesn't feel shiny and new. It feels comfortably right."

Chapter 23

Ryder

As Ryder unwrapped his fourth and last condom with a grin on his face, his phone vibrated with a buzzkill text: I have further information.

"Reality." He sighed, flipping the condom onto the nightstand. He pressed his palms against his forehead and groaned as he recalibrated.

Ryder rolled over to kiss Sabrin.

Her sleepy disappointed eyes, looking up at him… God, she was *so* beautiful it hurt.

Making love to her through the night had been mind-altering. Ryder had had no idea what he'd been missing. He didn't want this moment to end, afraid he'd never recapture it. Sabrin was satisfying in the most amazing way imaginable. And yet. "Duty calls."

"Honey?" she asked.

"Yep, he says he has something new."

She came up on an elbow. "From Sven?" The sleepiness fell away, replaced with anticipation and trepidation.

"One way to find out." Ryder sniffed and pulled himself up to sit with his back to the headboard. His hard-on quietly deflating as he shifted into work gear.

Ryder tapped his phone.

"Honey here."

"Ryder and Sabrin on speaker phone in our hotel room."

"Good morning. I caught you very early, my apologies," Honey said.

"Not at all." Sabrin leaned toward the phone. "We were awake, anxious to hear word."

"Sven has been out tracing Ketil's normal walk. He discovered eight motion-detection game cameras along the path."

"Did Sven trigger any of them?" Ryder asked.

"We don't believe so. Sven was walking parallel to the path, so not in the line of sight of the camera lenses. An interesting thing he discovered, some of the trees had pieces of blue duct tape on the backside. With further investigation, he found speakers, all of them posted at the same height, approximately thirteen feet off the ground."

"Two-meter ladder," Ryder said. "Two-meter bloke with his arms over his head."

"It wasn't for recording nature sounds?" Sabrin asked. "Bird songs for research?"

"Sven's question, too," Honey said. "Here's why we're tossing that possibility. The only place that the devices were found was along Ketil's path. They were two-way communications so that they could speak, and they could hear a response. They weren't in the same places as the cameras. If the cameras and comms were set out as part of a research project, the two elements should be in proximity."

"Ketil has done environmental research on his own since he left the university." Sabrin pulled the sheet up to cover her breasts, tucking the fabric under her arms to hold it in place. "He's not necessarily rational. Could it be his equipment?"

"Before Sven went out on his task, he spent more time interviewing Ketil's mother. He wanted to see if she mentioned this kind of equipment, so Sven would know about its placement in advance of his search. The mother said that Ketil's research consisted of him documenting the animals that naturally crossed his path or came into view as Ketil walked to the top of the hill that is at the end of his normal walking path. Ketil has decades of notebooks filled with tally marks. Sven's seen them. The mother said that Ketil isn't technically inclined and has conspiracy theories around computers. He won't touch one."

"Who would do such a thing?" Sabrin's frown was fiercely protective. "Tormenting a man in ill health that way?"

"A good question," Honey said. "It would certainly help to know the end game."

"Yesterday, Sabrin—" Ryder lifted the phone as Voodoo jumped onto the bed, circled, and lay down between Sabrin and him. "You said that our plans today were based on whether or not equipment was found."

Sabrin scooted down the bed. *"Just a second, let*

me get my notes. This passage is from the dictation on the bus. I've been working to clean this section up to make sense. So it's speculation. Educated guesses."

"Copy," Honey said.

"Possibly even a little magical thinking. Though given the circumstances, I don't think that necessarily throws us off course." She came back to her spot and laid a hand on Voodoo's head, holding the pages. "Reading: *The heart of the country. Rounded bosom. Grandmother trees of ancient wisdom.* Okay, from that section, maybe central Slovakia, with a mountain range that's not as tall as the Tantras. Grandmother trees could refer to the old-growth forests that are protected right up the street from where Ryder, Voodoo, and I are now." She stroked her hand over Voodoo's head. "Reading the next section—and I can have Ryder send you my annotated notes."

"Thank you," Honey said.

"Reading: *Borrowed limbs sing songs with the fujara.* I'm pretty sure that's what the computer tried to spell. I'll explain *'fujara'* in a moment. *Beautiful. Soul-filling. If there is such a thing as god, this is the manifestation. If I were to commune with such a thing as a god, it would be here. I must protect her. If there's any hope, I must do what the trees have been telling me must be done. Loudly, they called to me. The ten laws. The ten laws. The ten law*—Remember, this is what we talked about earlier, *Janteloven.* I just wrote it out this way to be in English."

"The tenets for egalitarian living that Ketil extended to flora and fauna," Ryder said.

"Exactly. Reading again: *The trees bellowed and barked. They sent me here. It's unfolding exactly as I was told. Exactly. Isn't that crazy? I had no idea that I would be a prophet. As a scientist, as an atheist, I scoffed. But with the booming words. With the unfolding of this experience, I weep not just at the majesty around me. I take an oath to go to the shadow of the castle. I will find my bride's veil in nature."*

"Bride's veil in nature?" Honey asked. "Shadow of the castle?"

"This passage comes after he talked about Huldra, the long-haired siren-like mythological figure. I am theorizing that he's speaking of a waterfall. And there is a Zvolen Castle very near where the Ukrainian survivors were recovered. Reading again:—and again, this is possibly about the idea of the Huldra—*She is everything that is beautiful, and I will never leave her and never be unfaithful. The children circle around her skirt and dance to the fiddle music. Ah ho, fossegrim."* She pulled a breath through her nostrils and let the exhale escape her mouth.

"Okay, this means things to you," Honey said.

"It's the map I suggest Ryder and I follow for our hike today. Let's start with that last bit, *fossegrim*. In Norway, the *fossegrim* is a fiddler who can make the sounds of nature—the wind and water—rise in the notes of his fiddle playing. The tune of the *fossegrim* is a bit similar to the Huldra. But where the Huldra lures men to satisfy her lust, the *fossegrim*, according to some takes on the folklore, lures women and children to streams where they drown. Some of the stories say that it can lure men as well. But mostly, they're called to streams—mmm, not just streams but to the waterfalls—by the music. Possibly a bit like the Pied Piper."

"Okay," Ryder asked. "From the passage, does it

sound like that's how he wants to kill the researchers? Drown them? There were the Ukrainians that were released. Despite the mentions of the *Huldra* and the *fossegrim*, Ketil may not be intent on murdering the researchers."

"And there may be more releases today," Honey said. "France fulfilled its task."

Ryder's body tensed. "What was the ask?"

"It was for France's president to go on television and say that the environment had to be humanity's priority."

"And he did?" Sabrin asked.

"Yes, he added it into his speech at the EU last night. It was televised," Honey said.

"And? Nothing this morning?" Sabrin asked.

"The American Embassy contacted me last night about the demand that was met. I know they're hoping to get a call that the French citizens, seven of them, are found. The police have BOLOs—be on the look out—for people on the side of the highways, they've increased highway patrols."

"We're down to twenty-three hostages plus Ketil," Sabrin said, "who seems to be a victim here as well. Have they made a demand on the United States yet?"

"Nada," Honey responded.

"If it's Ketil in a car, seven is a lot to transport." Ryder stroked a hand over his chin. "Though, I suppose if they're unconscious, he can pile them in, put some in the trunk."

"Won't they die of carbon monoxide back there?" Sabrin asked.

"That depends on how far they drive, among other things," Honey said. "Sabrin, I'd like to continue with your thoughts on the dictation."

She pulled her knees up toward her chest and wrapped her arms around them. "Ryder, do you remember lunch yesterday? We were listening to the band in the park?"

"I do."

"There was a guy there who was playing a Slovakian instrument called the *fujra*. It was that long wind instrument that the guy balanced on his thigh while he played it."

"Yeah, I know what you're talking about."

"The *fujra* is played by shepherds as a way to talk to nature. The *fujra* was only played in a small, mountainous area in Central Slovakia in the Polana mountain range. It's about a half hour east of us. So the Ukrainian hostages were found in Zvolen, about a half hour west of our hotel. That would be an hour from a protected landscape that includes an old-growth forest. Remember, the old-growth forest was referenced in that passage I read, and the bridal veil was, too. There are waterfalls there. There's a very famous one called *Bystré*. It could fit." She tipped her head left the right. "Might not. Reading: *I take an oath to go to the shadow of the castle. I will find my bride in nature.*"

"That's where you want to go today? Hike to the Bystré."

"Yes, I do." She rested her chin on her knee. "There's another place that might be interesting, the caves. Let me…" She looked down at the pages lying across the bed. "Yes." Her finger came down on a sentence. "Here's another passage: *And now look. Now, look! Huldra sang her song. That's what happens. I will say my goodbyes. Whether I can satisfy her or not will be seen. But she calls me into her vagina.*" Sabrin cleared her throat and pinked. "Uhm, that's the literal translation of the Norwegian word. Continuing: *I will do as I'm told by the spirits of the pine. Take heed. Don't you see? We will be trolled! And yet, everything comes to pass as it was told to me. I will do what was demanded. And I am not afraid. We will be gifted with our needs.*"

"And you think that the vagina reference might be caves?" Ryder asked.

Sabrin shrugged. "It makes some sense."

"So he doesn't expect to return to his home," Honey said.

"I guess because when the folklore Huldra calls, that's what happens. Once she calls, you leave the life you were leading. You live if you satisfy her sexually. You die if you don't. So that's one thing. Vagina could be a cave, especially because he said he's being trolled, and trolls live in caves. And again, the trees talking to him and his needs being met. Which, for me, begs the question, how did Ketil travel to Slovakia? You mentioned the possibility of a car, Ryder. How did Ketil get hold of one? Someone has to be helping him. He didn't get from Norway to the Tantras where he boarded the research bus on his own." She paused. "Honey, do we know how he got to the dam in March?"

"Yes," Honey said. "He used his mother's credit card. She said that she put security on it, and that can't happen again. And you're right, Sabrin, from the time Ketil went missing to the time he took the bus and the hostages was less than twelve hours. He had to have had help."

"And that bus must have been chosen specifically," Ryder added.

"A reason we don't understand yet," Honey said. "But Panther Force is working on that angle. We need you and Sabrin—Sabrin, if you're willing—to keep doing what you're doing. Once the sun comes up, go check out the waterfall today. See if there's anything of interest. Just an FYI, I have scent samples from each of our four American hostages. They arrived last night, and I shipped them to your present hotel under the name Tucker. You'll have them sometime today. Maybe Voodoo can pick up something when we come up with tomorrow's plan."

"Thank you," Sabrin said. "And I've been assigned to assist. I'll do my best to do that."

"Tomorrow, perhaps we can think about caves," Ryder suggested.

"Sabrin," Honey asked, "are you familiar with the caves in that area?"

"Yes, they're very popular with tourists. That's why I would think that would be a no go, too many people wandering about. Someone would have seen something, except... I have notes..." She paused as she rifled the pages. "Yes, there's one that is temporarily closed to tourists. It doesn't say why."

"Which one?" Honey asked.

"Bystrianska Cave. It would be perfect—limestone chambers keep a constant temperature, underground streams, so the water is readily available, and the formations would make it seem magical for Ketil. The only problem is that it's too far north. Two hours' drive?" She looked up at the ceiling, calculating. "I'm guessing that's right. No, it's got to be something closer."

"I can research that today while you two are out.

Any signs of your four friends since the one was spotted in the pub yesterday?"

"No," Ryder said. "We might have shaken them off our tail. New car. New credit cards, thanks to Uncle Sam."

"He has his uses," Honey said wryly.

"One less worry, hey?"

"Exactly," Honey said.

"So we'll just clean up and get our kit together," Ryder said. "Grab a bite of breakfast and head out. How's connectivity in that area?"

"It's reading as a big fat zero today. Low cloud ceiling, but the storms should hold off until tonight. Ryder, I need you to log your trails with Nutsbe. If you need to deviate, you mark it with tracking signs. Though, we've kept Ridge in Vienna, so Zeus is available if we need to come in and track you down."

"And on that jolly note," Ryder said, "we're going to get rolling with the day."

"Good luck. Out." Honey left the call.

Ryder leaned over and kissed Sabrin. That's what he wanted to do today. Lie around in bed playing with Sabrin.

"That was a first—a naked mission meeting." Sabrin smiled. She didn't look like she wanted to get out of bed either.

Someone needed to bite the bullet.

Ryder propelled himself from under the sheets. "Shall I shower first, or would you like to?"

"Let me run in and use the bathroom quickly, then you can shower first. I wanted to lie here and think for a bit." Her expression clouded.

Ryder hoped this was mission-related thinking and not Sabrin rethinking their night together in any way.

After all, their making love had started as a joke experiment to appease the sex-rays and stay mission-focused.

Had it worked?

Was she done?

Chapter 24

Sabrin

When Ryder shut the bathroom door, Sabrin pulled on her robe, then chose her hiking clothes for the day. Layers were always the best way to go.

Voodoo trotted over and caught the loose cuff of her sleeve in his mouth and directed Sabrin over to one of the suitcases, released her robe, and sat, tail thump, thump, thumping on the ground, focusing intently on the bag.

Sabrin looked toward the bathroom. She could hear the water starting up, the shower curtain sliding shut. She looked back down at Voodoo.

He stomped.

"Okay, buddy, what's in here?" She unzipped the case and tentatively lifted the top. It was full of Voodoo things, toys, vests, his bag of dog food. Voodoo's nose came over the rim, and he pushed at his food bowl.

Sabrin lifted it to show Voodoo. "Is this what you want? Are you hungry?"

Voodoo bowed, his tail in the air, wagging. And he popped up to sit again.

"Okay." She looked toward the bathroom. "Usually, you eat in there. Let me see." She laid a towel down on the rug and placed the bowl on it. "That should keep things clean, don't you think?"

Voodoo's tail thumped the ground.

"I don't know how much you eat." She scanned the directions on the food bag. "You're about sixty pounds, right? Oh, there's a scoop in here. Two cups, yes, okay. That's right." She called out. "Hey, Ryder, is it okay if I take care of his food?"

"Yeah, thanks," Ryder called back.

She sat down beside the bowl, scoop in her hand. "Okay, I know you're supposed to get a command." She poured the kibble noisily into the bowl.

Voodoo stepped up to the bowl and sent her a "please?" look.

"Yes, go ahead. Uhm... Tuck in. Is that right?" It must have been right because Voodoo started gobbling his food down. She laughed at his enthusiasm. Sabrin was scratching Voodoo's ears when Ryder burst out of the bathroom door, covered in suds.

He stopped on a dime, his arms out, fingers splayed, looking like a football player ready for the tackle. Naked.

Sabrin started laughing.

Voodoo licked his bowl clean, then licked her cheek.

Ryder clutched at his heart. He put his hand on the wall and rested his head against it, breathing heavily.

"What?" Sabrin asked.

"You fed Voodoo." The sound was all air, like his voice got trapped in his throat.

Sabrin was so confused. "You…you said I should. I asked before I did anything."

He pointed his finger at her. "You asked if you should take care of the food. I thought you were going to order room service breakfast like yesterday."

"Oh, okay. I'm sorry. I…meant feed Voodoo. He said he was hungry."

Sabrin had to swallow down her laughter as Ryder stood there naked and dripping, looking completely befuddled, a cap of shampoo bubbles ridiculously on his head.

"How did he do that exactly?" he asked.

"He led me to the case and showed me his bowl, then bowed as if asking me for food. I mean, I thought he was communicating pretty clearly. He was hungry."

Ryder lifted his brows and squinted his eyes at Voodoo.

Voodoo turned around to sit in Sabrin's lap.

"You're turning him into a lap dog, are you?" Ryder's hands came to rest on his hips. "He's supposed to be a fierce security dog."

"Aww, he's just a big baby." Sabrin stroked her hands down Voodoo's side and rested her head on his back.

"With very sharp teeth, yeah? You need to be careful. We need to talk about Voodoo and food before you feed him again, right?"

She kissed Voodoo. *"Malý zamilovaný."* Little lovey. Voodoo rewarded her by licking her fingers.

"I'm going back to get these suds off, but here's the rule. No more talking to Voodoo in a language I don't understand, yeah? It's like whispering to someone's kid. It just isn't done."

"I apologize. I didn't mean to be rude. It's just when I talk lovey-talk I do it in Slovak."

"Lovey talk to my *war* beast?"

Sabrin didn't think she'd ever heard Ryder sound more male.

Still, he looked ridiculous, and she didn't know why he'd sprung himself from the shower like that. "Hey, Studly-suds-a-lot, you're dripping shampoo bubbles all over the carpet."

He turned and headed back to the bathroom, muttering to himself about fangs of death as he closed the bathroom door.

"What was all that about, Voodoo?"

"I'm surprised we haven't passed anyone on the trail yet today," Sabrin said. "I think it's the mud. Admittedly, this climbing's been treacherous after the storm. It's an unpleasant mess. I'd avoid it if I was just craving a day hike and stay where there's pavement."

Ryder looked around. "Are you okay back there?"

"Yeah, I was thinking, though, I'll have to check with the motel about hosing Voodoo off outside. He's been having a good time rolling in the dead things."

"K9 perfume."

"That's so gross. Oh, hey, look!" She pointed at the sky where two eagles had locked talons and were spinning toward the earth.

"Eagle death spiral." Ryder tipped back to watch. "If

they survive the fall, they'll mate for life." He caught her eye.

"That sounds like a metaphor for love right there. It's all about surviving the fall…"

"Sabrin," he said, his voice husky with emotion. "Last night meant a lot to me."

She paused. Froze. "Me, too." This was going somewhere.

He pointed up at the screaming birds, spinning ever closer to the ground. "Those eagles aren't a metaphor for us."

"Okay."

"We can just decide what we want for *us* and reach for it," he said. "We don't need to chance a crash and burn. We don't have to make things tough. It could be as easy as just deciding." He put his hand over his heart. "I've decided. *I* want a future with you beyond the mission. I hope you're with me on that."

"Yes." She exhaled. It wasn't the "this was fun, catch you on the backside" speech.

"Just to be clear—"

Crap. She'd exhaled too soon.

"When I say future, I'm not talking about, let's get dinner when we get back to Washington. I mean, I'd like to see if our lives can line up on the same pathway if we can't hike the trails into the sunset together."

Sabrin snorted. Her hands came up over her mouth, covering her grin. "Oh my god, that was so corny."

"Yeah, that was pretty bad." He chuckled. "I don't have any experience with these feelings. They're brand new to me. It might take me a little time, you know, to figure out how to be sincere without causing you to actually snort…"

Sabrin snort laughed. "Sorry." She held her hands out as if to erase that. "Sorry!"

"Still…you're a linguist, you can figure out the sentiment, yeah?"

"I can. I did." She pulled her hands in to cover her heart. "I share your sentiment. That makes me very happy."

If they hadn't been on a rocky climb with only enough space to ascend in single file, she'd insist on a kiss. As it was, she'd just have to focus on his butt as he climbed ahead of her.

Not exactly a hardship.

"We're getting close," she called. "I think at the top of this hill, we should be near that place that we were looking at on the map, where the trail comes in from the military site to the fire break. Flat ground, easily walked. If the hostages are up here. I agree with you. That would be an easier way to get an unconscious body to a vehicle. Too bad it wasn't open to the public, and we didn't have to heft ourselves up the mud mountain."

"We're going to have to be cognizant of daylight," Ryder called back to her. "Keep an eye on the clock so we can get back to the SUV. With no phone bars and another storm coming in. We need to be off the mountain before we're part of the problem instead of part of the solution."

"Okay. Hey, do you have any gorp in your pack? My blood sugar's starting to drop."

"Dunno. I have food. Describe gorp."

"Uhm. Good old raisins and peanuts. Trail mix."

"Yeah, I'll dig some out at the top. But we call it scroggin."

"Scroggin…?"

"Sultanas, Chocolate, Raisins, and Other Goody-Goodies Including Nuts."

"Sultanas—a wife or concubine of a sultan?"

"Ha. No. Sultanas are seedless raisins. And I know you're teasing me."

"Scroggin has chocolate. I'll do scroggin instead of gorp from now on."

Breathlessly at the top of the climb, Sabrin sat on the rock and took a sip from her water bottle.

Ryder dug in his pack for his scroggin, and she looked at the map.

He came over and sat beside her on the outcropping. "Weather's starting to change up. Temperature's dropping. I'm going to cut our trail time. Last night's storm was too violent to mess around with."

Ryder pulled out his compass and looked around them, focusing on the different ridgelines, while she dug into the snack bag.

"I think we're here, and the military base here, the fire road is up there." Sabrin walked her fingers over the map.

"I'm going to disagree. We're here, and if we go around that boulder right there, we should be looking down on the fire road as it comes through here." He tapped the intersection.

Sabrin squinted down. "Okay, how about this. We go around the boulder and look. And when the path isn't below us, we'll go over here." She circled her finger up the trail.

"If it makes you happy," he said.

"Where's Voodoo," she asked as they stood, gathered their packs, and started off again.

"He's looking around. He never gets but so far out from me."

They walked ahead, around the boulder, down the trail, and squatting, Ryder pointed down below them where there was a wide fire line—a space cleared as a way to help stop forest fires from spreading out of control.

"Huh," she said. "You were right."

Ryder tapped his ear. "Say it again."

"You're right?"

"Such a lovely ring." He moved over to search for the best way to get down to the other trail. He tipped his head back and whistled for Voodoo.

"You're one of them?"

"I don't know who *them* is. But I am someone who likes to be right—not to rub someone's nose in my bloody rightness, but to actually *be* right. I put a lot of study and effort into my capacity to be right—because lives often lie on the line. My being wrong can be a death sentence."

Any joking between them slid away.

A heaviness descended.

They *had* to find the hostages.

Chapter 25

Ryder

"Hey, look at this." Ryder was squatting on the ground, squeezing his lips between his thumb and his knuckle. A thinking position. "Careful, come straight over to me, step where I did." He tipped his head back and whistled for Voodoo.

Voodoo hadn't been back to check-in for a while.

Sabrin came up behind Ryder, putting her hands on his shoulders and leaning over to see what he wanted to show her.

"There are some interesting tracks I've been following."

"Tracks after last night's storm? I'm surprised they weren't all washed away."

"The people were walking in muddy conditions, so

they left a hole to fill with water. But this seems to be a stop before a reset."

"I'm a linguist, not a tracker. Can you tell me what you're seeing?"

"There were three sets of tracks that all seem to be the same age. Though, it's almost impossible to tell in these conditions. I'm saying they're concurrent because two days of rain would surely obliterate any trace. So we have a center track that, from the shape of the toe and heel, was probably in hiking boots. Steady gait. A couple of twists and turns, one would suppose as the person is looking around."

"Okay."

"And then these two sets, here. They're a meter apart. One here, the other over there, see it?"

Sabrin looked out about the distance of a yardstick, and sure enough, yes. Parallel foot-size puddles. "Are they walking sideways?"

"Sort of. It looks like they're carrying something heavy between the two of them, bodies angled, walking with their feet crossing."

"Carrying someone out?"

"These tracks are bringing something in. And typically, if you're carrying a person, someone has the feet, and someone else takes the head."

"If they had something heavy, why not just drive it back here?"

"Dunno. But look, it seems like they dropped it. See this?" On a slight hill of land, where no water accumulated, there was a dent in the clay soil that, even to Sabrin's untrained eye, looked like the corner of a cube hit down hard.

"Then," he pointed to the puddles, "the two pivoted and took off running."

"How can you tell that?"

"Guessing, especially in these conditions, but I'm looking at the lack of heel strikes and length of gait."

"Okay, oh reader of forest leaves, why did they run, and what happened to the box?"

"Yeah, that's interesting. I think they were chasing the person in the boots. The boot prints scuffed and turned. There was a smear of mud like someone was pressing off the balls of their feet. And as to the box, that's another curious thing. I want you to walk backward four steps and wait for me, please."

Sabrin complied.

Ryder joined her and put her hands on his hips. "Walk in my footsteps, please."

They moved a couple feet down the trail, pivoted, and walked straight out at a right angle, ending up just in advance of the deep indentation.

"Two sets of prints, tennis shoes, same length and shape as on the other side of the dent, walk side by side, peel off to the meter distance, and then that same foot over foot."

"I don't know what that means."

"They chased the guy up the hill and came back for their crate."

"A crate, though?" Sabrin said. "Up here?"

"Interesting, right?"

"Bootleggers?" Sabrin shrugged. She pointed at one of the puddles; a piece of plastic stood up in the center.

"Is there such a thing here?" Ryder went over and pulled the plastic out, holding it aloft. "Good find,

Sabrin. Why the heck is there an IV bag out in the middle of nowhere."

"I have no idea." Sabrin looked up the fire trail. "I bet Green could get it analyzed. Or have someone do it. Is there a label?" She went over and read. "Saline solution, and I don't know what the other things are."

"In the commandos, we'd go out for a hard night of partying and hook ourselves up to saline drips, so we'd be hangover free in the morning."

"That's a terrible story."

"I'm just pointing out that it's weird *and* doesn't necessarily mean anything."

"Do you think that was what was in the box? That would be really heavy. Two pounds per liter, to mix measurement types. Figure three feet by three feet? No wonder the men were walking funny."

"*If* that's what it was." Ryder opened a plastic Ziploc bag and put the IV bag inside, sealed it up, and put it in his backpack.

There was a rustling above their heads.

"Come here, Voodoo. Trace."

"What is the trace command?"

"Trace your way to me. Trace your way down the cliff. It's basically a 'figure it out, I want you here' command."

"Thank you." That Voodoo and Ryder had their own language was very interesting to Sabrin. She liked it.

Voodoo ran down the almost sheer wall and leaped the final six feet. He was sopping wet and stank to high heaven.

Sabrin pinched her nose.

Voodoo padded over to Ryder, sat down, and put his paw on his nose.

"Bloody hell." Ryder exhaled, then looked up the hillside.

"What's that signal?" Sabrin's face told Ryder that she'd guessed it was bad.

He held out a hand to her. "Come on." He looked down at Voodoo. "Lead."

Sabrin's body became rigid; she didn't step forward with him. "Lead where? What's happening?"

"Voodoo's alerting on a cadaver."

She pulled her hand back. "But it could be a deer or something, right?"

"Unfortunately, no. Voodoo's trained on the scent of decaying human remains. Having said that, anything that leaves the human body decays. Someone could have cut themselves and left some blood. That would give off the scent that Voodoo searches."

"But it would have to be a lot of blood, right?" She seemed to have gotten over her initial freeze and was walking with him now.

"K9s can detect a drop of gasoline in a pool of water. No, it doesn't have to be a lot. It could be as small as a child's tooth that they were carrying back home for the tooth fairy, and it fell from their pocket. We'll know when we get there."

Voodoo always seemed to intuit human limitations. When Ryder asked Voodoo to lead, Voodoo always found a path that Ryder could access. Voodoo could scale this hill easily. They had passed a couple of spots that Ryder could have gotten up. Voodoo must be taking Sabrin's smaller stature into consideration.

They finally reached a section of hill that Voodoo deemed manageable for them. He scampered up the bank and stood over the top, barking encouragement.

Ryder stuck his hands under Sabrin's ass and hefted her up. She was doing fine on her own; Ryder did it because he loved the feel of her ass.

Ahead of him, Sabrin dragged herself tree to tree until they were at the top. She bent with her hands on her knees, catching her breath.

Ryder pulled out their map to orient himself. "We're right back on the trail we left an hour ago."

She pulled her water bottle from her side pocket, took a swig, and handed it to him.

Voodoo wandered over and sat beside Ryder, wrapping one paw over his nose, looking pitifully like he was crying.

Ryder signaled to wait.

"Do you need to catch your breath for a couple of minutes?" Ryder asked Sabrin. "This might be the time to eat something." What Ryder didn't add was that, once they found the cadaver, appetites could get squirrely. Ryder knew it wasn't just a spot of blood or a found tooth. Voodoo's whole body said he was proud of his find. It was the look Voodoo got when he found a person who was deceased. Had they been alive, even just barely, Voodoo would have sat, put his paws together as if he were begging.

"No, I think we should keep going," Sabrin said, looking at the sky.

She was right. Whatever was about to happen would take time. There were waning daylight and impending storms to deal with.

Ryder signaled, and Voodoo trotted ahead of them on the trail, then came Ryder, followed by Sabrin. Ryder tried to keep himself squared in front of Sabrin. If he was the first person to see the body, he could keep her away if it were too decomposed or gruesome.

Ryder lived a life filled with dead bodies.

He couldn't imagine that was true for Sabrin and her linguistics career. He'd protect her from getting those pictures into her psyche if he could.

"There's a waterfall just ahead. Do you hear it?" Sabrin asked.

"Voodoo, lead." Voodoo was back again. He would run out in his excitement of the find, then track back to check on Ryder's progress. Normally, Ryder would jog along to keep the enthusiasm up for Voodoo. The find should always be a happy celebration full of fun for the K9, so they liked to do that job. But now, Ryder was watching tracks. The boot guy had been running from the tennis shoe guys.

Voodoo yipped and plunged into the stream.

Bloody hell.

Ryder waded into the water behind Voodoo at the top of the small waterfall.

Voodoo stopped, caught Ryder's gaze, then barked.

There, the bottom of a boot.

Ryder knew it was futile, but he ran forward, scooping and pulling. He got a man's form up, then settled it back in the water.

Ryder climbed from the stream. "Come on, Voodoo. To me." He reached into his pocket for the celebratory toy that Voodoo got when he made a find and started a game of tug of war with him with high-pitched reward praise.

Sabrin was staring at the form, shaking. "Could it be one of the researchers?"

"I don't know," Ryder said. "I'll take a picture and

send it to Honey to see if it is. I doubt it, though. That's the boot tread we've been tracking. I think it was a local hiker who saw something he wasn't supposed to see." He arrived in front of her, arms crossed over his chest. "Sabrin, we have some tough decisions to make."

Chapter 26

Sabrin

"**A**re you hanging in all right?" Ryder asked.

"I'm conflicted. Though, there's nothing else to be done, is there? I mean, we don't have the equipment to get the man down the mountain. We had to leave him. It's just…" She put one hand on the boulder and another on Voodoo's head, so she didn't trip over him as she climbed over the tricky spot. "Yeah, for sure, we couldn't have gotten him down this. Part of me is glad that we left him because carrying a decomposing body—" She gave a full-body tremor. "I'd do it if I had to."

Voodoo wasn't running off this time; he stayed right by Sabrin's side, even on the tight spots where barely one fit comfortably. Sabrin didn't mind. She knew Voodoo was there with moral support.

She'd seen dead bodies before.

Well, one.

It was all just…the families and friends who would be getting terrible news. The grief that would follow. The pain.

Wrong place, wrong time, Ryder had said. There had been blows. This was a murder.

Sabrin and Ryder came to the heart-wrenching decision that with lives on the line and a possible direction to search, those unrecovered hostages had to take precedence.

They left the man in the water.

Even there, he might not be safe from the bears and wolves in the area.

They couldn't carry the man out by themselves. They couldn't be involved.

Police. Detectives. Questions. Detainment?

There was work for Ryder and Sabrin to do, finding those hostages. And practically speaking, there was no way they could get down the mountain with a body before the storm. Already the sky was turning that bruised, angry color it had been last night.

They'd call it into John Green and get a directive.

Especially because those tracks were the best lead they'd had so far.

At least, it was the thing that stood out as odd. That and the IV bag.

Sabrin tuned back in when Ryder said, "I know you would. And I know you don't like leaving him there. I'll tell you what. We parked under that overhang. How about I climb that and see if I can't get a sat phone connection and call the embassy from there, instead of waiting until we got back within cellphone range."

"Would you?" She sent a glance back over her shoulder. "That would be better, I think. It'll be too dark and the storm too dangerous to go after his body tonight. But, there's a family feeling desperate. I mean, I remember how upset I got when one of Mom's cats didn't come home—and those were cats. Can you imagine if this is your husband or son? At least, if a missing person's report is out, this might give them a sense of what's happening. That's better, right? And the sooner that call goes out, the better it will be for the family."

Ryder wore a bemused smile on his face. "Well, that answers that question. You're not a badass, super-secret CIA spy. You're just too tender."

Sabrin scowled. "This doesn't bother you?"

"I'm not indifferent. Let's just say that this is a fairly common occurrence in my life. It doesn't have the same emotional charge as it does for you."

"Because Cerberus Tactical K9 does all of that charitable work, going into mass disasters around the world and trying to save people?"

"Trying our best. Yes."

Sabrin stopped. From here, she could see the path to the SUV and a path up the rocks, where Ryder might be high enough and clear of tree interference to get a connection with the satellite phone. "I think I'm going to climb down and wait for you in the vehicle." She pointed below them to where the rental was parked. "Is that okay? Do you want me to take your pack?"

"I'll keep the pack. I'll just be a minute, hey?"

Voodoo ran ahead and checked the vehicle, turned, and ran back to join Ryder.

Sabrin was looking forward to getting in the SUV and untying her boots.

Down the path, onto the parking area, grit under her sole, she rounded to the back of their vehicle—the only vehicle here. No other hikers braved the muddy climb.

Keys in hand, Sabrin pressed the button, and the system *beep-beep-beeped*—a warning as the hatch slid up automatically.

A car pulled up behind her as she sat on the ledge to wrestle her pack off her weary shoulders.

Tweedle Dee was pointing a gun at her.

For the first time in days, the low level of fear that had hummed through Sabrin's system was silenced.

Sabrin slowed her breath and worked to get free of her pack. "What exactly do you want, waving that gun in my face?" she asked in Slovak as the man climbed from his car.

Barrel chested, he was a good six inches taller than she and weighed an extra hundred pounds.

Her frustration with this man's interference heated her system.

And now a gun?

"Where's the dog?" he growled. His tone pitched to make her fear him.

"The dog? Where's the dog?" She brought her hands up, showing the flats of her palms as if she were his prisoner.

Yeah, he brought a gun. And he held it sideways like a thug. It wasn't having its desired effect on her.

Quite the opposite.

His threat brought anger to a simmer in her veins.

"What do you want with my dog?" She took two steps toward the man, making sure she had her weight on her back leg as she came to a stop. This was muscle memory, going to the mats at The Farm.

Feint and strike.

One hand slowly lowering to be parallel to the gun. The other hand letting the fingers curl over naturally.

"Your dog," he growled. "I *want* him."

"Well, you understand, that dog belongs to Iniquus, not to me." She raised her voice, hoping it would carry toward Ryder in the wind. Not for him to come down and save her, but that Ryder should be aware that bullets might fly. "Voodoo is *not* a pet."

She took another two steps forward. "Why are you bothering us about the dog?"

Two more steps. Sabrin was within striking distance now.

And the guy let her. It spoke to his level of training. She imagined drunken bar fights and street brawls. Slapping women into submission.

She let her gaze slide over the man's shoulders as if she was focused on someone walking up. With a slow nod, Sabrin pretended to agree to a stratagem with the fictional person behind them.

When he turned his head to look, both of Sabrin's hands shot out. Her left hand gripped around the gun barrel, holding the slide, lest he tried to fire a shot.

Voodoo and Ryder were out there.

She jammed the knuckles of her right hand into the guy's windpipe.

Her leg swung up between his legs, her anger energizing that kick.

He hadn't let go of the gun, though he gagged at the vomit that caught in his throat. He reached to grab at her with his free hand, trying to fling her to the side.

She was sure if that happened, he'd shoot her out of

spite. The sheer audacity of her not quaking and suc-
cumbing to him.

That's *not* who Sabrin was. She didn't supplicate.
Her father's courage formed her spine. Her mother's
tenacity built her bones.

Sabrin reached over to press her thumb into the soft
spot on the guy's gun hand, and holding tightly, she pivoted. Chambering her leg, Sabrin thrust into the guy's
leg. "Eight pounds of pressure snaps a kneecap," she
parroted her fight instructor.

They weren't taught the pretty martial arts, the flying kicks with long air time.

They were taught to fight for their lives, fast and dirty.

The man's leg bent in the wrong direction.

He howled, managing to catch his balance on his
one good leg. His fingers reached into her hair, drag-
ging her head backward.

Control of the head meant control of the body—a
danger to having long hair.

Sabrin flipped her hands over, rotating the guy's
arm, so it locked at the elbow. One hand gripping that
gun slide to keep the bullet from flying, the other hand
came up over her head. She jumped into the air and
slammed her palm into the locked joint of his elbow.

Pop.

That arm lost all power.

She raised her fist and slammed it down onto his
left collar bone, then right.

Snap. Snap.

With his clavicle broken, he'd be unable to use his
arms without excruciating pain.

Adrenaline did its brain-trick, making this a slow-
motion dance of destruction.

In real-time, seconds had passed.

When the guy tried to plow a shoulder into Sabrin, she conjured the Monty Python film with the knight still trying to fight with his limbs severed.

This wasn't funny, though. It needed to stop.

She grabbed his hair with her free hand and slammed his head into her knee, sending blood flying as she broke his nose.

He tipped and fell to his back.

Sensing movement above her, Sabrin threw her head around.

Voodoo sailed down from the rocks. Front paws touching the ground, he bunched his muscles and, with a single leap, sprang over to her, sinking his teeth into the man's gun arm.

Sabrin had never heard a scream like that from a man before.

She stepped back, stunned by the violence of Voodoo's attack.

At the K9 competition, the men in the bite suits would yell in obvious pain, but this scream was high and shrill. It carried terror in the warble.

Sabrin knew this guy was seeing his life flash before his eyes.

She had no idea how to call Voodoo off.

Voodoo was too intent on the joy of the bite to hear anything she had to say.

This morning when Ryder had vaulted from the shower in terror, he'd mumbled about fangs of death. Sabrin hadn't understood.

Voodoo was precious and goofy and such a cuddly lovebug.

But Voodoo was also a killing machine.

"Away," Ryder's voice boomed. "Voodoo. Away. Here to me."

It had been all of thirty seconds. It had been so viciously brutal. Sabrin knew Voodoo was attacking in defense of her because the arm Voodoo latched onto was the one that still had the gun in the man's hand, his finger stuck in the trigger guard.

Thank god, Ryder had exquisite control over Voodoo.

One command, an immediate reaction.

Voodoo released the man's arm and dashed over to sit at Ryder's feet.

Sabrin could see a flash of white bone amongst the man's shredded muscle tissue.

She fought back nausea as she knelt beside the man who writhed beside his car.

Her phone out, video recording. "You're going to tell me exactly why you're here. How did you find me?" she growled in Slovak. "Tell me, or I'll have Voodoo bite you again."

"Please!" he sobbed. "Please. The hospital."

"Why did you point a gun at me?"

Ryder stood the whole time with his feet wide, his hands across his chest, and his head on a swivel, watching for anyone on foot or vehicle to come on this scene. It was growing gory as the guy bled into the dirt.

She rifled through his pants and took his wallet, flipping it open to make sure he had ID.

"I've got what I need," she said to Ryder. "He's too woozy to be coherent, now."

"I don't know. You look so cute and sweet," Ryder said, "and the next thing, I'm peeking over the rock to see what the noise is, and you're breaking a guy into pieces like kindling for a campfire." He put his hand to his chest. "You kind of scare me."

"Shut up."

"You know the store policy. You break it. You buy it." He pulled off his ball cap then stuck it back on his head, adjusting it in place. "We could maybe stick him in the garage for a rainy day when we feel like tinkering. Maybe put him back together. Sell him on eBay."

"Stop!" Sabrin looked down, assessing the situation. They couldn't call any authorities, that was for sure. "Look at this. He got his nose blood on my pants. These were my favorite hiking pants."

"Really rude on his part, I'd say."

Voodoo went over to sit on Sabrin's foot.

"So before any cars drive by, what are we going to do with him?" Ryder asked.

"If you load him into his car, I can drive him to the hospital. You could follow, and we could just leave him outside the emergency room?"

"Okay, how about I get him in the car." Ryder scooped up the gun, checked the magazine, checked for a round in the chamber. "Locked and loaded. He meant business." He bent to kiss her. "Good job. I'm proud of you." He slid the gun into the back of his belt. "*That* was bloody impressive." He grabbed the guy by the shirt and lifted his semi-conscious body up to a seated position.

Squatting, Ryder dragged the guy, moaning his agony, across Ryder's shoulders. "He say anything important?"

"Not about the hostages. I'll translate the video for you later. I'd like to get Nutsbe involved."

Sabrin ran over to open the passenger-side seat of

the man's crumpled sedan. She sighed out some of the energy swirling through her body. Adrenaline pumped through her system. And she was exhausted…by all of it.

"Voodoo can ride with you," Ryder said. "I'll leave this guy in front of the emergency room door and walk to the exit. If you could meet me there?"

"Yep."

"I'll contact Nutsbe to arrange a new car and a new room."

Sabrin nodded. "And we have to find somewhere to give Voodoo a bath. He smells gross. I'd like a shower. Food. And hopefully more answers."

Chapter 27

Ryder

"This is a three-way conference call. This is Nutsbe in Panther Force war room in Washington. I'm alone in the room."

"Honey here, I am alone at my location."

"Ryder and Sabrin here. We are alone in our newest hotel room," Ryder said.

"Thank you, Nutsbe," Sabrin said. "Your coordination has been seamless, and I've been very comfortable."

"Yes, ma'am," Nutsbe said. "If we're all set, let me start with information that you sent in on the dead man from the trail."

Ryder glanced up to check on Sabrin. He thought the fight as they'd come off the trail had muted her angst about leaving the guy in the water. But she'd been pretty quiet all evening.

"A message was sent from a Slovakian cell phone to the police. Some hikers had found a body on the trail. Map coordinates and time of day were included in the communication. The authorities are aware that there is a body that needs to be recovered."

"Good." Sabrin tapped her chest, and Voodoo jumped on the bed and curled up in front of her crossed legs.

"Our AI system found a missing person in the Zvolen area," Nutsbe continued. "There were social media posts about Ivan Tichý. In the pictures that I received of the deceased, there was some facial decomposition from being underwater for, say, twenty-four hours. Despite the decomposition, the computer indicates a high probability that the deceased is Ivan."

"What's being said on social media?" Sabrin asked.

"I depend on translation software to understand the Slovak. If it's of mission value," Nutsbe said, "I can put together a file, and you can read it in the original language."

"Thanks, Nutsbe, just the gist. Not for operational use...just morbid curiosity." Sabrin was kneading her anxiety into Voodoo's shoulders, and Voodoo seemed to be enjoying it.

"Yes, ma'am. It says that Ivan didn't show up at work, which was unlike him. A co-worker went to his house to check on him. Ivan's dog had not been fed or walked. The dog had gone to the bathroom by the door. The co-worker called the police, who took a report. If any friends or family knows what might have happened, ring the police."

"What did Ivan do for a living?" Ryder asked.

"Advertising, graphic arts."

"So no obvious tie to anything," Honey said.

"He was hiking in the middle of the week?" Sabrin said at the same time.

"His office was closed because of an electrical problem. According to the website, they'd opened back up for business today."

"Well, that all makes sense. Poor guy."

"With the storm activity in your area, I'd imagine they'll get a rescue crew out there in the morning," Honey said. "Ryder, I'd like you to steer clear of that pathway and from parking your vehicle anywhere near there. Speaking of vehicles and parking." He paused, and when he spoke again, Ryder could hear the grin in Honey's voice. "Congratulations, Sabrin, on your Rambo tactics. I'm sure Voodoo appreciates you taking down the dognapper and keeping him safe."

She bent to kiss Voodoo. "As if."

"Sabrin," Nutsbe said. "I sent the identification and video through the system. In the video, the guy was sobbing too hard between words to get a clear read. Did you understand him?"

"Right so, if his ID was real, his name is Milan Komársaid. Milan said he needed Voodoo as a peace offering. That was all. He didn't want to hurt anyone. Possibly also taking Ryder. Capturing Ryder would have been icing on the cake." She shot a look at him that said the idea of Ryder being captured was ridiculous.

Which he appreciated, but a gun was a gun, was a gun.

Apparently, Sabrin didn't ascribe to that line of thought.

"Interesting," was all Ryder said. He and Sabrin

hadn't had time to go through all of it as they disposed of the guy, cleaned Voodoo up, and changed logistics. *Icing on the cake, huh?*

"He said that he'd found us because he was showing a picture of Voodoo around, asking if anyone had seen his stolen dog. He said *we* stole *his* dog. He stopped at a gas station right after we'd filled up, and the guy was able to say what SUV we were in. Milan found our vehicle parked and waited for us at the bottom of the trail."

"And he thought you'd just load him in his car?" Nutsbe's voice was incredulous.

"Him who? Voodoo or Ryder?" Sabrin smiled. "Nah, I wouldn't let Milan take either. I've fallen in love," she caught Ryder's eye and added, "with Voodoo. I don't think Milan thought it all the way through."

"Yeah," Nutsbe said. "Okay, our readout said, 'Peace offering. Heads on a platter. They'd like this.'"

"Do you know who would like it?" Honey said.

"Me?" Sabrin asked. "No, Milan was pretty incoherent. I thought having his ID would get us some of those answers. He's one of four. He didn't say if the other three are looking for us or not."

"Heads on a swivel," Nutsbe said. "Okay. I do have some information and an educated guess."

Ryder slid back on the bed to sit beside Sabrin and wrapped his arm around her shoulder. She snuggled in against him.

"Milan," Nutsbe started. "I checked with two FBI sources, Steve Finley and Rowan Kennedy, who both deal with issues in the Slovakian region. Finley says this guy plays on the fringes of the Zoric family. Milan is not a Zoric. He's a wannabe. He keeps trying to find a way to make the cut and be on the team. Finley gave me a few names… I'm putting pictures up on the data screen to see if you can't pick these guys out of a crowd. Can you see if any of those faces are familiar?"

Ryder and Sabrin bent in. "That one there with the funky nose," she said.

"And that one with the scar on his chin."

"Yup. That's Milan on the bottom right… This one here," she pointed for Ryder, "could be the fourth."

"Look at this guy. The cowlick and the eyebrow."

"You're right." Sabrin nodded. "He was driving the yellow car."

"Nutsbe, we're saying the four are 1A, 2D, 3A, and 3D," Ryder said.

"Okay, that lines up with Finley's best guesses," Nutsbe said. "Milan has failed the upstanding citizen awards. The men you picked from the line up are his known associates."

"What was he in trouble for?" Sabrin asked.

"In broad strokes, he looks like he enjoys beating the shit out of people, stealing cars, and petty stuff mostly to do with drugs and gambling. Fun times," Nutsbe said. "Do you want copies of the photos?"

"I think we'll recognize them if they show up again," Ryder said.

"Let's move on to Rowan Kennedy's take on this. It's interesting in that it lines up with Sabrin's translation. Kennedy thinks the guys were at the championship this last week watching the Iniquus dogs. Low-level wannabes in the Zoric circle, they'd need to do something that they thought would ingratiate them."

"Sabrin actually mentioned something about this when we first met. The Zorics make a game of stealing things for the fun of it."

"And to show power. The Zorics like to play at psychological warfare. Kennedy said that there's a thing in Native American culture, and I can't remember which tribe or region, I apologize, but that a sign of bravery was called a 'counting coup' where the warrior went up to their enemy, and hit them, then rode away. Not to say that these four are anywhere sophisticated enough to imagine such a thing."

"But I could imagine they'd say, 'Hey, Iniquus is Zorics' enemy.'" Sabrin's eyebrows were up in her hairline. "That's not a big secret. Here were two Iniquus members right over the border in Czechia with their dogs."

"How would they know that?" Ryder asked.

"There's nothing on the Internet about you or Ridge," Nutsbe said. "There are mentions of Cerberus Tactical K9 in the articles about the competition. If anyone had an Iniquus alert on their computer, it would have come up."

"And they thought, steal the dogs and become a favorite with Mrs. Zoricova?" Sabrin's voice trailed off.

"What was that thought?" Honey asked.

Sabrin shifted around. "Remember that they brought that bottle to the campsite, Ryder? What if it was laced with Ketamine or some other date rape drug? What if they had steaks laced with sleepy drugs for the dogs? All they needed was for us to welcome them to the circle and drink."

"But you were pregnant and not drinking," Ryder said.

"What?" Normally warm and mellow, Honey's voice was the most agitated Sabrin had ever heard.

"Not in the real world, operational cover," she clarified. "My pregnancy being true or untrue, the four saw their plan wasn't going to work, and they've been following us around."

"They chased you on your way to the embassy," Nutsbe said.

"With guns. So they hold up a gun, and they take Ryder's dog?" Sabrin shook her head as she sent Ryder a look of incredulity.

Honey and Nutsbe started laughing. Yeah, that would never happen.

"Did Ridge have any issues?" Sabrin asked.

"He was able to get a hotel room when some of the contestants who didn't progress on the competition field vacated them. He paid some guy to go get the RV back to the rental place. No issues on his end," Nutsbe said.

"So why do you think they targeted Ryder and not Ridge?" Honey asked.

"I'd guess that I made Ryder vulnerable," Sabrin offered. "We were improvising. They just drove up from the farmer's field. I pretended to be Ryder's girlfriend when the men started hitting on me. And I turned down their drinks because I was pregnant. I'm sure that the men believed that as Ryder's girlfriend, pregnant with his baby, Ryder would defend me before he'd defend Voodoo. Same at the car. If Milan had a gun to my head, Ryder might just load Voodoo into the back seat and let him drive off."

"One would surmise," Ryder said.

"Not true?" Sabrin pursed her lips.

Ryder felt an intensity of purpose swelling his chest. "I would defend you to the death, Sabrin." His voice thick with conviction. "That doesn't require you to be pregnant or vulnerable in any way. The surmise was about Voodoo. He might think Voodoo would just load up and get carted off when a gun was near you. You saw what happened earlier. Voodoo leaped thirty feet to the ground to get to you."

"When Sabrin was fighting Milan?" Nutsbe let out a long low whistle.

"Yeah, mate, I've never seen Voodoo like that. I mean, I've seen him jump astonishingly long distances, but to get to you, Sabrin..."

She put her hand to her heart.

The conversation came to a standstill when a knock sounded at their door.

Ryder stood to go check who it was.

"I'm fairly comfortable with the idea that this Milan guy and his pals have nothing to do with our mission. They're just clutter we picked up along the way." She looked up. "Listen, our dinner just arrived, and Green is on his way over. One last thought before Ryder wheels the cart in." She sniffed. "Okay, look, I need to be clear here. The thing that happened today at the car that *isn't* my gig. I'm trained in case things go terribly wrong, but I'm a translator. Please don't depend on my tactical skills. Translation is all I want to do. Except, of course, save the hostages."

Chapter 28

Sabrin

They'd been eating in silence.

Sabrin had ordered comfort food in the hopes that it would put her into a food coma, and she could just curl up in Ryder's arms, with Voodoo tucked in tight, and sleep without the dead man's face haunting her dreams.

She'd seen photos before of the dead in various stages of decomp.

Movies…

It was something quite different to see Ryder desperately pulling Ivan out of the water on the off chance they could blow life into him. But, of course, once they saw his face, they knew he'd been underwater for far too long.

Sabrin thought about the *Huldra* and the *fossegrim*. How ancient families would find their loved ones and blame the seductive powers of mythological figures to kill.

But this wasn't folklore. Ivan had been chased, beaten, drowned, and left.

Ryder had tried to keep his body between her and the corpse, trying to protect her from witnessing it.

Still, she'd seen.

There were men in the woods that chased and killed. Even with the incredible skills of Ryder and Voodoo—and to some extent herself—

Maybe Green had some answers. This was just *not* what she did for the CIA.

Sabrin had zero desire to be a special operations officer. Zero.

She looked over at Ryder. "What are you thinking?"

He looked at her for a long moment. He seemed to be weighing his response. He wiped his mouth. "The story goes that when we die, we walk toward the light, and your loved ones will meet you there to welcome you across. Help you get acclimated. I was thinking about the man Voodoo found today. I hope he had someone there with him in those last moments."

She rolled her lips in and canted her head. That seemed like the outer layer. Truth-lite.

"I wonder what happens if you have had no loved ones who have crossed over," she said. "I mean, my paternal grandmother passed away, but I barely knew her. I didn't love her because I didn't have the time to love her. She's tacky Christmas sweaters and cat slippers in my memory. Cigarettes and coffee mugs. All my other relatives and friends are still around." She swirled her fork in her plate, not looking at Ryder. "It might be odd if one of my old schoolteachers or someone showed up."

"Wow, that's...dark."

"Tell me you don't consider your death." Her gaze came up and caught on his. Maybe he didn't consider death, given his choice of careers. Maybe he decided to set that subject on a shelf and close the cabinet door.

"Yeah. Sure. Thoughts come to me. Sometimes because of events, like today. Searches where I see that someone was in the midst of their everyday life and that was blunted by the disaster. Moms with their laundry basket in one hand and their child in the other. Dead in the street."

"God."

"I'd imagine that once you get to the other side, you're good. It's the transition that might be the hard part." He set his fork down. "Why are we talking about this?"

"I'm a little off-kilter. Sometimes it helps to face the boogie man."

Ryder nodded.

Sabrin picked up her fork and scooped up a bite of her dumpling. "Who do you think will show up for you?"

"I think that when I die, my mum is going to meet me and welcome me home."

"Did she pass recently?"

"When I was four."

"Such a tender age. I'm so sorry. That must have been disorienting. Do you remember her?"

"Flashes. She used to smell like lemons. Or, when I smell lemons, I think of her."

Sabrin put her elbows on the table and leaned her chin onto her hands. "In what sense? Fresh or sour."

"Fresh."

"If I were to die, and my child were to remember

me through life as the smell of lemons, I think I'd like that."

Ryder slid down in his chair, looking comfortable with one hand resting on his stomach and the other resting on Voodoo's head. "I remember her from photos. I see a photo of her, and I think I remember that outfit or that smile. It's one of the reasons I wanted to come to America. Gran—everyone says my mum and my gran are carbon copies. This is my chance to absorb what I can. I need that."

"I'm wondering about your dual citizen status."

"Mum and dad met while she was doing some surfing in Australia. A trip after she graduated from college. She took the summer off before she started her career."

"What did she do?"

"She was a nurse. When she got home to America, I was the surprise souvenir."

"Wow."

Ryder grinned. "Right? I imagine that was what she thought. After she passed, my dad came and got me and took me back to Australia, where I grew up."

"With the baker's dozen of kids, eleven girls, two boys. Where are you in the pecking order?"

"Let's see, I was the number nine kid but number thirteen to join the ever-revolving nest of ankle biters that moved between the various parental houses. My dad's hobby was marriage, followed by divorce. He's in the skulking phase of the moon right now."

"How many wives?"

"Six, last count. But who knows? By tonight, we could be at number seven. My mum wasn't one of them."

"Bit of derision in your voice."

"Imagine that."

"Okay. Sour topic. I really don't mean to pry." Sabrin picked up her glass of water and drank it down.

"Your mom's Slovakian, your dad American, how did they meet? How did you get your dual citizenship?" His tone changed back to neutral.

"So, I was born in Slovakia—when it was Czechoslovakia—when my mother was visiting her dad—end of life visit. I came early. Surprise." She smiled. "How did my parents meet? My dad was on leave from his ship. He decided to visit Czechoslovakia because he liked the architecture. And they fell in love. The fabled love at first sight."

"Do you believe in that?"

"It worked for my parents. I fell in love with Voodoo at first sight." She leaned down to look at him. "Didn't I, sweet boy?"

"Yeah, yeah. None of that. We don't want to lower his testosterone and make him a mama's boy."

"Love at first sight?" Sabrin turned to look out the window into the stormy night. She turned back to Ryder. "Yes, I believe in it. I just…yeah, it's a confusing sensation, surprising, and maybe a little overwhelming." This. Whatever was between them. It felt like it might be what her parents experienced. Except maybe they embraced the adventure while she had been pushing it away. Maybe she was just confused by the upheaval since her plane landed in Bratislava. She'd like a little peace to be able to take her own temperature.

Ryder reached for her hand. "I'd say—"

When the knock sounded at the door, they both spun to look.

"I've got it." Sabrin stood and went to peek through

the eyehole. She unlatched the safety locks and pulled the door open.

John Green walked into the room, his eye on Voodoo, a little wariness. He looked around for somewhere to sit, and Sabrin indicated the chair where she'd been eating. She moved her plate to the chest of drawers. "Can I order anything for you? Get you something to drink? I have water, tea, and coffee in the room."

"I'm fine, thank you."

Sabrin sat on the end of the bed, spine rigid. "Did they find the French hostages?"

"No. And that's one of the reasons why I wanted to talk to you." He pulled a map from his briefcase. "A trying day today for you two. But helpful. We're moving forward at a fast clip."

"Good," she said.

"The table's not very big. I'll spread this on the bed." He walked over and laid it out. "This pink highlighter is your path today. Does that look right?"

Ryder came to lean over and look at the markings with Sabrin. "Yes," he said. "This is a much better map than the one we had available."

"I got this from a Slovakian military asset of mine who works in the area. This is the road that you two considered as the path for someone to bring a vehicle for resupplying and transporting hostages." Green said, "My asset found the bus."

"What?" Sabrin's eyes stretched wide. "Where was it?"

"Here, there's an indentation in the cliff wall. They backed the bus in, threw a camo cloth over it. It's in a place with zero traffic. Like that, if no one was looking, it wouldn't be found for maybe generations."

"Anything left on the bus?" Ryder asked.

"Clues to the why?" Green tipped his head. "Nada. The only things on that bus were puddles of piss."

"It's a military base. Did they bribe their way on? Is it someone who works there?"

"We think someone who works there took a sizable payment. My asset is gathering data on who was on duty, etcetera. We're running it down."

"They'd need to be on duty every time they needed access," Sabrin said. "Not impossible."

"What *is* impossible, though, is vehicular access to that road now," Green said. "In the storm the other night, they had a lot of trees come down in the high winds. There are, according to my asset, four trees that cross this road, now. First, that means no more hostages can come out, no matter what the different nations do to fulfill the ransom."

"Well, at least they can't come out in a drugged state like the Ukrainians were," Sabrin countered.

Green nodded. "Second, they'll have to foot the supplies in."

"Did they analyze the IV bag?" Ryder asked.

"It's exactly what's on the label. Saline and a cocktail of drugs, typically used during operations that contain sedation medications, go to sleep medicines as well as anti-anxiety medications that have an amnesiac effect."

"They tested the Ukrainian survivors' blood?" Sabrin asked.

"The substances in their blood are consistent with what's in the IV—versed and fentanyl."

"We're close." Sabrin grinned. "Twenty-four more victims. The twenty-two researchers, the bus driver, and I assume they'd have to drug Ketil as well. They'd have to keep him alive so he could take the downfall. I can't imagine who would do this."

"But you're going to find out," Green said. "Does your GPS unit work up here at all?" He pointed toward the map at the spot they'd found where the crate had dropped.

Sabrin shook her head. "It didn't yesterday. The weather might change that. I don't know."

"I have my asset ready to assist you tomorrow at zero-five-thirty hours. He's going to bring you through the gate on foot, and he's going to wait and let you back out again at the end of the day." He put his finger on the map. "When you make the find, you're going to go back and tell him. He's going to be the one to call it into the authorities."

"The Slovakians will go in and save the hostages if we're successful in finding them? Good," Sabrin said. "That's good. As long as everyone gets out healthy."

Ryder was silent.

"That's his get. He gets to be the hero. We get to keep American diplomatic ties calm. The hostages get saved." Green drew his finger along the fire break. "You'll be walking. It's a little over ten kilometers, so six miles in, six miles out. Make sure you have the necessary supplies." He moved his finger to the cliff's wall with topographical rings so tight they looked like the map had been painted pink. "Easy walking, just make sure you're not seen. That didn't go so well for the hiker yesterday. This right here is not on Slovakia's subterranean maps because it's a manmade cave. It was a hiding spot during World War II. My understanding is that the entry is hidden. It might take a K9 to find it," Green said then paused. "Sabrin."

She jerked her head up.

"This is *very* important. *Extremely* important. Based on the intelligence you brought in today, we think this is where the hostages are being held." He tapped the map. "If they aren't, contact me. We'll keep trying. *If* they're here, you are not to try to rescue them. You are in place for reconnaissance. Observe. Video, if possible. Think strategically. Look for ways that a rescue could go sideways. Count heads. You know what to do."

"Yes, sir," Sabrin said. She was trained on what to do. But that was years ago. This was *not* what she did. Sabrin translated and did word puzzles.

And she *only* had control of herself. She had zero control over what Iniquus decided to do.

Ryder would do what Honey ordered.

"Here's the most important part," Green continued. "One of the researchers had a backpack that has IFF glow patches on it."

"IFF's your BFF in a night op," Ryder said.

The IFF patches would glow when seen through a night vision illuminator. It let units know who was a friendly, so they didn't get shot by mistake. This was exactly what Sabrin had thought from the beginning. One of the four Americans was there doing extracurricular activities, using the research trip as cover.

Green lifted his chin toward the bag he'd left by the door. "That's your equipment." He looked toward Ryder. "I included you and Voodoo, just in case you were to tag along." He focused back on Sabrin.

She figured out Green's game. It wasn't subtle.

"Sabrin, I need you to find a way to get that bag out of there *before* we can send in rescue. It may take you some time to figure out how to do it. I don't care how long it takes. That backpack has to be in our hands before anyone else goes in."

What the heck is in there?

"How much does it weigh?" Ryder asked.

"I'd imagine less than twenty pounds."

"You lied to me." Sabrin stared at Green.

"I didn't lie. From interviewing our assets, we see no Russian and no Zoric involvement in the hostage-taking. And this has zero to do with that Syrian op you brought up. Put all of that aside and focus on what I'm saying. Here's what is an absolute: That backpack's contents *cannot* be reviewed by the Slovakian government."

Chapter 29

"How many languages do you speak?" Sabrin asked. They were jogging fast enough to make time, slow enough that she could still speak.

Some of their speed had to do with the hostage-takers no longer having an easy route to supply their crime and provide for the researchers. That was *if* they were in this WWII hideaway that Green had pinpointed for them.

Some of it was that it was chilly out.

A lot of the reason they were running was that Voodoo was a little nuts this morning and needed to burn some energy.

Okay, a lot of it was that Voodoo was hyper this morning.

Ryder said that Voodoo picked up on the prevailing energy, and she needed to do her best to keep her systems calm.

Easier said than done.

Obviously, after over a decade of experience handling K9s, Ryder had that Zen down pat. Sabrin couldn't imagine Ryder getting riled.

"I told you that with my French language skills, I can get by in Italian and Spanish. True story, I was in Italy hanging out with some people I'd met. I was very impressed with my ability to slip into the Italian language. With their hand gestures giving me context, I could keep up with the language basics—'survival Italian plus,' I'd call it. But after about an hour of talking to these people, I realized I was speaking French and just adding 'O's and 'A's to the end of the words. So it was a non-language language, but they understood me a bit, anyway, enough to keep chatting."

"*Manger* in French, *mangiare* in Italian. *Fenêtre* window in French, *finestra* in Italian. It could work as long as you were communicating with someone who often spoke with people speaking Italian as a second language. Listening to a foreigner speak in your language is a learned skill. Even though we both speak English as a native language, you and I come from different points of geography. We have different vocabularies as well as different viewpoints."

"When you speak to me, you censor some of that to make yourself understood, like when you explained 'circling the wagons.'"

"It's reflexive. You do it, too."

"Yeah? When?" Ryder was jogging along with not a drop of sweat. He wasn't even breathing heavily, and he was the one carrying almost all the weight. Her backpack only had her survival ten. The ten items everyone should have on them when they're in the woods to stay alive, fire, water, food, shelter, navigation…

"Sometimes, I hear you talking to Voodoo without that censor, and I have no idea what you're saying. It's not just the thickened accent, but it's also got those interesting twists of the Australian language babyfying some words—barbie for barbeque and sunnies for sunglasses. Nick off and fair go, I can make out. 'I lived out woop woop.' I'd be guessing."

Ryder chuckled. "When I take you out to my family's station, you'll completely understand what it means to be out woop woop. Why are you asking about this?"

He was talking about going to Australia and her meeting his family. That was a major relationship leap forward. "Oh, I don't know." Sabrin shrugged. "Maybe, I'm just trying to distract myself from the blister on my heel."

He stopped and pulled off his pack. "We don't mess around with feet. No feet, no way for us to go forward." He pointed to a rock, and she went over to sit down.

As she reached for her boot, Ryder took a knee and began unlacing her boot just like he had when she'd come back to the hotel room in distress from the storm.

That was the night their relationship shifted to this new place. Scary and exciting. And maybe a little tender as it unfurled like a sprout emerging in spring.

He looked at her face. "That's a curious expression."

"I've been running. Just…you're fussing with my sweaty feet."

He ignored her embarrassment as he rolled down her sock. Peeled it away. "Sabrin," he scolded. "You should have said something earlier."

"I'm not a complainer."

"I get that. And I appreciate that." He cut a piece of mole skin. "But we try to take care of things when they're small, so they don't become big and debilitating."

"A stitch in time?"

"Yeah, something like that." He continued his ministrations.

"I'm a big girl, though, Ryder. I don't need a mom." She said it quietly, soothingly. It wasn't meant to chastise.

"I know." He kissed her on the nose. "But I want to care for you."

Sabrin was, in fact, enjoying his gentle attention.

"He's using you. You realize that, right?" she asked.

"Green? Yeah, we know. Honey and I went over it."

"I don't have anywhere near the skills to do an operation like this. I'm okay with the gathering intel part, but sneaking by kidnappers to retrieve a bag? I can't imagine being successful. I bet Green couldn't imagine that either. He thinks you'll follow me in and do the deed. And you doing the deed keeps any blowback off the US and squarely on Iniquus. If anything bad were happening, Iniquus was in there trying to save the four Americans as part of their contract. Green put you in the crosshairs. I'm not down with that."

"Okay, so we agree on his play. Like I said, we figured. My orders are to go in and look around. If I think it's doable, do it. If I think I need the Panthers, Ridge and Zeus, they're all mobilizing toward us now. They'll be here by dark. We just exit and wait for our backup to come in. And most importantly, Honey agrees that I will do whatever is required of me to keep you from performing your orders, even if that means gagging you and throwing you over my shoulder to hike you out."

"Voodoo would *never* let you do that to me," she said confidently.

"You might be right there, but you're not to put yourself in danger because doing so risks all the hostages. Better we get ourselves out, and report to Honey, bring the team in, and based on our intel, do this the right way."

Ryder wore Ranger beads on his shirt. A series of cords with beads on them. As he counted their paces, he'd pull a bead down. It helped him calculate exactly where they were on their map—old school.

Ryder lifted his dog whistle to his lips and gave three short bursts of sound that Sabrin could barely hear standing right next to him.

Voodoo launched out of the woods and came to his side.

Ryder signaled Voodoo, and in turn, Voodoo crouched down and slowed his stride, stalking.

Ryder caught her eye and bladed his hand toward a rock formation.

This must be it.

Showtime.

Sabrin touched her elbow to the Glock at her hip. Part of the supply package that Green had provided.

They searched around the outcropping and found a door-size space in the curve that would go unseen if you weren't actively looking for it. The height and width were too obviously manmade to be mistaken, though there had been a nod made toward helping it blend into nothingness.

Ryder pulled out the night vision gear.

Moving single file into the space, they found themselves in a long dark corridor.

Ryder was mapping hiding crevices and marking them with a kind of chalk that glowed in their night vision but would be invisible to the naked eye. If someone were chasing them, they could dip into one of these.

There was light up ahead.

Surely, this was the place.

Green was right.

Sabrin was both thrilled that they were progressing toward saving the hostages and scared out of her mind. This was her training, but not her regular gig.

They crouched and advanced in careful, slow movements.

Voodoo was left back a few yards in a down-stay, ready to leap forward on his handler's command.

They came to the end of the tunnel. There were three steps down into a large room. The center was lit, and five men, dressed in warm clothing, sat around a table playing cards and drinking beer, even at this hour of the day.

On the far side of the cave, there were two lines of cots. Twenty-four people were tucked in sleeping bags. IV poles dangling waning bags of fluid. Off the sides of one of the beds hung a catheter bag mostly filled with yellow urine.

Three cots were empty.

On the other side of the cave were five other cots. Empty sleeping bags in disarray. A pile of day packs.

There was a small fridge in a very basic kitchen—a teapot. A fifty-five-gallon barrel that Sabrin assumed was their water source. And another barrel with an X and a frowning face that looked like it was the waste-water.

Sabrin trembled from cold and adrenalin.

Ryder looked back at her.

She gave him a thumbs up.

Slow as molasses, Ryder reached into the tactical pocket on his thigh. He waited for a burst of laughter to hide the rasp as he pulled the hook and loop closure and tugged out a listening wire. He handed an earbud back to Sabrin, who coiled it into her ear canal as Ryder snaked the mic forward.

As soon as she could make out the men's words, she tapped Ryder's leg, and he held steady.

"Women, so many women. I'm not a beautiful man." The guy with a rounded belly petted his hand over his paunch. "But a couple of millions in the bank will entice enough girls, especially in sunny island countries. I will make myself a harem of women to take care of my every need. Rub my feet as I read the paper. Suck my cock as I watch football."

The men laughed.

"Where will you move, Petter?"

"Me? Bali, maybe? Thailand."

"Yeah. Yeah. Petter likes ladyboys. And Thailand is the place to find them. The best of both worlds. Yeah, Petter?"

"It's almost time to change the bags. I did the piss last time. I'm doing IVs this time."

"Last round, then we're out of supplies. What's the plan?"

"Halvard said they'll pack in enough to keep us through the next twenty-four hours. What time is it?"

The guy on the left tipped back in his chair. "Just

now turning seven o'clock. You know I can get used to this life of beer and cards for breakfast."

"He'll be here around ten," he said. "He wants to watch the trail and see if there are any searchers going out to look for that guy. Sucks the hiker turned up like he did."

"How long did they say we had to stay underground? I don't like being down here without a little fresh air. A little sunshine."

"They'll let us know. It depends on the guy in the water."

"As long as we can keep them asleep, I'm willing to put up with the discomfort." The man nodded toward the hostages. "Glory days come soon enough."

"Halvard is bringing in our back up plan if they can't manage the IV bags."

"Yeah? What does that look like? I didn't hear this."

"Shackles and blindfolds are what he said."

"And the catheter bags?"

"He didn't mention those. They'll have to piss in their cots like they did on the bus."

"You know, that might not be a bad idea at the end of this anyway. Three more weeks of this shit."

"Sucks so bad. But the reward—I'll *live* under the golden sunshine warm and happy for the rest of my days."

"What were you saying, Jarle, about maybe that's not a bad idea?"

"So boss man's coming in to save the day, right? He finds the hostages and goes and calls it in. Says he's bloodied up two guys and ran away. The men are gone when the authorities get there, and the hostages are fine. I think we clean up the medical equipment, shackle 'em up, put on the blindfolds, and let that be the thing that the authorities focus on. How did they keep the hostages alive, and why don't they remember anything?"

"It would look better for the boss man, too."

Sabrin lay there listening hard, even though the comms would record everything. She wanted to understand just why these people were taken and held here in the bowels of the Slovakian hillside.

And after an hour of listening, she had her answer.

Chapter 30

Ryder

When the men got up to move about, changing catheter bags and IVs, Ryder tapped Sabrin's leg. The men probably wouldn't be saying anything now, and Ryder wanted to know what Sabrin had heard.

They squirmed backward until they were farther from the mouth of the cavern, rose slowly to their feet, and signaling Voodoo to come with them, they made their way outside.

On the way, Sabrin touched Ryder's back.

Ryder turned as she pointed to a thin black wire. That must be how they had electricity running inside for the lighting, the kitchen, and the three area heaters—near the kidnappers' cot area, one near their table, a much larger one over by the hostages held in their medicated comas.

Sabrin and Ryder followed the wire out of the cave. It wrapped up the side of the hill. They climbed along beside it, up to the very top. There, in a space open to the sky, were solar panels and batteries to store power.

"Can you get a satellite connection here?" Sabrin asked. "I'd like to call this in."

Ryder pulled his pack around and dug through. "How'd you come to look for that wire?"

"They were saying that they hoped when resupply came in, that they'd bring enough battery back up to at least run the lights."

"Not the heat?"

"I'm guessing the sleeping bags are rated for the arctic. They looked that way."

"What language?"

"Norwegian," Sabrin said.

"Yup. It didn't sound like Slovak to me." Ryder bladed his hands on his hips. "Did you get an idea what's happening?"

"They're planning their after-crime lifestyle of abundance. Lots of sex with young women, booze, and sunshine. They have a three-week window, then their boss man is coming in to save the day and be the hero."

"Interesting. Bloody ridiculous, three weeks?"

"They're worried about the supplies."

"Yeah." Ryder shifted his pack off. "So they didn't come out and say what this was all about."

"Though, that would have been nice. No."

Ryder drank from the hose on his camelback, and he bumped Sabrin to remind her that she should be hydrating, too.

She pulled out her water bottle. "But I got a pretty good picture, I think." She took a long swallow. "Imagine this. You're a Norwegian oil company big wig. Norway is a prosperous country, mainly because of its offshore drilling."

"Right."

She screwed the top back on and put the bottle away. "The political climate in Europe is to become a hundred percent renewable, and oil is the big bad evil. How do you change that dynamic?"

"By becoming a hero and saving a bunch of researchers?" Ryder shook his head. "Does that make sense?"

"Depends on whom you save them from, doesn't it?"

"What if the scientists were taken hostage because the bad people were eco-terrorists?" Ryder asked.

"Exactly." Sabrin pointed her finger at him. "The pressure is taken off the oil company as they say, 'You think we're bad? At least we aren't snatching buses of scientists.' Anyway, that's the general feel of what they were saying. Laughing about. Not only that. But do you remember last summer about this time, there was a group of scientists that were taken hostage in Africa?"

"The terror attack on the hotel in Ngorongoro?" Ryder asked.

"That's it—that impacted scientists. Many of whom questioned whether they wanted to do fieldwork. I've seen some of those discussions cross my desk. The science impacts US policy."

"This is a copycat," Ryder murmured as if puzzle pieces were falling into place.

"It worked. Like I said, it impacted the scientific community. It was a topic of discussion all over the world. Go with strategies that have been proven successful."

"How sure are you that it stems from Norway's oil fields?"

"They were using the company name."

"Okay, we're sure."

"Let's talk about the plausibility of getting that pack for Green before we leave and call this in. I'd like to end this now if possible. The men said they were hanging the last of the IV supplies. The satellite phone didn't work?"

"Cloud cover," Ryder said, putting the apparatus back in his pack. "The problem…well, there are a lot of problems getting that pack Green wants so badly. But the main one is that we don't know which one it is. The IFF works with night vision. It's too bright in there. I tried while you were listening."

"This is their power source." Sabrin gestured toward the battery.

"If we cut the power, I could figure out which one it is. But it would have to be cut for a split second. Off then on."

"They might not think much about that," Sabrin said. "But that second would pinpoint which bag is my target."

"Our target. My orders are to assist."

"Your mission, as I remember you telling me, was to gag and overwhelm me." She popped her brows. "Hypothetically, the target bag is located. Then what?"

"Twenty pounds, Voodoo can get it."

"Just how would that work?"

There was no way for them to communicate effectively from outside of the cave to inside the cave, so they'd come up with this: Ryder reached around and gave two tugs on the string that attached via easy release knot around his ankle.

Up top, Sabrin had the same knot, securing the string to her ankle. Grab, tug, run—if necessary.

Running would end up in bullets flying, and bullets were last resort.

Ryder felt a tug, tug on his ankle, indicating that Sabrin was about to detach the electrical wire from the battery. Ryder aimed his night vision toward the pile of bags, and one lit up as the room sunk into sudden black. Ryder put his laser dot on the bag just as the lights flashed back on.

The men looked around, confused. They jabbered in Norwegian. Ryder had no idea what they were saying. But it sounded like they were talking each other out of their concerns.

They went back to their game.

Ryder checked the time.

They knew that there was a resupply coming in. They didn't have all day for tactics. He lay there on the cold-assed rock for an hour, Voodoo panting next to him helped Ryder stay functionally warm.

The Norwegians looked sleepy and lazy now, maybe a little buzzed as they kept downing their beers.

Ryder kicked his ankle twice.

Immediately, he felt Sabrin tug twice back.

The room flashed to black.

"In you go, Voodoo."

From zero to sixty, Voodoo took two leaps, and Ryder could see he was in the pit looking around. "Silence. Go left. Left. Left. Shadow," Ryder whispered into the comms on Voodoo's neck. This radio would work as long as Ryder was line of sight. Those commands put Voodoo over toward the men's cots as Sabrin cut the lights back on.

This second time, the men weren't as agitated. They'd seen that the lights had come back on last time and that they'd been fine for a while. Ryder imagined that they were telling themselves that their resupply guy could check.

Sabrin had said that they were told not to leave the cave lest they'd be seen by one of the rescue crew that might be out searching for the lost hiker.

When Ryder had told Voodoo to shadow, it meant he was to get himself into a dark space and disappear. No noise, no movement, nothing that would call attention to himself.

This was a challenging task for Voodoo, but he always got an extra special reward when they practiced for the extended periods—the amount of time that Ryder deemed sufficient training for just such a scenario.

Voodoo would be thinking of his raw steak he would get later.

Again, Ryder waited for the men to settle.

"Voodoo," he whispered into the comms. "Slow snake. Slow snake to the dot." Ryder swirled the laser beam over the bag, defining Voodoo's trajectory.

Voodoo searched the room until he locked on to the bag. "Slow snake to the dot."

Voodoo lifted his belly an inch off the ground. Slowly. Stealthily. Voodoo crept forward.

Ryder circled the laser with one hand and clasped his gun, pointed at the leader's head in the other. If anyone noticed Voodoo, Ryder planned to tap the leader and watch him fall. The sheer unexpectedness of their leader being shot dead would freeze up the men, giving him enough time to get Voodoo and that bag out of there and get their team of three into the woods.

"Slow and steady there, mate."

Voodoo continued the fluid stalk until he arrived at the bag.

Slow and steady was hard as hell. But it kept people alive and missions on course.

"Slow there, mate, grab it and freeze." That told Voodoo to get his teeth in and stop there.

Voodoo was perfection. *Two steaks for you tonight, mate.*

Ryder slid his gun into his holster and reached for the string.

Taking a deep breath, he tugged the string twice, and once he felt the return tug, Ryder pulled the knot to release it from his ankle.

And just as planned—three, two, one. The cave was plunged into darkness.

"Bring to me. Bring to me, Voodoo."

Here was the tense piece. Would Voodoo come by himself or come with the bag. If he came out without the bag, Ryder would race in and grab it.

The men had their rifles stacked against the cave walls.

Ryder imagined that the men wouldn't have their cell phones on them in the cave—no receptivity down there. No one could yank the cell from their pocket and karate chop their flashlight on.

Never say never.

The men were yelling this time. More than the second of black sent them into action.

Voodoo landed almost on top of Ryder.

Ryder grabbed at the bag in Voodoo's mouth, and they ran from the cave, scrambling toward their exfil target where Sabrin was supposed to run after she'd gathered the string.

Voodoo and Ryder raced hard for the mark.

Once they got around the boulder, Ryder found Sabrin bent in two, still panting from her own race.

They collapsed victorious into each other's arms.

Epilogue

Green knocked on the door. When Sabrin opened it, the first thing he said was, "The bag?"

Sabrin knew he would, so she had it in her hands. She thrust it toward him, and he received it with a grin. "Fantastic."

Scooping her arm to invite Green in, Sabrin then shut and locked the door behind him. "We're watching on the news. They're saying that the hostages all have acceptable vital signs and will be transported via ambulance as soon as they can get the downed trees clear."

"A huge success," Green said.

"Your asset was thrilled when we told him it was a go." Sabrin gestured for Green to take a seat.

"And I will have control of him for the rest of his career," Green said with a grin. "As I said, a huge success. You two pulled it off." He moved the chair to a place where he could watch the TV then sat.

Sabrin went back to her place on the bed that she'd just vacated. She curled herself back into Ryder's arms with Voodoo moving up to position himself so he could keep a watchful eye on Green. Meh. She was on vacation. She could do as she pleased.

Green nodded and turned toward the TV.

They watched until the twenty-four-hour news channel took a weather break.

"What about the king-pin? The Norwegian oil guy who set all of this in motion and was going to come in and be the savior, pulling on his hero's mantle?"

"We have your video and translation, Sabrin. I don't have any doubts that those men are going to make a deal and hand over all of their evidence so their prison stay will be shortened. You should be reading about the man's arrest—or possibly, his flight from justice—in the news in the next few days."

"A positive conclusion all around, then." Sabrin smiled.

Green patted his hands onto his thighs. "Listen, you're not done, Sabrin." He turned his focus to Ryder. "Ryder, you'll get instructions from Honey. But we've conferred. The two of you need to stay around for another five days of playing tourist to solidify your cover for the sake of diplomacy. If Ryder leaves out right away, they'll know Iniquus was involved."

"Yes, sir," Sabrin said.

"We have a car for you outside and reservations in Bratislava. Lay low for two days or so, then you can venture out sightseeing."

"Yes, sir."

"Oh, and Sabrin." He cocked his head to the side. "Nice job working over the dognapper. He'll be hospitalized for a while. And my sources say that was the final straw with the Zorics. Far from making them happy, the family has made it clear that repercussions are heading his way."

"As if he hasn't had enough already," Ryder said.

"Are we still Mr. and Mrs. Tucker?" Sabrin asked.

"Cut up those credit cards," Green said. "There's no more funds on them. No, you're Mr. Kelly and Ms. Harris. What you want to do about changing that is up to you."

And that was how Sabrin found herself standing here, a year to the day after the hostages were rescued, at the main entrance of CIA headquarters paying the Mr. Hale tax.

Here, at the statue of Nathan Hale, of "I regret that I have but one life to lose for my country" fame, Sabrin fulfilled the obligatory nod to CIA superstition. Before embarking on a mission, the CIA officer places seventy-six cents at the feet of the statue. This would convey good luck and safe passage to the officer and her family.

Not that Sabrin felt like she needed more good luck.

But it was tradition.

As she stood from arranging her coins, Sabrin put her hand on Voodoo's head and smiled at Ryder.

"Mission ready?"

"Absolutely." She spun the first of what would eventually be a total of three wedding rings on her left finger.

This first ring that she wore, Ryder had slid on her finger at their first wedding, the one here in DC for their American friends and family, two days ago.

The second she'd be given when she married Ryder in front of her Slovakian family in Dedko and Babka's backyard in four days' time.

The third, she'd get in the ceremony they'd have on Ryder's family's station next week.

Once back at their home in Northern Virginia, the jeweler would fuse the three circles into one whole ring. A commitment to their marriage and to their families on three continents.

Ryder tucked Sabrin under his arm as they made their way to the car, heading to the airport for Bratislava.

"Three weeks, three weddings, I wonder if that's a record," she mused.

"Dad's had six."

Sabrin looked up. That was always going to be a sore spot for Ryder. Commitment and effort were cornerstones to his makeup.

"Yes," she said. "But your father's were all to different women. You get to marry me all three times."

"My one and only love."

Sabrin wrinkled her nose. "Still corny."

"I'm working on it." He put his hand to his chest. "The sentiments are sincere even if the words are off."

"The only thing I care about," Sabrin said, lifting to her toes to offer a kiss, "is your conviction and sincerity." She took a few more steps. "I just think of it as 'Ryder language.'"

Voodoo pushed between them.

Ryder reached down to scrub a hand down Voodoo's

back. "Voodoo, you picked our Sabrin right out of that competition crowd. Bloody amazing instincts. Thank you, mate. One thing I can say is, I will *always* trust my dog."

* * * * *

Get 4 FREE REWARDS!

We'll send you 2 FREE Books plus 2 FREE Mystery Gifts.

FREE Value Over **$20**

Both the **Harlequin Intrigue®** and **Harlequin®** **Romantic Suspense** series feature compelling novels filled with heart-racing action-packed romance that will keep you on the edge of your seat.

Get 4 FREE REWARDS!

We'll send you 2 FREE Books plus 2 FREE Mystery Gifts.

FREE Value Over **$20**

Both the **Harlequin® Desire** and **Harlequin Presents®** series feature compelling novels filled with passion, sensuality and intriguing scandals.

HARLEQUIN
PLUS

Announcing a **BRAND-NEW**
multimedia subscription service
for romance fans like you!

Read, Watch and Play.

Experience the easiest way to get
the romance content you crave.

Start your **FREE 7 DAY TRIAL** at
<u>www.harlequinplus.com/freetrial</u>.